Praise for

A Gardin Wedding

"*A Gardin Wedding* is full of tender moments that pull at your heartstrings. Rosey Lee has penned an inspiring tribute to the power of second chances."

—RUTH P. WATSON,
author of *A Right Worthy Woman*

Praise for

The Gardins of Edin

"The surprises and heart in this fast-paced family drama kept me turning pages late into the night."

—KJ DELL'ANTONIA, *New York Times* bestselling
author of *The Chicken Sisters*

"In a clever twist, debut author Rosey Lee plucks four women inspired by the Bible and sets them down in a tension-filled contemporary Black family struggling to find answers to messy and pesky questions. As they sort out relational fireworks, will they figure out how to stay a family and also be their best selves? It's a loving and lovely journey from an exciting, talented new author willing to explore the meaning of family in intriguing ways."

—PATRICIA RAYBON, Christy Award–winning author of
the Annalee Spain Mystery series
and two critically acclaimed memoirs,
My First White Friend
and *I Told the Mountain to Move*

"Rosey Lee's *The Gardins of Edin* testifies to all that it means to be family. It conveys the passion, heartbreak, faithfulness, and conflict that come with loving the people closest to you. Readers will wish they owned a cottage on the Gardin estate or lived close enough to witness first-hand all the goings-on in Lee's fascinating saga."

—ROBIN W. PEARSON, Christy Award–winning author

"Nothing complicates a family more than a family business. *The Gardins of Edin* by Rosey Lee is a gorgeous debut that freshly examines the painful past of two sisters and their matriarch, their cousin by marriage, and their successful peanut farm. With courage and ambition akin to the casts and epic dramas of Tayari Jones, Lee has written a page-turner of grief and hope."

—MELISSA SCHOLES YOUNG, author of *The Hive*

"With complex and intriguing characters reminiscent of their biblical namesakes, Rosey Lee's *The Gardins of Edin* provides an allegorical look at friendship, family tension, and the concept of forgiveness."

—KIMMERY MARTIN, author of *Doctors and Friends*

Also by Rosey Lee

The Gardins of Edin

A
Gardin Wedding

A GARDIN WEDDING

A Gardins of Edin Novel

Rosey Lee

WATERBROOK

WaterBrook

An imprint of the Penguin Random House Christian Publishing Group,
a division of Penguin Random House LLC

1745 Broadway, New York, NY 10019

waterbrookmultnomah.com
penguinrandomhouse.com

A *Gardin Wedding* is a work of fiction. Names, characters, places, and incidents are the products of the author's imagination or are used fictitiously. Specifically, Edin, Georgia is a fictional town. It is not based on the actual town of Eden, Georgia, which is located in Effingham County near the South Carolina border. Any resemblance to actual events, locales, or persons, living or dead, is entirely coincidental.

A WaterBrook Trade Paperback Original

Interior illustrations, Adobe Stock: title page flower arch, Olga Linespace; title page flower cluster, Maryna; chapter opener single flower, Мария Минина

Trade Paperback ISBN 978-0-593-44551-8
Ebook ISBN 978-0-593-44552-5

The Cataloging-in-Publication Data is on file with the Library of Congress.

Printed in the United States of America on acid-free paper

1st Printing

The authorized representative in the EU for product safety and compliance is Penguin Random House Ireland, Morrison Chambers, 32 Nassau Street, Dublin D02 YH68, Ireland, https://eu-contact.penguin.ie.

BOOK TEAM: Production editor: Laura Wright • Managing editor: Julia Wallace • Production manager: Sarah Feightner • Copy editor: Cara Iverson • Proofreaders: JoLeigh Buchanan, Rachel Kirsch

Book design by Diane Hobbing

To their moms.
(They know who they are. And so do their sons.)

A
Gardin Wedding

Chapter One

Mid-June

Martha swept the sandalwood fan in her hand back and forth, not to cool her brow but to tame the nervous energy brewing inside her. Although almost everything was going according to plan, she couldn't shake the notion that things were about to get messy. Martha placed her mason jar on the coffee table and scooted closer to Oji. His constant reassurance had proven right so far. The day had gone exactly as he said it would. And now they were in the homestretch, chatting on a sofa like they did most evenings at his home or hers. But their surroundings were different on this cloudy late-spring evening as they sat on a rented sofa that was part of the lounge vignette at her aunt's outdoor wedding reception near the lake pavilion on the Gardin family estate.

"The Garden and Games theme is a big hit," Martha said, mindlessly repeating the same comment she'd just made as she slowed the speed of her fanning and scanned the east portion of the property. The wedding planners had turned the area into a floral wonderland in shades of pink and orange. Flowers lined the walkways leading to the pavilion and cascaded down its posts from the ceiling.

Oji gave her a comforting smile. "Want to go for a walk around the grounds to let off some steam?" he asked.

Martha coyly held the fan, a favor from the wedding reception, up to her face like a woman in one of the Regency-era dramas Oji pretended he didn't like to watch with her. "I would love to go on a promenade with you around the grounds, sir. But when we pass by one of those big lawn games, I'll have to beat you again. Which game do you feel like losing *this* time?" she asked.

"I kept letting you win because I'm a gentleman," Oji replied, smirking.

"Whatever you need to tell yourself to make it okay," Martha teased.

Oji burst out laughing, and Martha joined in, reveling in the serotonin release. *He always knows what I need,* she thought.

"That's all right. I'd prefer to stay here and talk with y'all," Martha said, accounting for her sister and her cousin by marriage, who sat chatting among themselves across from Martha and Oji. The women maintained an easy balance of having their own conversation, engaging with Martha and Oji, and watching the other attendees enjoy the festivities.

With only ninety-six guests, the reception felt like the laid-back Juneteenth cookout the family hosted each year, except both the venue and the attendees were more spiffed-up. Following a dress code described as "comfy cocktail attire," wedding guests looked chic as they posed for photos in front of a massive floral wall. A few groups of people congregated at the reception tables or at one of three lounge vignettes overlooking the lake, but most rotated among the array of giant games—checkers, Jenga, Connect Four, and Etch A Sketch—spread across the grounds. Bursts of laughter filled the air as some men and women played like children, and other adults introduced their kids to the games they grew up with. But Martha fretted because the joyful occasion served as the first meeting for her family and Oji's since the couple began dating three months prior. And Martha wanted it to go perfectly.

Laughing with Oji assuaged Martha's anxiety for a couple of minutes, but it soon returned. She folded the fan and placed it on her lap as she leaned toward him. "I didn't expect your mom to talk so much to the other guests," she whispered. Her deep-brown skin glowed against the tangerine dress she wore. "I was looking forward to bonding with her as she got to know my family, but she's spent the whole reception meeting people instead of spending time with us."

"Since she and my dad don't get out as much as they used to, she can't help herself. She's just doing her thing," Oji replied in a hushed tone. "She likes you. I promise," he continued, squeezing Martha's hand.

"Okay," Martha replied as she caught a glance of her sister. She swung her head to her right, where Mary leaned back in a burnt-orange wingback chair that faced the lake. "What are you laughing at?" Martha asked in a perky voice. The long swoopy layers in her pixie cut framed her oval-shaped face perfectly.

"You two are cute together. It's good to see you happy," Mary said. Her hair cascaded down her back as she readjusted her body in the chair and smoothed the fabric of her flowy magenta midi dress.

"That's sweet of you to say," Martha said, blushing.

Because of their similar physical traits and fashion tastes, the sisters had embarked on extensive discussions regarding their maid-of-honor dresses and hairstyles for the wedding to ensure they didn't end up with similar looks. This was intended to prevent guests who didn't see them regularly from confusing them as the same person. But mostly, it was important to Martha that everyone was clear about which Gardin sister was dating Oji Greenwald. She and Mary had the same complexion, prominent eyes, and pouty lips, but Martha was two years older at thirty-eight.

Oji stood and lifted Martha's mason jar from the table. The ice clicked against the otherwise empty glass. "Thanks, Mary. She makes *me* happy too," he said with a big smile. "I'm gonna get Martha another lemonade. I'll bring one for you and Ruth if you'd like."

"That would be great!" Mary said.

"No thanks," Ruth replied from the vintage chair positioned next to Mary. "I'm still working on mine."

As Oji walked away, the women made kissing faces at Martha behind Oji's back. Martha blushed and playfully rolled her eyes, but she didn't utter a peep to her sister and cousin-in-law until Oji was a safe distance away.

"Y'all are so embarrassing!" Martha whined. "You would swear I've never had a boyfriend before."

"It has been a while," Mary teased.

Martha turned her head to the side and narrowed her eyes at her sister.

"I have no plans to stop picking on you anytime soon. This is too much fun," Mary said, twirling her hair around her finger.

Ruth smiled. "I like that he's being so supportive. I've still got my eye on him, but he might be okay after all."

Martha sighed, but it wasn't because she was upset by the comment. She appreciated that Ruth was still willing to look out for her. The woman was a model of forgiveness in action, given Martha's previous attempts to wreak havoc in Ruth's professional life as well as in her personal one. She and Ruth were still in the rebuilding phase of their relationship, but they were on solid standing. "He's a good guy. I'm not worried about him. It's his parents. How do y'all think it's going?" Martha asked.

"It seems like it's going fine to me," Ruth responded. "It's not like the Greenwalds are total strangers. Well, today was our first time meeting Adam, but we met Eve at the Gardin Family Enterprises Christmas party. We got along smashingly then, and she's been just as personable today."

"I know, but I wasn't there when y'all met. It's different this time," Martha grumbled.

"You really should calm down. You don't want Oji to see the snappish side of you, do you?" Mary teased.

"Oh, I bet he knows. She hasn't changed that much," Ruth said. The curls in her Afro shook as she laughed.

"Ha, ha, ha . . . Yes, he knows," Martha said. She attempted to hold it in, but she laughed too. And it felt good to let go. Even Martha could admit that she'd mellowed out since dating Oji. Her family teased her about it every chance they got. As proven by her stress over the meetup between the Gardins and Greenwalds, Martha hadn't totally abandoned her high-strung personality. But she was much more bearable, and her family was grateful.

"Mrs. Greenwald has always been kind to me when Oji takes her calls while we're hanging out," Martha continued. "And we've picked up his parents for lunch a couple of times too. It's gone well, but she's never invited me inside or had me over for dinner. It's odd because they're such a close family. I think Oji would've at least hinted if his mom didn't like me at all, but maybe she's saving a home-cooked dinner for someone she likes more."

"It's just been a few months. Give it a little more time," Ruth said reassuringly. The confidence in her voice should've calmed Martha down, but it soothed her only a little.

"How much time does she need? It's not like I'm expecting Oji to propose anytime soon, but I don't have time to waste," Martha bemoaned.

"Hey, I'm on your side," Ruth said, placing her hand at her collarbone and running it across the neckline of the orange and magenta A-line dress she wore as matron of honor.

"I know you're just trying to help. And it *is* helping, as hard as it might be to see it from my responses. I'm just nervous because I don't want anything to mess up what Oji and I have going."

"That's understandable," Ruth said. "I don't know if you've noticed that you two have been getting lots of admiring stares from people today. They're watching y'all almost as much as they're gazing at the couple who actually got married. Is that getting to you at all?"

"It's very thoughtful of you to notice," Martha replied. In the preceding months, she had grown accustomed to the endless inquiries about her future with one of Macon's most eligible bachelors, but attending a wedding with him in her neighboring hometown of Edin seemed to increase the usual interest in the couple. "Oji and I pick up on the looks too. I don't mind them so much, but it is a little weird when people make comments to us. Can you believe Sister

Johnson told us she expects to hear about another Gardin wedding soon? She is always getting in somebody's business. The first lady of the church should know better than saying that to us at a wedding, of all places! She—"

"Hold up," Mary said. "Have y'all started talking about getting married? As much as we've prepared for today, you never mentioned that. Not once!"

Martha thought carefully before answering. She didn't want to be untruthful, but she also didn't want to let on more than she was willing to share. Her sister and Ruth knew her well enough to read between the lines if she said too much, and she didn't want to seem shallow.

Although Oji hadn't explicitly agreed to it, they had talked about the future, and Martha had a feeling he was thinking about proposing. They had daily talks about issues that popped up in their families and in their relationship, as well as things at work. He had asked Martha's opinion about an offer he received to purchase his real-estate investment company, and he gave her objective advice about her role as the medical consultant for the teaching kitchen in Mary's new restaurant. Martha felt as if she and Oji had become each other's confidantes, and she valued the friendship at the foundation of their romantic connection.

Martha loved Oji, but, so help her, she also viewed their potential union as a fast track up the social ladder she so desperately wanted to ascend. Gardin Family Enterprises had done quite well over the past ten years, but Martha grew up comfortably not wealthy. She looked up to Eve, who had been born into one of Macon's wealthiest families. By marrying Eve's son, Martha would achieve her dream of being part of a power couple, which would provide the status and influence she craved. And those things not only would bring her personal prestige but also could help with her work. As a Black female physician, Martha faced a myriad of daily challenges in her quest to improve health outcomes among people who were disproportionately affected by health conditions and had very limited access to health services. She had learned early in her career that it took more than goodwill to make change. She needed to know the right people who could help open the right doors.

"I've dropped a few hints, and I think he caught them. He's started to say *we* a lot when talking about stuff. And remember him giving me this for my birthday?" Martha asked as she extended her arm to show off the gold bracelet with three large freshwater pearls that adorned her wrist. "It's by a brand named Isshi. And it's called the Someday bracelet. I found the website where he bought it from, and the description said something like 'Embrace what will be.' Do you think he was thinking about that and, uh . . . us . . . when he picked it out?"

"Maybe?" Mary said, with the inflection of someone who didn't want the responsibility of chiming in. "Or maybe he just liked the bracelet. I don't know."

"Time will tell," Ruth said. As she spoke, the string lights in the trees and those forming a canopy in the pavilion switched on, illuminating the expansive area on the estate under the cloudy skies.

"Talk about timing!" Mary proclaimed. "Apparently, Ruth is onto something," she said with a giggle.

Martha leaned back on the sofa. She clasped her hands and drew them to her chin. Everything she desired seemed so close that she could almost touch it. But she felt like it was just beyond her reach, and she suspected Eve Greenwald might have a little something to do with that.

"I've never dated a guy whose mom didn't love me," Martha said. "Usually, the mom is all in from the first time she hears about me, but the guy takes some time to figure out what he wants. Even when I made some recommendations about Mr. Greenwald's health, Oji's mom was polite but didn't warm up to me. I just can't get a good read on her. That's why I was hoping y'all would be able to help me figure her out."

"What did Oji say after you brought up the health stuff about his dad?" Ruth asked.

Martha tilted her head. "He actually said his mom and I are a lot alike, but I don't really see it."

"Is that so?" Ruth asked. "Most men are the last ones to see the similarities between their mom and the woman they're dating. So if he sees it and admits it, my guess is it's probably very true."

"SEE, HERE'S MARTHA, and this is where we're sitting," Oji said as he and his father approached the end of their assigned reception table under the lake pavilion, where a lush runner of pink and orange bougainvilleas draped off the table and pooled to the floor next to the spot where Martha stood.

The first notes of "Cha Cha Slide" played over the speaker, but it didn't prevent Martha from hearing the frustration in Oji's voice. His emotion was hidden under the superficial layer of politeness and pleasantry that might fool strangers but rarely worked on the people who know someone well. Something had shifted the lighthearted banter the father and son had enjoyed throughout the day. "Is everything okay?"

"Hey, Martha! Good to see you again. You having a good time?" Adam Greenwald asked. His voice was just as charismatic and melodic as it had been when he and Oji teamed up against Martha in a spirited game of checkers on the lawn before the two of them headed to the restroom. But given the mere fifteen-minute interval, Martha recognized Adam's response as subtle evidence of sundowning, a phenomenon in which people with vascular dementia may experience confusion, agitation, or other symptoms in the late afternoon or evening.

"Hello there. Yes, a lovely time, thank you," Martha said with a bright smile.

Oji leaned in close to Martha. "We had a little issue on the way back," he whispered, "but we're on the other side of it now. Let's just enjoy the rest of the reception. I'll fill you in later."

A half-hearted smile spread across his face, alerting her that he was beginning to rebound from whatever happened during their brief time apart. "Okay," she said as she squinted. Then she relaxed her facial muscles to remove the evidence of the apprehension building from not knowing what happened and how it might affect the rest of the evening.

Martha had never heard Oji use anything other than a pleasant tone with his father before. She wanted to know more about what happened to cause the sudden departure, but she resisted the urge to push for more information, deciding instead to trust Oji's guidance when it came to his parents. Always the respectful and dutiful son, he spoke very highly of them to anyone who would listen. He'd explained early on that with one brother deceased and another estranged from the family, he shouldered a lot of responsibility for his parents. Martha admired the way he looked after them, even if she thought he doted on his mother too much.

Oji held Martha's hand as they quickly made their way to their seats. Accustomed to the routine, Martha walked slightly ahead of him. The couple's positioning allowed Adam to stay in Oji's field of view while allowing him the independence of walking along the other side of the long rectangular table without a chaperone by his side. And being aware that Adam was sundowning, she also regularly turned her head to catch a glimpse of him.

Adam, a consummate Southern gentleman, greeted the sprinkle of wedding guests seated at the table as he strolled by them. "How do you do?" he asked each one with a nod although he'd already spoken with each of them several times over the course of the day. Martha didn't know if their seemingly pleasant responses meant they had picked up on Adam's diagnosis or whether they were just being kind, but watching the interactions warmed her heart regardless.

Having arrived at his seat with a few moments to spare, Oji kept an eye glued on Adam. As Oji watched, his head moved as if he were guiding his father's footsteps past the remaining open seats until he came to the chair across from the one where Martha had settled.

The DJ continued his stretch of line dance songs, and the packed dance floor erupted into the Electric Slide. Martha called Oji's and Adam's attention to the newlyweds, who executed all the steps flawlessly. But Martha had never doubted they would. Naomi and Nicholas always seemed to be in sync. After a whirlwind romance, they chose a wedding date two months after they became engaged. They opted for a simple church ceremony and a reception that prioritized fellowship and fun. After a seated meal, the couple's closest family members and a handful of special friends enjoyed a scrumptious three-tier lemon cake with sculpted ganache flowers descending across the front.

"They look good!" Adam exclaimed.

"They should," Martha said, laughing. "They made us practice the steps with them all week!"

"I forgot about that. Do you want to join them? I can stay with Dad," Oji said.

"I don't need a babysitter, Oji," Adam said firmly. "I'm ready to go anyway. Your mother is around here somewhere, and we're going to head home as soon as she gets here."

"It's fine. Everything is okay," Martha said, looking back and forth between the Greenwald men. "I'm having a good time sitting with y'all." She rubbed Oji's arm.

"Thank you," Oji whispered.

The trio watched in silence as the DJ transitioned to "Wobble," but it wasn't long before they were all moving in their seats.

As if on cue, Eve Greenwald sauntered up to the table as the song wound down. She walked with the confidence of someone who thought that everyone's eyes were on her, and she was usually right. Eve commanded attention everywhere she went. Tall and curvy, she maintained her figure with a rigorous fitness routine, and her elegant wardrobe choices accentuated her hard work without being too showy.

"Did y'all miss me?" she asked as she approached the chair next to her husband.

Adam grinned as he jumped to his feet and pulled out the chair for her. "You know *I* did," he said, gazing at her.

Martha imagined that he used a similar line on his wife when they first met. It was obvious that Oji owed his suave demeanor to years of studying his father.

Eve blushed as she settled into her chair. "Thank you," she replied in an endearing voice. The floral appliqués on her off-the-shoulder dress glistened under the string lights strewn across the pavilion's ceiling.

"Mr. Greenwald, do you think Oji will still look at me like that when we've been together as long as you and Mrs. Greenwald?" Martha asked.

"If he knows what's good for him," Adam replied.

Eve turned toward her husband. "Hush now, Adam. I think it's much too soon for anyone to be talking about marriage," she said as if Martha and Oji weren't sitting across from them.

"If you say so." Adam shrugged his shoulders.

Martha felt like she'd been stabbed in the heart, but she maintained her composure despite the unexpected verbal blow. "We definitely don't want to get ahead of ourselves, but it's nice to have such good role models," she said without missing a beat. Her voice was as sugary as the remnants of sparkling lemonade in the mason jar that sat between her and Oji.

Eve smiled and tilted her head toward Martha. Her gaze

was cool, but at least it acknowledged Martha's presence. "That's a good point, dear. Very good indeed," she said.

Martha briefly made eye contact and smiled softly. Then she turned her attention to the middle of the lake pavilion, where the newlyweds walked to the dance floor.

"Mom, it's getting dark. Don't y'all want to head home?" Oji suggested pleasantly. There were no signs of the frustration he'd exhibited only a few minutes earlier. "Dad mentioned that he was ready to go."

Oji gently placed his hand at the center of Martha's back, but she didn't turn around. She was too afraid she would cry. *How could he be so aloof? After all our discussions about marriage, why doesn't he know that what his mom said hurt my feelings?*

"I said that?" Adam asked. "I guess it *is* getting late."

Just as Adam finished speaking, the DJ made an announcement. "Calling all single ladies to the dance floor. It's time for the bouquet toss."

Martha slowly rose from her chair as she contemplated the direction of her next steps. She wanted some time to herself, but she didn't want to disappoint Mary, who had already made it to the dance floor. And she especially didn't want Eve Greenwald to think she'd gotten the best of her.

"Fine. We'll leave after the bouquet toss," Eve mumbled.

MARTHA WASN'T THE type of woman who cared about the wedding tradition of catching the bouquet. She just couldn't get behind a belief that a bunch of flowers landing in her hands would bring her good luck, much less a groom. Martha didn't believe in luck. She believed in blessings. She believed in hard work. She believed in planning and strategy. But social pressure was a force she could never resist. So as the sun began to set over the lake of the Gardin family estate, she glided toward the faux parquet squares in the center of the lake pavilion.

As Martha stepped onto the dance floor, her eyes fell upon Naomi, who giggled as Nicholas playfully pantomimed from the periphery how the bouquet should be thrown. Naomi stood in the middle of the dance floor, beaming in a stunning chiffon Hanifa gown. Its structured shoulders, along with the train formed by its dramatic white cape, made her look like both a bride and a superhero. With her hair pulled into a halo of bouncy gray curls, she radiated joy. It was contagious, and it was just what Martha needed.

Martha laughed along with her aunt and tucked her exchange with Eve into the back of her mind. She would process the uncomfortable conversation as soon as she had a moment alone or, better yet, discuss it with Oji as soon as she had a moment alone with him. It wasn't lost on Martha that sometimes men didn't pick up on the same cues that women detected. But she had seen, or possibly caused— depending on whom you asked—enough family drama to know that these sorts of things needed to be nipped in the bud so they wouldn't snowball into years of strife. Oji had some explaining to do. But now was not the time to sort through it. Much unlike the bouquet toss, figuring out how to handle Eve Greenwald and her son was not for public viewing.

"Last call for all the ladies who want to catch the bouquet," the DJ announced.

Martha spotted Mary, who stood front and center among a group of four women who had scattered in self-selected spots that ranged from about six to ten feet behind Naomi. Martha braced herself as she walked toward her sister. To everyone else, Mary looked like she was merely gearing up to catch the bouquet, but Martha knew better. And she wasn't fooled by the fake smile on her sister's face. It was there just because everyone was watching.

"It took you long enough to get here," Mary said as Martha reached her, but Mary maintained a pleasant look on her face.

"I got up from the table as soon as the DJ announced it," Martha said. The words flew out of her mouth before she realized it would only further irritate her sister. *Mrs. Greenwald sure has knocked me off my game.*

Mary's eyes widened and her pretend smile fell away. "We agreed that no matter what came up, you were supposed to meet me by the dance floor at seven-thirty so we could get a good spot. And I texted you a reminder, so there had better be a good reason you're late. On second thought, never mind. That won't help us. We need to focus on where we are now. Are you sure you don't want to take off your shoes?"

"I told you I am not walking around barefoot just to catch some flowers," Martha scoffed. She had already compromised enough by agreeing to wear the slingback Shekudo mules that Mary chose instead of a shoe with a stiletto heel. The sculptural wooden block heels were supposed to give Martha some stability if she needed to scramble for the bouquet, but she liked them because the heel reminded her of the fancy finials on antique staircases and furniture.

Mary chuckled. "All right, all right. Here, I saved your spot."

"Thanks, but you can stay there. I'll just stand next to you."

"Martha, we've been over this twice," Mary said, her voice returning to a serious tone. She moved about four feet to the right, creating space for Martha to assume the spot directly behind Naomi.

Martha hesitated. Out of the corner of her eye, she noticed two of Nicholas's nieces standing a few feet behind Mary. They inched toward the space that Mary had saved for Martha. Martha chuckled and squinted at them. They retreated, giggling.

"Three times. We've gone over it three times. I understand your marching orders. I promise," Martha said. Although Mary had become annoying, Martha was secretly tickled by her sibling's preoccupation with her catching the bouquet. After weeks of Mary's persistent nudging, Martha had finally agreed to participate in the bouquet toss, albeit begrudgingly. While Martha had not been moved by Mary's initial argument for solidarity with her and the other four unmarried women who surrounded them, she believed her threat to drag her to the dance floor if she didn't show up.

"Everyone ready?" the DJ asked.

Naomi pretended she was about to toss the hand-tied Biedermeier bouquet of pink and orange poppies, zinnias, and peonies over her head.

The women cheered.

"Okay," the DJ continued, "I'm gonna count down, and the bride will throw the bouquet. Let's go. Three . . ."

A rush of excitement overtook Martha. She tried to ignore it, but she couldn't. She locked her eyes on the bouquet. With its brilliantly colored blossoms arranged in rings of alternating bands, the bouquet resembled a bull's-eye, and she felt like a skilled archer focusing on her target.

"Two . . ."

I'll just get ready in case it comes my way, Martha thought. She widened her stance and planted her feet. Her arms shot up in the air.

"One!"

Naomi leaned forward and flung the bouquet backward with both hands. But instead of it going straight, it veered to the right.

Maybe I can try a little bit. Martha kept her gaze locked on the blur of petals flying through the air. She lunged to the right and nearly lost her balance as the palm of her right hand made contact with the soft flower petals. She quickly made a fist, clutching the victory.

"I caught it! I caught it!" Martha yelled. With the petals still squished in the palm of her right hand, she supported the bunch of blooms with her left hand as she jumped up and down.

Mary, who stood with outstretched arms between Martha and one of Nicholas's nieces, rushed forward and wrapped her arms around her sister.

"I didn't think I'd care about catching the bouquet, but I do!" Martha said with her eyes squeezed closed.

"You did so great! I wish you could've seen yourself!" Mary exclaimed amid applause from the wedding guests.

"Thank you for coaching me!" Martha said, clutching Mary tightly. Although the duo still squabbled from time to time, they had mostly smoothed out the kinks in their relationship. With Martha no longer jealous of her sister's new restaurant near the hospital where she worked and comfortable with their collaboration on its teaching kitchen, the bouquet victory represented an acknowledgment of their progress. She kept her eyes closed, savoring the moment.

"Look! Martha, turn around," Mary said. Her voice sounded like a whisper against a round of cheers that broke out across the lake pavilion.

"Huh?" Martha said, opening her eyes.

She pivoted as instructed, and there was Oji on bended knee before her. Both his hands rested on his right knee. His lips were moving, but Martha couldn't hear anything he said.

She leaned down close to his ear and said, "Are you proposing? Is that what this is?"

Oji nodded and smiled. The cheering got louder.

Martha stood still. Her eyes blinked quickly. The bright flash from the wedding photographer's camera reminded her that she and Oji were surrounded by Naomi and Nicholas's wedding guests. Martha looked up at the camera. It flashed again, triggering a wave of dizziness. She tried to think quickly.

"Yes," she said breathlessly.

Chapter Two

"It looks like we have a proposal on the dance floor! And she said yes!" the DJ announced in a booming voice over applause from the wedding guests.

What is happening? Martha wondered as Oji rose to his feet. She couldn't make out what the DJ said next. His voice sounded muffled. She stared at Oji, focusing on his face. His smile was energetic and bright, but it reflected a different element than the usual delight he displayed when they spent time together. He looked happy, but there was something else there. She just couldn't quite put her finger on it. Nothing made sense to her in the flurry of events. How had she swung from half-hearted acquiescence about catching the bouquet to suddenly wanting it so badly? And how did she go from actually catching the flowers to not being able to string together a coherent thought after getting the proposal she had dreamed about for so long?

I have to hold it together. Did he really just ask me to marry him? And I said yes, didn't I? Okay, I should smile too. Martha contracted her facial muscles, but Oji leaned his face toward hers before she could fully lift her lips and cheeks to expose her teeth for a smile.

She closed her eyes and leaned forward. Their lips connected in a light kiss, grounding her in the moment. *Now, this feels real.* Then Oji wrapped his arms around her and held her close. Martha inhaled the woody scent of his cologne, hints of vanilla and nutmeg wafting through her nose. She exhaled and time seemed to slow down. Oji released his arms from her body and grabbed her hand. She interlocked her fingers with his and opened her eyes.

A small crowd comprised of Martha's family members and a few of the women from the bouquet toss gathered around the couple. The words she'd heard finally registered in her head. "Awwww!" Mary exclaimed. She grabbed Martha and Oji for a hug. "I can't believe it!"

Naomi and Ruth squealed as they accompanied Mary into the joyful grouping.

Nicholas stood talking with Ruth's son, M.J., as they waited their turn to congratulate the couple. They were a dapper duo in matching black linen suits, as M.J. had served as Nicholas's best man. "Oji certainly is full of surprises!" Nicholas exclaimed with glee.

"That's for sure. And who would've thought I would go from being the only man left in the family to finding out you're my granddad and now we're getting Oji for reinforcement? This is great!" the twenty-seven-year-old replied as he put his arm around his elder.

"We're still outnumbered, but we're catching up at record speed," Nicholas said, playfully commiserating with his grandson, who frequently joked about the female dominance in the Gardin family.

As the group hug among the Gardin women dispersed, Nicholas and M.J. went straight to Oji. But Martha didn't mind. She lingered with the women awhile longer, delighted by Oji's warm welcome into her family. She couldn't yet sort out what to make of the unexpected and very public proposal, but having her family close by helped her begin to recover from the shock of it all.

Other guests soon chimed in with their best wishes.

"I'm so happy for y'all!" said Nicholas's niece who had been standing behind Martha during the bouquet toss. "I was ready to fight you for those flowers, but I realized I wouldn't have stood a chance when I saw how you jumped up for them. Not that Mary would have let me get close anyway. Did you see how she blocked me?"

Martha laughed. "She told me she was going to do that. I tried to convince her not to, but she never listens to me," she said before turning toward her sister. "Wait a second. Did you know Oji was going to propose?"

Mary shook her head and moved her hands like opposed windshield wipers. "I had no—"

"I didn't tell anyone," Oji blurted. "Not even my parents. Speaking of my parents, where are they?"

With everything happening so fast, Martha hadn't had an opportunity to realize that the Greenwalds had not joined her family in congratulating the couple. Dread crept into her mind. *I hope Oji's mom didn't stomp away because he proposed.*

Martha looked around the lake pavilion. She stared at the reception table where she had sat with Oji and his parents only minutes earlier. Then she scanned the other seven rectangular tables positioned around the border of the dance floor. "They have to be around here somewhere."

He sighed. "I don't see them either. Maybe Dad had to go to the restroom again." His voice dripped with concern.

They quietly scoured the area and she gripped his hand.

"Is everything okay?" asked Naomi, who stepped away from Ruth and M.J. to inquire.

"Yes. Everything's fine," Martha replied reflexively. Her tone was reassuring and confident, and it seemed to work. After Naomi returned to her conversation without additional questions, Martha beckoned to Nicholas, who stood a few feet away chatting with some friends from Philadelphia. "Please excuse me, Nicholas. It's just about time for you and your lovely new wife to leave for your honeymoon, isn't it?" She nodded as she met his eyes.

"Uh, yeah. Got it. It's about that time," Nicholas responded, returning the nod. "I'll get Naomi."

Thank you, Martha mouthed as she discreetly nudged Mary.

"Hey, we're gonna step away," Martha whispered to her sister. "We need to find out where Oji's parents are."

"Oh, no. I hope everything's okay," Mary said.

"Me too."

MARTHA FEIGNED A smile and flailed her right arm in the air. Her mounting apprehension wouldn't let her fully focus on the last milestone of Naomi and Nicholas's wedding, and she didn't want it to show to the sea of wedding guests who stood on the grass with her and Oji to bid farewell to the newlyweds.

"Can you check your phone again?" Martha whispered to Oji. "I can't believe we still haven't heard from your parents. Do you really think everything is okay?"

The taillights on the flower-adorned golf cart carrying Naomi and Nicholas disappeared down the road connecting the lake pavilion to the rest of the Gardin family estate. Oji pulled his phone from his pants pocket. After a quick look, he shook his head. "Nothing, but it's only been ten minutes since I last checked it. They're probably just driving through an area with poor cell service on their way home." His voice sounded like he was trying to convince himself as much as he was trying to convince his new fiancée.

As the wedding guests began dispersing, Martha again scanned the group of people who stood on the stretch of grass closest to the road, where two well-lit potted trees marked the entrance to the serpentine aisle of florals, lush greenery, and flameless candles that forked to the lake pavilion and the associated body of water. She needed to reassure herself that she and Oji hadn't somehow overlooked his parents. Martha and Oji had already walked around the entire lake pavilion, covertly searching while accepting best wishes on their engagement. Then they inspected the game areas and lounge vignettes on their way to witness the newlyweds' departure.

A crowd had gathered to watch, and Martha's eyes landed on Ruth, M.J., and Mary. How relieved she would be if she found Oji's parents talking with her family, but the Gardins were chatting with Nicholas's nephew and nieces instead.

"Hopefully you're right," Martha said. "And thank goodness Aunt Naomi and Nicholas decided to have their honeymoon send-off tonight instead of having a breakfast or brunch tomorrow. That gives us time to make sure your parents are okay without worrying the bride. Aunt Naomi can always tell when something's wrong, and I wouldn't be able to keep my fear from her if the reception weren't winding down. I would've felt terrible if I had anything to do with her being upset on her special day."

Oji shifted his weight. "Huh? Why would it be your fault that we can't find my parents?" he asked with a puzzled look.

Martha glanced away. "What if . . . Never mind. I'm just rambling," she replied. It would hurt too much to say aloud what she had been thinking. *Perhaps it could be a coincidence that we can't find Oji's parents minutes after he proposed, but what if they left because they don't think I'm good enough for him?*

"Let me try calling my parents again," Oji said, looking at his phone.

Martha let out a quiet sigh. "Good idea," she said, looking up at the stars shining in the dark sky. As she said a silent prayer to hear from Oji's parents soon, a faint but familiar voice interrupted.

"Oji, is that you over there?" Eve asked as she walked up the slight incline from the main road onto the grass where Martha and Oji stood. She sounded as if she'd run into a friend she hadn't seen in a long time.

The couple walked quickly to meet her, taking care not to draw too much attention to themselves.

"Are you all right? We've been looking all over for you and Dad. And I've called you a million times. Where is he? Why isn't he with you?" Oji asked. His speech was pressured, but he didn't raise his voice.

"My phone died. But yes, I'm fine. I'm sure your father is fine too," Eve said calmly. "We can talk about it on the way home. I'm going to ride with you."

"Mom, did you let Dad drive home?" Oji asked. While still speaking in a respectful tone, his voice grew more intense with each word he uttered.

Martha remained quietly locked in the background of the exchange until she heard someone yell her name.

"Bye, Martha!" exclaimed a nearby voice.

Martha spotted Naomi's tennis partner flailing her arm from the driver's seat of a convertible beside the valet stand.

"Thanks so much for coming," Martha replied.

"I would never miss a Gardin wedding! I'm looking forward to yours, too!" she said.

Martha glanced nervously at Oji and Eve, who both looked unfazed. "Yes, ma'am. Please drive home safely." She waved and then returned her attention to the mother and son as the car took off. "Let's step away from everyone to finish talking."

She grabbed Oji's hand and guided him several feet in the direction of the lake pavilion.

Eve followed. She briefly nodded at Martha but otherwise looked at only Oji as she spoke. "You know how your dad can be when he gets his mind set on something. He must've been carrying a set of keys with him, because our car is gone. I attempted to be discreet and look for it on my own, but I eventually had to ask the valet team for help. They couldn't find the car either. And—"

"But we took them. We took all of his keys," Oji protested.

"Well, he must have found a set somewhere. But don't worry. He's probably halfway home by now," Eve replied. The tone of her voice stood in such sharp contrast to Oji's that she almost came off as nonchalant.

"How do we know? He's not answering his phone. What if something happened?" Oji asked.

Martha's heart broke. She could feel Oji's worry and frustration with each word he uttered. *I want to help, but I don't want to come between him and his mother. It's a no-win situation.*

"I called him before my phone died, but I doubt if he has his phone with him. He can never keep up with that thing," Eve said.

"Mom, could you take this a little more seriously, please?" Oji asked.

"Oji, let's not do this here," Eve replied, her eyes darting between her son and Martha.

Of course. Now *she looks at me,* Martha thought.

"Martha is about to be part of the family too, Mom," Oji said firmly.

Martha took a deep breath. She had determined to stay silent as Oji and his mother spoke, but she couldn't bite her tongue anymore. "Why don't y'all head home and see if he's there? Then we can decide our next steps, if needed," she said sweetly.

Eve looked her straight in the eye. "Thank you, dear. I appreciate your concern, but everything will be fine. We will head on home, but I'll decide what happens after that."

For the second time that night, Eve's words cut Martha like a freshly sharpened knife.

MARTHA SQUEEZED HER already closed eyelids and threw her head back into the plush cushion of Ruth's sofa. As she lay supine on the couch, the oversized half bow that cinched the rear bodice of her dress dug into her achy back muscles. Any other time, she would not have tolerated the discomfort, but it paled in comparison to the emotional strain she bore from the night's events.

"I hate to see you so upset," M.J. said, slouched in the armchair in front of the fireplace.

Mary sat on the sofa opposite Martha. "Do you want to talk about it?" she asked.

"Which part? There are so many things," Martha replied, dragging out each word for emphasis but also in an attempt to buy herself a couple of extra seconds to sort through what was okay to say.

While the personal components of her situation were the most obvious to her family members, Martha also weighed an issue of professional ethics. As a physician, she was accustomed to supporting Gardin family members through any health issues that arose, and she had a policy of getting approval before talking about the situation with others in the family. Because she always seemed to be held at arm's length by Oji's parents, she hadn't had an opportunity to share her concerns about Adam's health with them, but she suspected they would want to keep things as private as possible. And even as she processed the risks and worries that surrounded Adam's disappearance, she could rely only on what Oji had confided in her. But how much of that was actually reliable? Martha sometimes wondered if Oji had held details back, and she more often wondered if he passed on any of her other advice to his parents.

"Mr. Greenwald might be at home. Please try not to think the worst," M.J. said.

"It's hard not to," Martha said, putting her hands over her closed eyes. The tears she held back during her conversation with Eve and Oji had fallen down her face the second she hit the threshold of Ruth's home, and the dampness still lingered. "And it's supposed to start raining soon. I was so relieved when the weather held up all day, but I didn't consider that it might be an issue once the wedding and reception were over."

"I agree with M.J. There's a good chance Mr. Greenwald is safe," Mary said, "so let's keep hoping and praying that's the case. And we can focus on your good news to help bide the time while we wait to hear about him."

"Mary's right," Ruth said, entering the room. "It hasn't been long since Oji and Eve left the reception to find him. There shouldn't be any traffic at this hour, so we should hear something soon. Here, drink this."

Martha removed her hands and opened her eyes. Ruth stood over her, holding a mug that matched the vibrant orange color of Martha's dress. A soft smile appeared on Martha's face, but it vanished suddenly as she sat up and reached for the mug. "Thank you," she said dryly.

"I thought it would cheer you up," Ruth said. The disappointment in her voice was palpable. She typically reserved the china, which featured the iconic Harlem Toile de Jouy design, for special occasions. Martha assumed Ruth had made an exception since Martha was having a tough time.

Martha cupped the dainty mug with both hands, covering the drawings of Black women in French ball gowns that adorned it. "Mom would've loved this mug. I've dreamed of putting the whole collection on our wedding registry."

"You're right. These are exactly Mom's taste. How have I never picked up on that before?" Mary asked.

"She'd have used them every day," Martha said flatly.

Ruth smiled. "And she'd have made you hand-wash them even though they're dishwasher safe," she said.

"Yes! She always said it built character," Mary said with a soft smile. "They'll make a sweet reminder of Mom when you and Oji get married. Oh, Martha. Is that why you sound so gloomy about the mug? Because they remind you of Mom but she and Dad aren't here today?"

Martha nodded. "Obviously, I think of Mom and Dad all the time, but it's harder missing them on special occasions. I've dreamed of putting the whole collection on our wedding registry because of Mom. The dishes make me think of her and how happy she would have been for me. But they're also a reminder of the stark difference between that response and Mrs. Greenwald's. It makes me sore about the fact that my fiancé's mother doesn't care for me. What if she tries to stop us from getting married?" Martha griped.

"She wouldn't do that. Right, Ruth?" Mary said. Her head swiveled toward Ruth, her eyes begging for agreement. "I can't imagine things not working out for y'all. *But* if somehow they didn't, you don't have to wait to get married to buy the collection. It could be a nice treat for yourself."

"No, I doubt Eve—" Ruth said before she was interrupted.

"I could've done that when the collection was first released," Martha snapped. "But I don't want to buy it myself. I've always wanted Wedgwood china on my wedding registry."

"Okay. I get it," Mary said, holding up both her hands.

Ruth pursed her lips and took a deep breath through her nose.

M.J. arose from his chair. "I'm headed to the kitchen for a snack. Do you want anything, Martha? I can transfer your tea to a different mug if that would help you feel better."

"No, I'm fine. But thank you," she replied before sipping her tea. "Mmm, this is good."

The hibiscus tea blend comforted Martha in Naomi's absence. She yearned for the maternal figure in her life after such an emotional evening, but she would have to settle for her aunt's favorite tea flavor paired with the presence of her cousin-in-law and sister.

"I'm sorry, Mary," Martha said, wiping moisture from her eyes. "I didn't mean to bark at you about the china. You're just trying to help, and I really appreciate it. I'm struggling to process everything that happened tonight. Between worrying about Oji's dad and missing our parents, I'm a mess."

"I know. It's okay. You're carrying a huge load. It's a lot for one night," Mary said.

"And Mrs. Greenwald. How could I forget about her? She hasn't congratulated me on the engagement," Martha said.

Ruth settled on the other end of the sofa opposite Martha. "Are you sure Eve knows that Oji proposed? I mean, was she even there?"

"Right," Mary chimed in. "She may have missed it, and since Oji didn't give you a ring . . . Ooh, my bad. I didn't mean to bring that up." She hung her head.

Martha rolled her eyes. "I was trying not to go off about it right now because Mr. Greenwald is missing. And I feel selfish thinking about myself, but it must mean we're supposed to talk about it now since you brought it up," she said with fire in her voice.

"Hold up," Mary said. "Don't put that on me. But it might be better for you to talk about it with *us* before you say something to Oji that you might regret later."

Ruth leaned forward. "But you're happy he asked you to marry him, right?"

Ruth always gets right to it. Aunt Naomi would never do that. She always eases into the tough questions, Martha thought. After taking a sip of her tea, she grabbed an antique brass coaster from the holder and placed it atop the large marble coffee table. Then she rested her mug on it. *Talking about this right now isn't a good idea after all. Maybe if I just sit here, they'll change the subject.* She stared at the wall behind Ruth and Mary, running her finger along the soft sofa seat while counting the four transom windows near the ceiling over and over again.

"Are you okay?" Mary asked.

Ruth leaned over to Mary. "Give her time," she said in a soft voice.

"Those sheer curtains make your vaulted ceiling look really tall," Martha said, determined not to go down without a fight.

"Come on, Martha. Spit it out," Mary pressed.

Ruth picked up the striped silk shantung accent pillow that lay on the sofa and playfully threw it at Mary. "I'm going to put some tape over your mouth."

As the pillow bounced off Mary's arm and landed on the empty cushion between Mary and Ruth, Martha finally spoke.

"Why would Oji propose at Aunt Naomi and Nicholas's wedding?" she asked slowly. "Why didn't he plan a real proposal, one that didn't risk his mother either running away or pretending she didn't see it? And where . . . where is my ring?" Her voice cracked as tears began to fall again. She hated the vulnerability she felt when crying in front of others. She preferred to cry alone, but it was a relief to let out the emotion she always fought so hard to hold in.

Ruth and Mary leaped from the sofa and rushed to console Martha.

"It's gonna be okay. I didn't mean to make you cry," Ruth said. She squeezed into the small space between Martha and the end of the sofa and placed her right arm around her.

"And I didn't mean to push you into talking about the proposal before you were ready," Mary said. She embraced her sister with her left arm as she sat on the other side of her.

"Do you know how many people asked to see my ring tonight—my nonexistent ring?" Martha cried. She leaned her head on her sister's shoulder before speaking again. "It was so embarrassing. And now I'm embarrassed having to admit that I'm embarrassed about it!"

Mary leaned her head against her sister's. "You don't have to feel embarrassed around us. We're not going to judge you."

"It's—" Ruth started.

"And can you imagine what my staff at the primary care center will say? 'Dr. Gardin got engaged, and she didn't even get a ring!' People will think it's so tacky that Oji proposed at a family wedding! Speaking of which, do y'all think Aunt Naomi was upset about it?" Martha asked.

"Oh, no, I don't think so. She's happy about getting married herself, and she just wants you to be happy too," Ruth said. She rubbed Martha's arm reassuringly.

"But, Martha, I understand what you mean," Mary said. "You wouldn't take it well if it happened at your wedding. But while I wouldn't like it if someone proposed at mine, I wouldn't make a big deal about it if it were someone I'm close to. So I agree with Ruth that Aunt Naomi probably doesn't mind." Her voice was full of the confidence and caution that came naturally to someone who had spent a lifetime choosing her words carefully as not to wake a beast that was easily aroused.

"Are you kidding me? I would have a fit!" Martha exclaimed. "A wedding should be all about the bride."

"And the groom," Ruth interjected. "Let's not forget about him."

"Yes, of course," Martha said without flinching. "But on top of all that, Oji proposed minutes after his mother said it's too soon!"

Mary gasped. "She said that?"

"Wait. Did she really tell you that, or did Oji pass it along?" Ruth asked in a heavy voice.

Martha took a deep breath. "It's a long story, but she actually said it to my face," she said, wiping her eyes with her hands.

"Humph! I heard Eve was a piece of work, but I never imagined her carrying on like that, especially at our family wedding. We didn't have to invite her, you know," Ruth huffed.

"This is a whole lot for one night. No wonder you're on edge," Mary said.

"Right! And his father just happens to go missing the night we get engaged! Hopefully, Oji will tell me soon that Mr. Greenwald is safe at home, but what kind of life are we going to have together with it starting off like this? Are we really supposed to be together?"

Ruth squeezed Martha. "I know you wanted everything to go a certain way—"

"Yes, and it's extra pressure because everyone was watching," Martha whined, interrupting Ruth.

"I know. But that doesn't necessarily mean you and Oji aren't supposed to be together," Ruth said.

"Are you sure?" Martha asked.

"What's most important is that *you* are sure," Ruth replied.

Chapter Three

The pitter-patter of raindrops on Martha's roof opened up into a harsh downpour. *Just because Oji hasn't called yet doesn't mean it's bad news, but this rain makes it too much like the night Mom and Dad died.* Drowning in a mixture of memories, worry about her future father-in-law, and regret about her outburst at Ruth's house, Martha needed something to nurse the steady ache at her temples that was growing stronger by the minute. Standing in the hallway outside her bathroom, Martha placed the palm of her hand on the door of a steel medical cabinet as if she drew strength from the coolness of the metal. In her bare feet, she stood three inches taller than the majestic family heirloom, one of the few items she'd kept from her parents' home. With its bronze-grayish color and natural patina, it was a daily reminder of her resilience and an emblem of her tendency to mix vintage and contemporary elements in her life.

Martha reached over the bath towels, toiletries, and other personal items to the top shelf of the cabinet. As her hand made contact with a warehouse club–sized bottle of ibuprofen in the corner, her phone rang, startling her. She quickly moved the bottle to the front of the thick glass shelf and retrieved her phone from the pocket of the Adidas x

Wales Bonner knit shorts she wore. "Hello! Oji!" she exclaimed as she answered the phone.

"Hi, babe. My dad's not here. And sorry I'm just now able to call. It took forever to get home because we ran into a storm," Oji said.

"Oh, no. I'm so sorry," Martha said.

"I want to hop back in the car and try to retrace where he might've driven, in case he had an accident or something. My mom wants me to wait until the rain stops. But I don't know. I feel like I should go now."

"It's storming here now, and I think it's supposed to rain the rest of the night. I'm really worried about your dad being lost, and the rain adds another scary layer."

"*I'm* worried too," Oji said. "I can't sit idly when he could need me out there."

Martha felt the weight of his silent thoughts as he spoke. "I know it's hard to wait, but it'll be tough on your mom to be worried about both of you driving around in this weather." She began to pace up and down her hallway. Afraid she would start crying again if she let on how overwhelmed *she* felt with worry about the Greenwald men driving around in the rain, she left that part out. She couldn't risk burdening him with her feelings. He was already managing his own and his mother's while looking for his father.

"That's just it. My mom is acting like it's not a big deal."

Shifting into doctor mode, Martha set aside her hurt feelings about Eve to come to her defense. "She's still in denial that your dad has dementia. It can take some people a while to accept that a loved one's memory is not going to return."

Oji let out a loud sigh. "But it's been years since he started showing signs, and she still keeps making excuses and questioning the diagnosis."

"We've got to just meet her where she is and try to support her through it. The most important thing right now is to find your dad," Martha said, still pacing.

"That's what I'm trying to do, but she won't let me. She just keeps saying that he always turns up eventually."

Martha slowed to a stop in front of the arched stained-glass window in the middle of her hallway. "This has happened before?" She placed her lower back against the windowsill and stared out the window. A bolt of lightning flashed across the sky.

"Yeah, it's been a while since the last time it happened, but that's probably only because I took his keys. Mom couldn't bring herself to do it, so it fell on me."

Martha fumed. *After all the conversations we've had about his concerns and my insight, he never thought to bring this up to me?* She needed to see what else he might disclose.

"Are you there?" Oji asked.

"Yeah, I thought you were about to say something else," Martha said, fighting hard to hold on to her patience.

"So, yeah, he's gotten lost at least two or three times before, but it's never happened at night or in the rain. That's what troubles me the most."

"Have you thought about calling the police?" She tucked away her anger and replaced it with concern.

"Nah, it makes me real nervous to call the police on my father. He taught me how to stay alive if they ever pulled me over, so it feels wrong to get them involved. But don't you have to wait twenty-four hours for someone to be missing anyway?"

"I understand, but this is an extenuating circumstance," Martha said. "We have to think about what getting assistance from law enforcement could prevent in this situation. Remember how you mentioned being concerned about an accident? Calling the police could prevent an accident or it could help find him if he's stranded somewhere because he had one."

Martha expected Oji to respond, but he didn't, so she kept talking.

"And if they happen to find your father driving erratically, the officers' knowing that a Silver Alert has been issued on his behalf could actually prevent them from jumping to conclusions or using excessive force. It could actually save his life."

"That's a good point."

Martha could tell she was getting through to Oji. "They have a special policy about how to handle it when an elder with dementia goes missing. They'll take a report, and they may be able to track his cellphone. But even if they can't, they use other steps to try to find him, like informing other police departments and 911 centers across the state. Talk to your mom and see if she'll go for it. It's called Mattie's Call here in Georgia, but just tell her it's a Silver Alert system. That's what they call it in most places anyway."

"Okay. I'll go talk to her now. I don't know how I would get through this without you. Thanks, babe. Love you."

"Love you too, but wait. Don't hang up yet. Do you want me to go to your parents' house when the weather settles down? I could keep your mom company or whatever you need."

"Let's see how it goes," Oji said. "Hopefully, we'll find

my dad before then, but I'll let you know. Okay, I gotta go. I'll check in with you later."

Martha leaned her head against the windowpane and clutched her phone to her chest. *Why so many secrets? But at least he finally told me,* she thought before she was interrupted by the sound of Oji's voice coming from her phone. She extended her arms and looked at her phone screen. The call with Oji had not disconnected, so she could hear him talking to his mother. Martha hit the mute button and listened.

"Mom, I just talked with Martha," Oji said. "She said there's an emergency system we can use to help us find Dad. She said it's called—"

"The Silver Alert system. Yes, I know all about that. Your father's doctor gave me some information about it, but that's not something we need right now," Eve said. "Let's just be patient and give your father time to make it home."

"But Martha said—"

"It sure feels like Martha is trying to control things in our family, and I don't take too kindly to that," Eve said in a measured voice.

"She's just trying to help."

"Is she? That's enough about this, son."

"Mom, I really . . . Oh . . ." The call ended abruptly.

"Aargh!" Martha shrieked. A roar of thunder erupted outside her window.

MARTHA SLUMPED ON the settee in the four-season room of her cottage as she waited for the ibuprofen to kick in, the dull ache at her temples having transitioned to a tight band around her head. She had expected to have showered and changed by the time Ruth arrived, but she was paralyzed by the conversation she had overheard between Oji and his mother. She mustered the strength to send a brief text to Mary. At Ruth's house, her sister had suggested that Martha might feel better if she went home to get refreshed, and she insisted that she and Ruth would go over to check on Martha at home.

Because of her long history of giving her younger sister advice that she didn't request, Martha had pushed back against the reversal of their roles over the past several months, but they had worked through it, and now she was grateful for the second time that day for Mary's intervention. Given her circumstances with Eve, Martha now needed a special kind of help that Mary couldn't provide, and the person she least wanted to ask for it was the one best suited to provide it. Although Martha felt desperate, she wasn't convinced she would've had the courage to ask for assistance if the arrangements had not already been made.

Sitting next to Ruth in the cozy space she usually reserved for herself made Martha feel all the more vulnerable, but she needed the safety the space provided in order to be able to share with Ruth what Eve told Oji.

"I am stunned," Ruth said after hearing the news. "So, on top of your worry about Adam missing in this weather and your memories about your parents, now you have to deal with Eve's drama."

"It's unimaginable," Martha said. "I keep praying that Mr. Greenwald makes it home safely."

"I'm also praying for them, and I'm adding Eve to my prayer list too."

"Thank you. I've been nothing but kind to Oji's parents. How much more must I do to make Mrs. Greenwald like me? I'm really at a total loss." Martha rested her arm against the back of the gray hammered-velvet seat.

"We'll help you talk through it. I . . . Oh, where is Mary? Is she on her way? Do you want to wait until she gets here to keep talking about this, or did you two already talk about it by phone?"

Martha's hand began to fidget in the empty space separating her from Ruth, so she ran her fingers along the boning of the sofa cushions. "I haven't talked to her yet. I sent her a quick text and asked her not to come over."

"Oh," Ruth said with confusion spread across her face.

Martha sat up straight on the sofa. "I wanted to talk with you alone."

"That's the last thing I expected to hear from you."

Martha bit her lip, still searching for the same words she had labored over since she decided to talk to Ruth without Mary. "This is tough for me to say, so I'm going to just say it," Martha confessed. "You put up with a lot of resistance from our family when you and Beau started dating. It leveled out over the years, but how did you do it? It's one thing to stumble into a lifetime of struggle, but it's another thing to knowingly sign up for it."

Ruth intertwined her fingers and rubbed her right thumb across the ball of her left thumb. "Leveled out over the years?" she asked before letting out a light chuckle.

"You know what I mean." Martha blushed.

"If you mean that you unjustly and passive-aggressively targeted me for years and then suddenly apologized last year after my successful father, who you respect, forced you to see the light—well, a glimpse of the light—then yes, I know what you mean." Ruth's voice was pleasant but firm.

"You aren't pulling any punches, are you?"

"I wouldn't go that far. I'm just trying to make sure we're clear. That's part of accountability. And, yes, I can see the similarity between our situations. It's pretty ironic."

"Indeed. But what do you mean a glimpse of the light? You make it sound like you don't think I'm being genuine."

"Do you really think you've been doing the work you need to do and for the right reasons?"

"I'm trying. You and I get along much better now, don't you think? I've been very intentional about doing my part to improve our relationship. But I actually feel like you still hold back sometimes."

Ruth squinted at Martha.

Heavy drops tapped on the triple-pane windows. *Maybe I went too far. I do need her help,* Martha thought as the rain outside picked up again.

"You've been through an awful lot today, and it's important for us to give each other some grace when we need it. But when this comes up again, I want you to remember this moment and whatever you're thinking or feeling right now. You have to start being honest with yourself if you really want to get to the place you say you're working toward."

Martha cast her eyes downward. "Okay. I hear you," she said softly.

"I hope so. If it feels like I hold back with you, it's because you haven't shown me I can trust you. We both know you only invited me here tonight because you need something."

She's not wrong, Martha thought, overwhelmed with the

intoxicating mix of vulnerability and embarrassment that she'd experienced so many times that evening. As she lifted her eyes, Martha sensed moisture forming in the corners of her right one. She dabbed it with her fingers. "I still have a lot to work on, and I appreciate your patience with me. I'll think about what you said. I promise. But, yes, you're right. I need your help. I hope you can find it in your heart to give me some advice about how to get through this situation with Mrs. Greenwald."

Since childhood, Martha had always found it difficult to ask for help. But in the thirty-one years since Ruth entered the Gardin family—when she married her first husband, Marlon, who was Naomi's son—Ruth had never denied Martha help, nor did she require that Martha ask for it. Ruth was just always there, serving as a buffer, a soft landing place, or whatever she thought would make things easier for Martha. And Ruth continued that support even though Martha did not return the favor after Ruth's first husband died and she later married another of Martha's cousins. Martha hoped that by making an explicit ask for Ruth's guidance this time, it would be obvious to Ruth that Martha recognized her contributions over the years.

Ruth nodded, wiping her eyes. "Of course," she said. "But this is probably not going to be as profound as you'd like it to be. As you know, someone's intentions can be appropriate and their heart can be in the right place, but you can't make another person accept that. All you can do is make sure your heart is really in the right place. Those are the things you can control. I couldn't convince you of those things about me. You had to figure them out on your own."

"But look how many years that's taken me," Martha whined.

Ruth smiled softly. "I know. I lived it. And trust me, I'm glad we're not going through the worst of it anymore. We're making progress, but—"

"I love Oji. I really do. He's my person. I want to spend my life with him, but I don't want his mom to make my life miserable."

"But you—"

"But I made your life miserable. I know. I'm sorry. I really am sorry." Tears streamed down Martha's face.

Ruth grabbed Martha and held her as she sobbed. "That's not what I was going to say. I had a wonderful life with Marlon. I was so blessed to find love again and have an amazing life with Beau until he passed away. And, of course, it's a joy to be M.J.'s mom. But thank you for acknowledging that you caused me a lot of grief over the years. It means a lot. And it's the first time I've really felt like you mean it from the heart. That reminds me of an important caveat that might bring you peace during your journey with Eve, if you can grasp it. Your relationship with her doesn't have to be perfect. It can be a work in progress."

THE RAIN BEAT on Martha's roof, and she tossed in bed like the leaves on the towering magnolia tree outside her window. Nearly two hours had passed since eavesdropping on Oji's conversation with his mother, and with no updates on his father, she was engulfed by the tension in her muscles.

As a million possibilities ran through her mind, she drifted in and out of sleep, falling short of reaching the depth that would allow her to feel like she'd had even a moment of rest. It was only when her phone rang, jarring her, that she realized she had fallen asleep.

"Hello?" Martha said in a slightly husky voice, her heart racing.

"They found him. The police found my dad," Oji said. He sounded like he'd been up partying all night, though Martha knew it was quite the contrary.

Martha sat up in bed. "Thank God," she said. "But I thought—"

"Hold on. I'll be right back. Don't hang up."

I guess his mom changed her mind about getting the cops involved, Martha thought as she waited for Oji to come back to the call.

"That was quick," she said when Oji returned a minute later.

"Yeah, that was just the police sergeant in Atlanta confirming that I'm coming to pick up my dad," Oji said, still sounding spunky.

"Atlanta?" Martha asked, her voice increasing an octave.

"Yep. Can you believe he made it all the way there?" Oji said before erupting into nervous laughter. "I'm just so glad he's okay."

"Me too. So, is he at a police station?"

"Actually, they brought him to the hospital to get checked out. He ran a bunch of traffic lights, and an officer pulled him over. And you were right about the Silver Alert. The officer had just heard it, so he figured out who my father was pretty quickly. Dad was confused, but they wanted to be sure his confusion wasn't caused by an urgent medical problem. So far, everything has checked out. I'm just about to get in the car now."

Martha swung her legs to the side of the bed and popped to her feet. "Okay. I'll get dressed. I'll be ready when you get here."

After a few seconds of silence, Oji spoke. "Thanks, babe, but you don't have to come."

"Oh . . . Got it . . . Your mom's going and she wants time with your dad. That makes sense," Martha said, thinking aloud.

"No, she's not coming," Oji responded coolly. "I told her to stay home and get some rest. And *you* should rest too. I'd actually like some time alone with my dad if you don't mind."

"All right," she said begrudgingly. Then she lowered her body to her bed. She gathered the pillows, propped them up against the headboard, and leaned her head against the soft silk pillowcase.

"Thanks for understanding," Oji said.

"Of course." She bit her lip, endeavoring to regroup and think quickly. "You never told me what happened when you and your dad went to the restroom earlier tonight."

"Oh, that's right. We didn't talk about that. It seems like it happened days ago." Oji sighed. "Dad needed a little extra time in the bathroom, so I stepped outside to wait for him. After a while, I went in to check on him, but he wasn't there. I must've been talking to someone when he came out, so we didn't see each other. I figured he must've gone out to meet you like we agreed. But before I could make it to our table, I found him sitting with some other people that he didn't realize he didn't know. He thought that's where he was supposed to sit, and he was having a grand time talking to them."

Martha shifted and her head slipped against the silk pillowcase. "Wow. Now I understand why you were so upset when we met up."

"Yeah, that's never happened before, so it really threw me off," Oji said.

When Oji sighed again, Martha could hear the exhaustion and guilt that his excitement had covered up earlier. "This is not your fault, Oji. Please be patient with yourself. Your dad's illness is a big life change for all three of you. And I'm here to help you figure out what resources are available. We can talk more about that later."

"Thank you. And you've already been so helpful to me. My mom takes a little more time, but she'll come around . . . Hey, I hate to go, but I need to head out to pick up my dad."

"Please let me know when you make it to Atlanta. And, of course, when you get home, too."

"I will. The rain has slacked up here, so hopefully the weather will be smooth for the whole drive. Love you."

"Love you too."

Chapter Four

Martha replayed Oji's morning text over and over in her head. *"Boarding the plane for Denver."* *That's all I get after not seeing him yesterday? I can't deal with this now. Maybe I can process it after my treat.*

Still struggling under the weight of the ups and downs of an emotional weekend, Martha needed her Monday morning pick-me-up more than ever. She would've loved to crawl back into bed, but she couldn't bring herself to cancel at the last minute on her patients, some of whom caught multiple buses and walked lengthy treks in the summer sun for treatment at the primary care center. When Martha had begun kindergarten, her mother allowed her to have hot chocolate on Monday mornings before school to soften the blow of the start of the week. Now, as an adult, her weekly hazelnut latte did the trick.

Martha relied on the tasty coffee and jolt of caffeine to add some pep to her steps, and a few minutes in the vibrant and welcoming atmosphere at Edin Coffee and Smiles had turned her day around on more than one occasion. And she was depending on it to do so this morning.

As soon as Martha opened the door, the purple, pink, peach, and gold hues of the ombré daybreak wall mural brightened her day. "And still we rise, Martha!" said Sunny, the café owner, who was known for saving her most inspiring morning greeting for regulars who looked like they especially needed it.

Martha crouched forward when she reached the counter. "Do I look that bad, Sunny?" she whispered.

Sunny stared at Martha, slowly tilting her head in a way that made it seem as though the geometric patterns formed by her cornrows were moving. "I've seen you look worse. That was last year when Mary was sick. But I have a feeling your day will look up. Just keep pushing," Sunny whispered perkily.

Martha didn't know what she valued more, Sunny's coffee or her unusual mix of outspokenness and optimism. Talking to her was like spending time with your ninety-year-old grandmother who could get away with saying anything because she said it so sweetly, except Sunny was only thirty-two.

"I can deal with that," Martha said, nodding like she was hearing a new diagnosis for the first time and letting it sink in.

"I didn't expect to see you today," Sunny said. "I thought you'd be recuperating after your aunt's wedding. It was beautiful, by the way! I'm still surprised I was invited."

"It's a busy time at work, so I have to go in today," Martha said with a shrug. "But of course you were invited. You and the café hold a special place in my aunt's and Nicholas's hearts since they spent part of their first date here."

"Yep, right over there," Sunny said. She pointed to the table in the corner among the white laminate tables flanked by metal chairs with alternating yellow and orange bases and legs. "I remember like it was yesterday. They come in all the time and we have the best chats, but I never expected to get invited to their wedding. I sure hated that I had to leave the reception right after dinner. All the lawn games and everything looked so fun. But seems like you had your fill of partying this weekend, huh?"

"Thanks, Sunny," Martha said, holding in a laugh at Sunny's unintentional criticism. "But that's one way to put it."

"You're doing great, hon. What can I get for you today? Your usual?" Sunny asked.

Martha paused to think. "Yes to my usual latte. But instead of covering just one extra drink, I should splurge a little, given all the excitement this weekend. Let's do a hundred bucks extra."

Martha's weekly inspirational treat had become a regular part of her life, and she suspected that others struggled with Mondays as much as she did. So when, at the café's grand opening five years earlier, Martha and Sunny got into a conversation about the impact of random acts of kindness, Martha commenced the weekly practice of covering a drink for someone else who could use a boost.

"Ooh! Fun!" Sunny exclaimed. "You will give a bunch of people a lovely surprise today. May the kindness you spread return to you hundredfold."

"Thank you," Martha said with an energetic smile. She gripped the shoulder strap of her Yvonne Koné bucket bag with one hand and felt around inside until her fingers hit her credit card sticking out of her wallet. *What am I doing?* Martha thought, suddenly remembering her plan to be discreet about showing her ringless left hand around Edin until she worked through her embarrassment about Oji not having a ring for her when he proposed.

Martha quickly scanned the coffee shop. Sunny was busy running her transaction. Ann, a member of the café staff, refilled a bowl of fresh fruit behind the counter. Most customers took their orders with them, so there were only a handful of people seated at the time: four men talking at a table near the window, a couple of individuals scattered at the two-seaters, and a woman adding sweetener to her coffee at the other end of the counter. And no one stood behind Martha in line.

Good, there's no one close by to worry about. I'm probably making too big a deal out of this ring thing anyway, Martha thought. But to be safe, she kept her left hand awkwardly inside her purse. Then she adjusted the purse with her right hand and quickly slipped her left hand in the pocket of her slacks. She didn't plan to keep up the protocol at work, but it felt like a reasonable strategy for her first stop as an engaged woman in a small town like Edin, where everyone knew her family and word traveled fast.

"Here you go," Sunny said, handing Martha back her credit card. "We'll have your drink ready in a few. Thanks again for spreading some cheer. Would you like to stick with the usual plan that I say an anonymous donor is gifting the kindness recipient with a smile?"

"That's perfect, and thank *you*, Sunny!" Martha hadn't had her latte yet, but she felt lighter already. *A random act of kindness goes a long way for the giver too,* she thought.

Martha stepped back from the counter to wait for her order. She felt frustrated with her and Oji's lack of communication all over again, and she shifted her attention to the table where Naomi and Nicholas had sat a few months prior. *They had some bumps early on, and now they're on their way to Bora-Bora for their honeymoon. Oji and I will be okay too. We just have to get through this rough patch.*

"Martha, your latte is ready," Sunny said.

"Thank you. It's right on time," Martha replied as she approached the counter.

"Enjoy! And I just heard that best wishes are in order for you and Oji. Ann told me you got engaged this weekend. You know how fast everything spreads in Edin. How wonderful! I'm so happy for y'all."

"Finished, and with several minutes to spare," Martha said as she rested her pen atop the executive notebook on her office desk. After a busy Monday morning seeing patients, crossing off the final point on the long list of discussion items gave her the flush of success that she would need to power through an afternoon of back-to-back meetings. She always looked forward to this twice-a-month talk with Mary to plan for the teaching kitchen in Mary's new restaurant, The Alabaster Plate. But given an eventful weekend and two restless nights, Martha was dragging through the day. She needed every ounce of motivation she could find.

"You're welcome," Mary said. She pursed her lips and clenched her jaw, but she let out a laugh anyway.

Martha leaned on her desk and rested her chin on her hand. "What's so funny?"

"Just how you run our meetings. Like it's a medical staff meeting or something."

"You said you wanted a firm delineation between our professional time and family time if we're going to work together on the new restaurant. And you're the one who suggested that we meet here or at Alabaster Lunch Box. Besides, our meetings are no different than a Gardin Family Enterprises board meeting. We're all family, but Ruth still keeps the meetings very professional."

"So you're emulating Ruth for real now? You two really have come a long way," Mary said with a grin.

Martha smirked. "What do you mean *for real*?"

"I remember what you said on Easter Sunday after Nicholas proposed to Aunt Naomi. You said you learned a lot watching how Ruth maneuvered her way into our family and business. Are you still pretending you weren't serious about that?"

"I keep telling you I was joking," Martha said with a mischievous grin.

"If you say so," Mary replied with a side-eye.

"Okay, there may have been a hint of truth to it back then. But I see now that Oji and I actually fit well together, so I don't need to maneuver my way into his family. It's not so much about their money and status anymore."

"Not so much? So, the money and status still matter. They can't hurt, right?" Mary teased.

"Mary!" Martha said, rolling her eyes. She wasn't in denial about what had initially attracted her to Oji. His good looks didn't hurt either, but Mary didn't have to make it seem like she was being shallow about any of Oji's attributes. Martha wasn't ashamed of her goals. Yes, she was strategic about climbing the social ladder. And no, she wasn't sorry that she happened to fall in love with a handsome man who was born into a legacy of wealth. Martha didn't like the term *new money,* but she was clear that the recent growth that Gardin Family Enterprises had experienced was barely enough to put her on the radar of upper-crust society. The modest Gardin family trust had provided one disbursement, and she used all of it to pay for college. She still had to work for the things she wanted, and she looked forward to a life with Oji where she wouldn't have to worry about her financial future.

Mary snickered. "Ooh, and she's touchy about it too!"

"But to get back to your earlier point, it was good to have Ruth around this weekend. I'm glad she and I are working through our stuff," Martha said, pushing past her sister's persistent teasing.

"Me too. And speaking of working through things, how did it go with Oji yesterday? Do you feel better since y'all have had a chance to talk?"

"Girl, he canceled. He said he needed to spend more time with his parents. And he didn't invite me over to *their* house either!" Martha exclaimed, temporarily forgetting she and her sister were in her office and not catching up on each other's lives at her kitchen table.

Mary didn't hide her shock. "Did he stay at their house the whole night, too? There should've at least been time for a phone call."

"He said he was tired and needed to rest. He flew to Denver this morning to meet with a potential investor. I get that he needed to be prepared for his meeting, but what about us and our fresh engagement?" Martha asked, returning to an office-appropriate volume.

Mary winced. "Yeah, that's tough. I would be upset about it too if I were you. But I'm sure y'all will talk soon."

"We'd better. I don't know how many more restless nights of overthinking I can take," Martha said before being interrupted by a knock at the door.

Mary rose from her chair. "That must be Jasmine. You said she's your two o'clock, right?"

"Yep. I can always count on her to lift my mood." Martha smiled. "Come in," she called out.

Martha's office door flew open with such force that it startled both sisters. A statuesque woman with cocoa skin stood in the doorway. "Hi, Mary. Are you two meeting about the new restaurant? I would love to work with you, if it's okay with Martha. I mean Dr. Gardin. Sorry."

"It's fine, Jasmine," Martha said with a chuckle. "Close the door and have a seat. Mary was just leaving."

With deep dimples in both cheeks that appeared whether she smiled or not, Jasmine brightened a room whenever she entered it. But Martha had gone back and forth about hiring her high school classmate as the primary care center's community outreach manager. Although she remained confident that Jasmine's graduate-level public health training, grassroots experience, and contacts across the county would pay off in expanding the center's community programming, she worried that hiring someone she'd known for so long might alienate some staff members and cause concerns about preferential treatment. But so far, that hadn't been an issue. The primary care center employees were so enamored with Jasmine that they quickly let her into their circle, which positioned her to keep Martha abreast of the latest gossip floating around the center.

"Hey, girl! It's great to see you," Mary said, greeting Jasmine with a hug. "Martha and I were just talking about you a few minutes ago. She told me you have some ideas for the teaching kitchen."

Jasmine's face lit up. "Yes. My master's thesis was on using community gardens and teaching kitchens for engagement in health programs, so I am ready. I've been peeking through the restaurant windows, but I can't see much. I'm itching to see the inside."

"They're ahead of schedule, so we've moved up the opening date," Mary said. "We're planning for it to be in a couple of months. Feel free to stop in if you see me there. Otherwise, Martha can show you around sometime."

"Sure thing," Martha said.

"The Gardin women don't mess around!" Jasmine said. "Y'all are always on the move. That's why I like working with Martha. She knows what she wants, and she goes after it."

Mary cackled. "Funny you should mention it. I was just telling Martha the same thing."

While Jasmine's back faced her, Martha cut her eyes at her sister.

"Really? Ain't that something," Jasmine said. "But everybody knows it's true. I keep my ear to the street, but you can't believe everything you hear. Oh, that reminds me. I knew there was something I needed to tell you, Martha." She pivoted from Mary to face Martha. "Somebody told me that you and Oji got engaged over the weekend."

I hoped to have another day or two before I had to deal with this at work, Martha thought. She leaned back in her office chair, being careful not to let Jasmine see her making eye contact with Mary. "Is that so? Care to reveal your source?"

"Do tell," Mary said, grabbing Jasmine by the arm.

"No, I couldn't," Jasmine said, waving her hands in the air.

"Come on!" Mary pushed.

"But if I told everything I hear, nobody would tell me anything anymore. And I can't have that," Jasmine insisted.

"Fine," Mary said with an exaggerated pout.

"People are always talking, but I know the engagement rumor isn't true because Martha would have a rock on her hand that I could've seen from the doorway. I bet it'll happen soon, though," Jasmine said.

She turned to Martha. "Oji Greenwald knows a good thing. He's not gonna let you get away. He's gonna make a move soon. So be ready. Like they say, if you stay ready, you don't have to get ready."

"That is what they say, isn't it?" Martha asked. Her tone was indifferent yet pleasant, but her true feelings were the exact opposite.

WITH HER FOUR o'clock Zoom call canceled five minutes before it was supposed to start, Martha expected to get a jump start on what she hoped would be a quiet Monday evening. Since Oji was in Denver for work, she planned on an early dinner and hoped to fall asleep after streaming a show that wasn't on their shared watch list. She was exhausted. Even though she wasn't sure how long she would stay asleep, she looked forward to trying. But an unexpected text from Oji sent her to his home office to look for a document that he had left behind.

Martha usually avoided the cluttered workspace tucked in the back of Oji's otherwise pristine loft whenever she visited, so she viewed her impromptu detour as a strong testament of her love. *I don't know how he works like this,* Martha thought as she reached the pony wall that separated the office from the living area. Nearly reaching all the way to the ceiling, it sufficiently hid the mess while allowing some light to pass through over the top of the wall. Three rows of boxes were lined up by an over-crowded bookcase. An old shredder collected dust in the corner. A bunch of baseball bats leaned against the wall next to a sleek stainless steel desk with a geometric frame and black finish. A curved-back office chair with vertical tucking and stitched accents was fit tightly under the desk.

When Martha first said something to Oji about the disar-ray, he complained that he didn't have time to unpack when he moved in four years prior. So the space became the de facto dumping ground for things he thought he might need later, although later rarely came. Martha suspected that it got worse with each month that went by, but she tried not to notice.

Amid the chaos, Martha sat comfortably sorting through the stacks of paper on Oji's desk, but she couldn't find the document. She texted Oji: *Tell me again what I'm looking for. There are ten piles of paper on the desk. Maybe I overlooked it.*

Oji's reply was instant: *No, it's on my desktop. The computer.* Then he sent another message: *The latest file. Called 1108 Projections or something like that.*

Martha shook her head. *Now, how would I know all that? Why didn't he say it earlier?* she thought. *He must be having a tough day too. Bless him.*

Password? she texted.

Martha noticed the three dots indicating that Oji was typing, but they disappeared. Then the same thing happened again.

Interesting. I guess he didn't consider that he would have to give me his password, she thought. While she waited, she powered on the computer.

Then a text came through: *0G$Martha.*

What a sweet password, Martha thought as she hearted the message. The creative take on their names reminded her of when she used to doodle her name, a heart, and the name of whatever middle school boy she liked at the time but lacked the courage to tell how she felt about him.

Martha typed the password and stared at the oversized monitor. She found the file Oji wanted exactly where he said it would be. *I guess he wants me to email it to him,* she thought. She clicked on the internet browser icon, and an existing window with at least fifty open tabs popped up. She gasped as she laid eyes on a vintage sapphire and diamond engagement ring in the center of the page. *Oh dear, I wasn't supposed to see this.* She immediately minimized the window. Then she remembered why she was using Oji's computer.

"Email! I have to send the projections document to Oji by email," she said aloud.

Martha's heart raced. She opened a new internet tab and logged in to her email, but her fingers jittered so much that it took twice as long as it should have.

When her phone chirped, Martha jumped in the office chair. *Everything ok?* Oji asked.

She hurried to send the document. Then she replied to Oji's text: *Sent via email. Need anything else?*

As she waited, she tapped her fingers on the top of the desk to distract from the urge to look at the ring again.

A minute later, *Received. Luv u babe.*

Love you too!!! Martha replied, and she added an emoji blowing a kiss, inspired by her excitement over the ring. Then she returned her focus to the internet window.

With her hands still jittering, Martha logged out of her email. As she closed the internet tab that she had just used, the vintage ring reappeared. *It won't hurt to look. Who could blame me for that? It's right here,* she thought. She scrolled the page to gather details about the ring, being extra careful not to click anything or interrupt the other tabs Oji had left open. *He knows my taste so well.* She looked at the ring again. The stunning platinum ring featured a cushion-cut sapphire weighing almost five carats framed by nearly three carats of similarly shaped but smaller diamonds. *That's enough. I really need to stop,* Martha thought before taking in another detail. But she was curious about the price, so she read a few more lines.

"Available upon request," she said aloud. And with that, she minimized the internet window and locked the computer. The only thing left to do was wait for the ring.

A MIXTURE OF butterflies and hunger swirled in Martha's belly as she waited for Oji to finish cooking dinner. Her mouth watered at the smell of french bread warming in the oven. Despite a full view of the six-burner range from the banquette table in the corner of her kitchen, Martha didn't try to figure out the contents of the large copper pot that commanded Oji's attention or the one sitting on the rear burner with a large colander on top. He had texted her that afternoon to say he would drive straight from the Atlanta airport to her house, where he would cook dinner before she got home from work. She knew that pasta was a given, as it was the only thing Oji knew how to cook, and he didn't have the patience to try one of the dozens of cookbooks that filled the long shelves on her kitchen wall.

Martha wanted to be surprised anyway—by the menu and by receiving the ring she had seen on Oji's computer the day prior. It was anyone's guess whether the ring's presence on the open internet browser tab meant Oji was thinking about purchasing that particular one, was in the process of buying it, or perhaps was even comparing it to another that was already in his possession. But she couldn't stop thinking about the ring, and she hoped to receive that exact one. She longed for a silver lining in her engagement saga.

The degree of surprise she would feign would depend on whether the ring came before or after they talked about

Oji's parents. And since Oji usually ordered takeout when it was his turn to be responsible for dinner, Martha liked that he was trying to make the evening special. Having missed lunch because her morning clinical duties ran over, she would have usually been hangry by the time she got home to find Oji still cooking. But she was saved by the treat she picked up on the way home: her second hazelnut latte of the week. She couldn't risk ruining the night. Too much was at stake.

Oji looked effortlessly handsome in a wrinkled linen button-up shirt and jeans, but he didn't look as good as the plate of steamy fettuccine noodles, tossed greens, and bread he placed in front of Martha. "Thank you. This looks yummy," she said.

He quickly returned to the table with his plate and sat across from Martha. When he stretched his arm across the table for Martha's hand and bowed his head, she followed suit.

"We thank You for this food, and we pray that You will bless it and every person in need who played a role in bringing it to our table," Oji said. "We thank You for Your grace and mercy over this past week, and we pray for Your guidance as we seek to find our way forward. Amen."

Please, God, with special emphasis on guidance as we seek to find our way forward, Martha thought. "Amen," she said. She opened her eyes, and they met Oji's. She smiled and lingered a second longer before releasing his hand.

"Hungry?" he asked. "I hope it tastes okay."

"Let's see," Martha replied. She twirled her fork in the pile of pasta, loading the noodles. Then she stabbed the plate twice to secure them while picking up a broccoli floret and red pepper. She dragged her fork through the creamy sauce pooled on the plate and lifted it to her mouth. "Mmm," she said as she chewed. "You seasoned it well. It's got a kick!"

"You've taught me well, or maybe it's because I used a very fancy copper pot." He chuckled.

"I'd like to be flattered, but since you don't own a complete set of pots, it's not hard to impress you," she replied, amused by the contrast between Oji's paltry cookware and her ever-expanding collection: aluminum, stainless steel, copper, cast iron, and even clay.

Because she had struggled with sharing since early childhood, it had taken Martha a few visits to warm up to having Oji in her space, especially in her kitchen. But she could understand why he preferred to cook at her house.

"I love that you feel comfortable in my home," she continued. "We've had a few bumps to get here, but we're good now."

"Thanks, babe. I'm glad we can joke about it now. I was so stressed about that pot. I thought we were done!"

"Whew! We came close," Martha joked.

"Over a pot," Oji said with a sheepish grin.

Martha giggled. "Yep, and I make no apologies about it."

Quite the contrary, Martha had discovered that she loved Oji after he ruined one of her copper pots. Never one to pass up a chance to shop for antiques, Martha had stumbled across an entire set of copper pots at an expansive estate sale in Danbury, Connecticut, after attending a medical conference in New Haven. She painstakingly cleaned and polished seven of the eight pieces on her own, allowing Naomi to guide her through caring for only the first one.

When Oji used one of the precious pots adorning her kitchen wall instead of the stainless steel ones she used every day, she didn't think twice—until she fell asleep on the sofa after dinner and awakened to the sound of her dishwasher. The copper pot Oji had used for dinner was inside instead of being hand-washed as required. The pot ended up significantly dull and discolored, but Martha discovered that she had patience for him that she had lacked in her previous relationships. Instead of hurling hurtful words and accusations, she asked questions and listened. She wasn't sure how this particular evening would play out, but she hoped that same love would carry them through the much-needed conversation.

"So, how was your day?" Oji asked.

"Nothing special. I'd rather hear about your trip. How'd it go?" Martha asked.

"I'm not sure," he said with a sigh. "I'd hoped meeting with me again in person would convince the investor and his team to move forward, but they're not fully on board yet. They said they're impressed with my previous projects and revenue, but they still want to vet the details of this project more. I can't help feeling they're making me jump through hoops they don't make other developers jump through, but you know how that goes."

"I understand."

"It happens all the time. That's why I couldn't believe I left the document you had to send me. And thanks again for that."

"Well, the past few days have been challenging. Don't be too hard on yourself. Plus, I was happy to help," Martha said between bites.

Oji shuffled the salad on his plate. "I also highlighted my success with the redevelopment near the hospital. They recognized that we cleared the zoning hurdles pretty easily and are finishing ahead of schedule, but that wasn't enough. They still want more assurances on a project that's a moderate risk, at most. But we'll see how it goes. I should know more by the end of the month."

Martha wanted to make Oji feel better, but she wasn't sure what she could say. Although she had never owned property on her own, much less a commercial-development company, she had experienced what it was like to have to work harder to get access to professional opportunities despite being far more qualified than her competition. And there were no magic words to make that feeling go away. "You've put a lot of work into this. I really hope it works out. I'll keep praying about it, but let me know if there's anything I can do to make you feel better."

"You always listen and encourage me. What more could I ask for?" Oji said with a grin. "But I've talked enough about myself."

"I asked. I wanted to know," Martha said, her voice teeming with concern.

"And I appreciate that, babe. But we're long overdue for talking about us."

"True," she said, softening her voice. "Well, would you at least eat some of this good food you cooked to butter me up?" she asked, smiling.

He laughed. "You picked up on that, huh?"

Martha nodded vigorously while she tore another piece of bread from the loaf and placed it on her plate.

"But I'm happy to see you're enjoying it," Oji continued as he looked at Martha's half-empty plate.

She blushed. "I sure am, and I'm proud of it." Then she loaded her fork with more noodles.

As Martha took another bite of pasta, the playful look on Oji's face faded. "On a more serious note, how are you feeling about everything?" he asked, with his tone shifting to match his words.

Here we go, Martha thought. She rested her fork across the top of her plate and took a quick drink of mango juice. "That's a big question," she said, placing the tall tumbler on the table. "This feels nice. You know, spending time together and talking. But this is the first real conversation we've had all week. Don't you think that's odd since we're supposed to be spending our lives together?"

"You're right. I should've made time," Oji said, nodding.

"Are you just saying that because you think I'm upset?"

He shifted in his seat. "No . . . But . . . aren't you upset?"

"I was at first. But now I'm more hurt . . . and confused."

Oji's eyes widened. "Confused? About what? You still want to marry me, right?" he asked in a panicked voice.

"It worries me that you didn't prioritize making time to talk to me. You're the first person I want to talk to when something happens. But when your dad was missing, you dealt with it with your mom. We barely talked."

He wrinkled his face as he pushed his plate away, which remained as full as it was when he brought it to the table. "But you told me about the Silver Alert. I wouldn't have known what to call it or what it involved if I didn't have you helping me figure things out."

"Yes, I suggested it, but I didn't know what you decided to do," Martha said, choosing her words carefully as not to let on that she'd heard Oji's conversation with his mother. "You never called me back to tell me what your mom said or if she agreed to the Silver Alert. Then, hours later, you called to tell me your father was found in Atlanta. Do you have any idea what it was like waiting? *I* was worried about your dad too. And I needed to know how *you* were doing. I needed to know if you were safe. Didn't . . . Didn't you think about how I might be feeling, especially after what happened to my parents?" she asked, her voice trembling at the end.

"*Your* parents . . . The weather," Oji said as the oversight registered on his face. He moved to the other side of the table, sat on the edge of the banquette seat, and put his arm around Martha's shoulder. She scooted over to make space for him.

"I'm so sorry, babe," he said as he pulled Martha closer. "The weather was fine when we first headed back to Macon, so when it started raining, I was just trying to get home to see if my dad was there. Then everything took off so fast and I didn't stop to think. I'll do better. Please forgive me."

Martha laid her head on Oji's shoulder. "Yes, of course. And I really appreciate hearing that. I feel like we would be okay if it were just the two of us, but we both have families—very involved families. We have to figure out how to do this." She wiped her eyes.

"It's not that hard. We'll figure it out," he said confidently.

She lifted her head from his shoulder and leaned away to make eye contact. "No, it's not that easy, Oji. Everything isn't just going to fall into place. Like you always say, we need to be on the same page."

"We *are* on the same page," he replied, his tone unchanged.

"Oji, come on," Martha said, thinking about the conversation she overhead between Oji and his mother but refraining from mentioning it.

"What?" he asked, pulling her closer, but she resisted.

Martha scooted several inches on the banquette seat until she faced Oji. She leaned back and folded her arms. "Okay. So, what's the plan for your dad?" she asked coolly.

"He has a follow-up appointment with his primary care doctor on Thursday, and—"

"And when were you planning to tell me that if I hadn't asked about it?"

"I figured it would come up."

"Well, it's come up now. Do you want my advice on what you should ask during the appointment?"

Oji inched toward her. He looked her in the eye and reached for her hand, slowly interlocking his fingers with hers. "Of course. We're in this together. I want your input and expertise every step of the way."

Martha fought the urge to smile. "You are always so smooth, Oji Greenwald. But I'm not letting you wiggle your way out of this." Her voice softened as she spoke.

"What are you talking about? We're just having a conversation. I'm just trying for us to be on—"

"On the same page. Mm-hmm. Yeah, I know."

He smiled. "So, you'll tell me what I should ask at my dad's appointment?"

"Sure, but what about your mom?"

"What do you mean?"

Martha locked eyes with Oji with her eyebrows raised, but she didn't speak. She embraced the silence as a tool.

After a few seconds, Oji gave in. "I'll handle my mom."

"So, are you ready to admit that your mom has a problem with me? Can we talk about that, too?"

Oji let out a deep sigh. "My mom is complicated. It's not that she has a problem with you. She's just not accustomed to sharing me."

And apparently she's not accustomed to shared decision-making, Martha thought, again recalling the conversation she overheard. But she kept quiet. She wanted to see what more Oji would say.

"It'll get better with time. Just be patient with her. She'll come around."

"I'll try, but I'm very concerned. She hasn't said anything to me about the engagement. Did she see the proposal, or was she looking for your dad? She does know that we're engaged, right?"

"Yes, she knows," Oji said, rubbing his forehead with his free hand. "We've just been spending time with my dad. We haven't really talked about anything else."

Martha shook her head as she released Oji's hand. "We've been engaged an entire week, and y'all haven't talked about it. Are you sure she knows? And why haven't you said something to her?"

"Babe, we're not like your family. We don't talk about everything. She asked if we had a date yet, and I said no. That was it. She wouldn't think of not showing up to the wedding or anything like that."

"Not showing up? It's that bad? The fact those words came out of your mouth says a lot."

"It's just an expression. You said you wanted to talk, so that's what I'm doing. Look, it's been a long week. I'm trying my best to help us reset and—"

"Get on the same page," they said in unison. It cut the tension that had built between them, and they both laughed uncomfortably.

"I don't think either of us wants to fight, but we shouldn't brush this under the rug. What do you think about starting premarital counseling?" she asked.

"Makes sense. I can't argue with that. And to show you how much you mean to me, I'll even find a counselor. If that's okay?"

Martha squinted at him. "Really?"

Oji nodded as he leaned toward her.

"Deal," she said, bending forward until their lips met in a sweet kiss.

Chapter Five

End of June

Although she wasn't a fan of getting her hands dirty, Martha had never been happier to find herself in a noisy construction zone. She liked making her sister walk around with her while wearing the teal hard hats Martha bought to match the planned accent color in the interior design at The Alabaster Plate, Mary's new restaurant inside Oji's redevelopment project next door to the hospital. One perk of partnering with her sister on the teaching kitchen was having the option to use part of their semimonthly meeting time to check in on the renovation progress. With the crew having just moved on to the hallway that led to the teaching kitchen, the sisters had some privacy to chat.

"We've come a long way," Martha said pensively as she examined the freshly completed drywall in the dining area.

"The build-out is going far more smoothly than I expected. Not that I'm getting preferential treatment or anything," Mary teased.

"I assure you that Oji runs all his projects efficiently. He goes the extra mile because that's just the kind of businessman he is. Not that I'm biased or anything," Martha said with a playful grin. Then her tone shifted to a more serious one. "But I meant the construction and also how far you and I have come. This restaurant is a physical representation of our progress."

When Martha had heard about the plans to redevelop the abandoned building near the hospital, she was certain it was the perfect place for her own high-concept restaurant, which would have a teaching kitchen for her community outreach work. But instead Mary was chosen for the space because of her success with Alabaster Lunch Box, her newly established restaurant in Edin. Martha initially had a tough time dealing with the decision, but she eventually came around when offered the opportunity to partner with Mary for the teaching kitchen. Given the sisters' history, only time would tell how the partnership would shake out. So far, they were off to a promising start.

"Being in walking distance of each other at home and work felt like a lot of pressure at first, but we worked out the kinks fairly quickly," Mary said. "It's nice now. I like working with you."

"Me too," Martha said. Then she let out an uncomfortable chuckle.

"What?" Mary asked.

"What if it's just because right now you only drop in for meetings and check-ins? It may be different when the restaurant opens and you start rotating between both restaurants and spend the entire day here. We'll see how you feel then . . . and how *I* feel too."

"I made it through working with your boyfriend, now fiancé, as the developer. The old Martha would've tortured me throughout the ordeal. You'd have blown through my boundaries without thinking twice about them. And you'd have popped up every time Oji was here—to see him and annoy me. But you haven't done either of those things. You're evolving. We'll be okay." While Mary was blunt, she wasn't wrong, so it still sounded reassuring.

Martha nodded. "You're probably right, and Oji will be done with his part soon. Speaking of which, have you confirmed the date for the grand opening?"

"Not yet. I'm stuck. I'm firm on the general timing, which is mid-August, but I'm still sorting through the best way for us to approach it. You know, since we have to show off both the restaurant and the teaching kitchen. Until I can figure that out, I can't nail down a date," Mary said with exasperation in her voice.

"I've been thinking about that too. What if we held two separate events? That way we could each do what we want and not feel constrained by the need to . . . uh . . . compromise. I mean, of course we would still coordinate our plans," Martha said hesitantly.

"How genius!" Mary exclaimed. "We've been so deliberate about collaborating in a respectful and peaceful way that we didn't think about the most obvious thing: having two separate events. That allows us to have the appropriate autonomy but still be thoughtful about how what one of us does complements the other."

"That's what I said."

Mary laughed. "I know. It just sounded better coming out of my mouth."

Martha chuckled. "I'm so relieved that you get it. I was nervous about bringing it up."

"I could tell. But if we're going to work together, we have to be good about saying what needs to be said . . . So I'm going to do it too."

"Uh-oh. Did I say something that offended you?" Martha asked, bracing herself.

"No, I'm sorry it came across that way. I was just thinking about Jasmine. You've never brought her by when I've been on-site, and I think you'd have mentioned if you two came some other time. Am I missing something?"

"You're correct. I've been busy, that's all," Martha said, looking away from her sister. She scanned the room for something that she could pretend caught her attention. Finding nothing, she paced around the area where they stood.

"Okay, why didn't you just bring her to this meeting? That would've been the efficient thing to do. We agreed ahead of time to start here and then walk to your office to go through the agenda. Every time you don't invite Jasmine to meet with us, you create more work by having to update her on what we discussed. Isn't your motto 'Work smarter, not harder'?"

"Thanks for reminding me. I'll add it to my to-do list before the next meeting. Promise," Martha said hurriedly.

Mary walked along with her sister, staring at her. "You didn't answer the question. What's the real issue?"

"It's not essential for what Jasmine does. If it were, we'd have had her at the meetings already. Once the teaching kitchen is further along, she'll have full access to the space," Martha explained.

"This is not about her work. Well, not directly," Mary said. "But I'm sure I don't need to lecture you about making your staff feel included, getting their buy-in, and all that stuff you've studied in your professional development programs. This is about keeping Jasmine at arm's length. You're going overboard with it."

"Jasmine is my old high school classmate."

"No, stop right there," Mary said. She stood still, and Martha followed suit.

Martha hadn't seen this side of her sister in months—since Martha attended Mary's counseling session at the high point of the strain in their relationship. Martha couldn't let herself backtrack down that road. She was trying to grow, even if it wasn't at the pace everyone wanted, so this time she ceased moving, looked her sister in the eyes, and listened.

"Jasmine was your friend. There's a difference," Mary said. "Mom and Dad didn't let us sleep over at just anybody's house, nor did they let random people come to ours. And as far as I know, you and Jasmine never had a falling out. Y'all just drifted apart. This is not how we treat the people we let into our lives."

"I respect your professional decisions, so why can't you respect mine?" Martha asked.

"Don't you see, Martha? Because we're not talking about a professional issue. I know you well enough to know that this is personal."

"I can see you're coming from a place of love. But just please give me the opportunity to work through this in my own way."

"I understand," Mary replied. "But I enjoy seeing Jasmine, and I could tell from our last meeting that *you* enjoy her too. It was like old times, when Mom and Dad forced you to let me tag along with you and Jasmine. You're comfortable with her like you are with our family members. And everyone knows you don't let your guard down easily."

"There are reasons for everything, Mary. Give me some time. Please, let's drop this."

"Okay, but don't get mad if you come to my cottage one day and Jasmine and I are hanging out," Mary said coolly.

Martha shot her sister a look that could melt ice.

"All right, all right," Mary said. "But maybe you should ask yourself why you're getting all sensitive about me building a friendship with Jasmine. You're already dealing with some heavy things right now, and I don't want to add stress to your life, so I'll respect your decision, like you asked. But I'm here if you decide you want to talk about what's really going on."

A STORM IS coming, Martha thought as she looked up at the gray clouds in the sky. Drifting back and forth in the egg-shaped basket swing on Naomi's back porch gave Martha a few more minutes to work through the nervousness that had built up in the preceding two weeks as she contemplated talking to her aunt about her engagement. She leaned her head against the headrest as a light breeze blew in, relishing the momentary escape while she waited for Naomi and Nicholas to join her.

With the swing's seat cushions coming up high enough to function as armrests, Martha felt cozy as she rocked. The swing itself had changed over the twenty-three years since she and Mary moved in with Naomi after their parents died, but the space remained her safe haven. From the first one Martha remembered—a white traditional wooden bench with spindles—to a fancier one made of cypress with a rolled back and contoured seat, she so often fought to have the swing to herself that Naomi had let Martha choose the current iteration. She selected a swing chair with a rattan wicker frame that had room for only one person.

"Are you sure you don't want dinner? We haven't put it away yet," Naomi asked as she closed the french door and stepped onto the porch.

"No, but I'm quite curious about this surprise dessert Nicholas keeps talking about. I can't imagine you had time to bake anything."

Naomi sat on the oversized rattan sofa while Martha kept swinging.

"You'll see in a minute. All he could talk about on the plane ride home was doing something special for you," Naomi said. "He should've been right behind me. If he doesn't show up soon, I'll have to run in to make sure he isn't standing in the kitchen eating all of it." She chuckled.

"You two are adorable," Martha said as a gust of wind blew in. "I probably should've given you a day or two to adjust to being back in town before I came over, but I couldn't wait to hear about your time in Bora-Bora. It really sounds like you had a wonderful honeymoon."

"It was absolutely lovely. Soon you'll be planning yours, too. But if you hadn't come here after work, we'd have certainly gone to your house tonight. I didn't have much of a chance to talk to you and Oji at the wedding, so I've been anxious to hear how you're feeling about being engaged. Oh, something just occurred to me!"

An ominous feeling came over Martha. *Uh-oh, what could it be already? I haven't said anything yet.*

"I must give you Valerie's information. Did you meet her at the wedding? She's been Nicholas's travel agent for years and has become like part of his family. She planned our trip to a tee. You and Oji should use her too!"

Martha breathed a sigh of relief. "Yes, I remember her. I'd love that," she said as she spotted Nicholas through the french door. She got down from the swing and hurried to the door, opening it in time for Nicholas to walk through without slowing down. Martha's face lit up when she saw the contents of the tray he carried. "Ice cream!" she exclaimed with childlike excitement.

"Watch your step," Naomi said as Nicholas crossed the threshold onto the porch.

"Thanks, honey," Nicholas said. "Looks like it's gonna rain soon."

Martha followed Nicholas to the round terrazzo coffee table, where he placed the tray in front of Naomi. Martha plucked a long-handled spoon from the tray and studied the three crystal bowls to determine which had the most ice cream.

Nicholas pushed a bowl toward Martha. "This one is yours. I added a little extra to it in honor of your engagement. The flavor is called 'bride's cake.'"

"Oh! This is the sweetest! You don't know how much this means to me," Martha said, blushing.

Nicholas sat next to Naomi. He placed a cloth dinner napkin on the table in front of the chair closest to Martha. "Here you go. Try it and tell us what you think."

Martha picked up the napkin from the table, but her excitement wouldn't let her wait to drape it across her lap. She dug into the frozen mound, scooping up one of the many chunks of cake that dotted the surface. The spoon darted to her mouth, where her taste buds delighted in luscious bursts of amaretto cream cheese icing and almondy ice cream with the soft cake.

"This is delicious," Martha said before filling her spoon again.

Nicholas picked up the two bowls and handed one to Naomi. "It's my new favorite flavor. Naomi would only let me buy a pint. She doesn't trust me with the half-gallon size," he said, playfully rolling his eyes.

"I'm just trying to keep you around as long as possible," Naomi said, digging into her ice cream.

Nicholas turned to Naomi as he lifted a spoonful of ice cream to his mouth. "Thank you," he said with a wink. His mingled gray hair and beard had grown woolier since the wedding, a contrast to his usual clean-cut appearance, but he still looked sharp.

Naomi smiled, then turned to Martha. "So, you were going to tell me how you're feeling about everything."

"Would you like me to give you two some privacy? I can take my ice cream inside," Nicholas said as he rose to his feet.

"Please sit. I'd rather like it if you stayed, if you don't mind," Martha said. She had come to rely on Nicholas's perspective, and she hoped he also might impart his wisdom to her. But first she had a question that required his input.

Nicholas nodded. "I'm happy to stay."

"You could probably tell that I was shocked by Oji's proposal. You were both so gracious about it. Did it bother you that he proposed at your reception? Please be honest, and don't hold back at all."

Naomi shook her head. "Not one bit. We assumed a proposal was imminent. While we didn't expect it to happen there, neither of us had an issue with it. But how do you feel about it?"

"*That's* what we care about," Nicholas said over a light rumble of thunder.

"I thought he'd do something more romantic and thoughtful, so I'm disappointed. But I'd never tell him that," Martha said.

Nicholas leaned forward. "What if Oji asks? Would you tell him then?"

"Probably not," Martha blurted out. "It would hurt his feelings."

"Honesty and communication are essential if you want to have a solid relationship. Your aunt probably thinks I'm too honest sometimes," Nicholas said with a light laugh. "But that's how we were able to get to this place of knowing each other so quickly."

Naomi nodded. "And it helped us work together, especially when Ruth didn't approve of our relationship initially. I don't know how else we could've supported each other to work through things with her. It was really rough for a season, but we made it through."

"That's another problem Oji and I have," Martha said.

Naomi frowned. "Are you about to say that Ruth is a problem for you and Oji? From everything I've seen, she's very happy for you. We just talked about it when she came home for lunch."

"I meant that we have a family member who doesn't seem

to approve, but I was talking about Mrs. Greenwald. I don't think she likes me, and she has a problem anytime I open my mouth. She hasn't acknowledged that Oji and I are engaged. Well, not to me anyway. But Ruth probably told you that and also mentioned that I asked for advice about how to handle her." She was still embarrassed about needing to go to Ruth for help about dealing with Eve, and she felt betrayed that she would speak to anyone about it without her permission. But instead of flying off the handle like she would've in the past, Martha quietly stewed.

"Eve . . . Now, that makes more sense. The jet lag must be getting to me. I should've let you finish what you were saying instead of cutting in. I'm sorry," Naomi said.

"That's okay," Martha replied softly while gathering herself after making conclusions about Ruth so quickly. *Ruth was right about me still having more work to do.*

"But Ruth didn't say anything about Eve causing trouble or giving you advice about it," Naomi said coolly. "She did update us about Adam. Nicholas was aware that something was amiss during the reception, but he didn't tell me until Ruth texted that Adam was safe at home."

Martha lowered her eyes. She was ashamed of herself for taking a step backward by jumping to conclusions about Ruth, and Naomi's measured response made her feel even worse. "I apologize for misunderstanding you," she said. Then she glanced at Nicholas and quickly looked away.

"On the positive side, I'm glad to hear that you asked Ruth for advice," Nicholas said. "From what I've seen, everybody in our family is on your side, even Ruth." His face was stern and his voice calm, evoking memories of the time Martha was called to the principal's office in elementary school for talking back to the cafeteria monitor who tried to make her eat her vegetables.

"Especially Ruth," Naomi said. "She suggested that we invite Eve over this weekend for tea. I assumed her intention was just a friendly session to get to know one another better and begin planning for the wedding, but I see she's actually taken a move from my playbook."

"Oh really? Ruth didn't say anything to me about that, but I love the idea," Martha said. "And thank you both for holding me accountable. You're right that she is always looking out for me."

"She wanted to run it by me first, since it would be most appropriate if I hosted. I'm still sticking to my policy of not meddling in everyone's business, but I will never shirk my responsibility to protect our family," Naomi said.

"I like the way you fixed that up. I'm still learning the ropes, so I may need a little tutoring. But that sounds like a double standard to me," Nicholas teased, chuckling.

"Hush!" Naomi said with a laugh.

Martha chuckled too as she dabbed her eyes with her napkin. "Thank you for lightening the mood, Nicholas. I needed to laugh. I don't know what I would do without the two of you. I missed you while you were away," she said, rotating her head between Naomi and Nicholas.

Nicholas nodded. "We missed you too. We both did," he said. Then he nudged Naomi.

Martha gave the couple a curious look. "What is *that* about?"

"The bride's family usually throws an engagement party. Nicholas and I started making a list on the long plane ride. But when we talked with Ruth earlier today, she said we should probably check in with you to see if you want one before we got too far into planning."

"You shouldn't have been thinking of me on your honeymoon!" Martha said.

"Why not? It's important to us to make this time special for you," Naomi said.

"And I missed out on all the father-of-the-bride stuff with Ruth, so I'm looking forward to whatever you will allow me to do for you," Nicholas added.

"Y'all are too good to me, but it's complicated," Martha said hesitantly.

Naomi inched forward in her seat. "What do you mean?" she said.

"Well, I don't have an engagement ring. And I don't know when it's coming. I'm reluctant to call attention to the engagement without it. I mean, with the reputations our families have in the community, what would people think?"

Nicholas sighed. "It doesn't matter what everyone thinks. Worrying about that will lead to a lifetime of heartache."

"I wondered if it bothered you that Oji didn't have a ring when he proposed," Naomi said.

"And two weeks later, still no sign of a ring, except for the one I saw on his computer," Martha blurted out. After the words escaped from her lips, she covered her mouth with her hand. She hadn't meant to let that last part slip, but she caved under the pressure of keeping it to herself.

"Cadence Martha Gardin! Don't tell me you went snooping for your ring!" Naomi exclaimed.

Nicholas shook his head quietly.

"No, ma'am. I stumbled across it. Oji asked me to find something for him on his computer."

Naomi leaned her arm on the sofa's armrest and put her chin on her hand. "And you just *happened* to see it? Seriously?"

"Really. I didn't go looking for it. I clicked on an open tab to email a document to Oji," Martha declared.

"Okay. Maybe I jumped the gun, but I know you," Naomi said. "Don't get any ideas. Your relationship should be based on trust. And snooping does not promote trust."

"You're right. I've thought that same thing. It's just that I have so many other pressures right now, and I would have one less thing to worry about if he would just give me a ring."

"You really should talk with him about how you're feeling," Nicholas said.

"How would I bring that up? I wouldn't know where to start," Martha asked, wrinkling her nose.

"You say something like, 'Can we talk about how I'm feeling about the proposal? I was a little disappointed that it happened at my aunt's wedding.' Or, 'I'm excited to marry you, but it feels weird to start celebrating before I have a ring,'" Naomi said.

Martha folded her arms and leaned back in her chair. "I couldn't do that," she said emphatically.

"Then maybe you aren't as ready to get married as you think you are," Naomi said.

"No, I'm ready," Martha said, waving her hands in the air. "I just don't want to hurt Oji's feelings."

"That's the second time you've said that," Nicholas said.

"It can't be your excuse every time you don't want to talk about something difficult. Being in a healthy relationship means you have to figure out how to talk to your partner about tough things. You can't bury everything that you don't want to deal with, Martha. Issues fester and explode if you don't talk about them."

"I hear you. I'll think about it," Martha said.

"Are you and Oji planning to do premarital counseling?" Nicholas asked. "It helped *us*. I wish it had been around before I got married the first time."

"Me too," Naomi said. "We don't want you to rush to get married before you're ready. We want you and Oji to put your best foot forward."

"I agree that counseling would be helpful. Oji is looking into it. I hope that gives you some reassurance about our relationship. We haven't talked about a date yet, but I'd like it to be this year."

"We're always here if you want to talk, even if you want us to just listen," Nicholas said.

"That's right. I'm getting better at just listening," Naomi said.

"Y'all are so good to me. It's really a blessing to have you in my . . . life," Martha said. Her voice cracked a little with the last word she spoke.

"This is a happy time, but I can imagine it's hard not having your parents here," Naomi said, her voice shaking.

Nicholas rubbed Naomi's arm.

Martha exhaled slowly through her mouth and shook her head as she fought to hold in her tears, but she broke with the first word she uttered. "Yes," she said, sobbing softly as a light rain began to fall.

Naomi's eyes filled as she stood and walked over to Martha. She held her niece as they both cried.

"I miss them so much . . . And it rained . . . while Mr. Greenwald . . . was missing . . . just like when my . . ." Martha said between sobs. Her pain wouldn't allow her to put words to the wound in her heart.

Tears streamed down Naomi's face as Martha's sobs grew louder. "I'm sorry you had to go through that, sweetie. I'm so, so sorry. And I'm sorry I wasn't there to help you through it."

MARTHA WALKED SLOWLY across the empty grass lot behind The Alabaster Plate, scribbling words in her notebook that she would likely not be able to decipher after her meeting with M.J. As he assessed the land, M.J. launched into an impromptu lecture about composting and soil temperature. Martha couldn't keep up with the technical agricultural terms he used or his strides, and M.J. didn't seem to notice. As she struggled to remember his last point, he veered toward the sunny area where she planned to grow herbs in raised beds.

The sides of her super-sized straw hat flopped against Martha's upper arms as she power walked to catch up with M.J. With each step she took, she felt like an elegant bird flapping its wings to take off in flight, until the brim of her hat unrolled and drooped over her face. As she lifted the long brim with the back of her hand, he turned around and burst out laughing.

As he got closer to her, his golden-brown skin glistened

in the sunlight. "You're the only person I know who would wear a hat like that out here," he said when he reached her. "You look like you're about to pose for a photo on a white sandy beach, not plan a culinary garden in red soil in downtown Macon, Georgia."

"You told me to bring a hat for the sun. I may have gone a little overboard, but I look good, so who cares?" Martha said. She struck a pose to annoy her cousin.

M.J. pulled his baseball cap further down over his boyish face, exposing more of the curly hair at the back of his head. "You, the Queen of Sheba, overboard? You would never. Wait. Don't move. Let me get my camera," he said in a deadpan manner.

"Ha, ha, ha," Martha replied flippantly.

M.J. and Martha never missed an opportunity to tease each other, usually endeavoring to outdo each other. With their eleven-year age difference and having grown up in close proximity on the Gardin family estate, M.J. was more like her little brother than her second cousin. And with the demands of his doctoral studies in agribusiness, she didn't get to see him as much as she liked. Their outdoor meetup provided a special opportunity for one-on-one time as well as the agricultural insight Martha lacked.

"I was just expecting you to give me some gardening tips, not a whole speech. You'll do great at your thesis defense," she said. She handed M.J. her notebook and pen. "Hold this."

"You're just used to bossing me around."

"True, but I listen to you when you know what you're talking about." She grabbed the sides of her hat with both hands. "So far, that only includes your thoughts on the latest hip-hop beef and anything that grows from the soil. You have a natural green thumb, like your dad." She loosely rolled the front portion of her hat and pushed firmly on her forehead to hold it in place while creating a large enough brim to shield her face from the sun.

He smiled. "Let's go this way," he said as he pointed to the area where the raised beds would be placed. "And I'd like to bring up one more thing, please, ma'am."

Martha extended her right hand, and M.J. placed her notebook and pen in it. "Sure. You think I need more raised beds?" she asked as she quickly turned to resume her note-taking.

He looked at her quizzically. "No, I didn't mean about the garden. I have one more addition to the things you consider to be my area of expertise."

Surprise registered on her face. "Okay. I'm all ears."

"When you were trying to kick my mom out of Gardin Family Enterprises earlier this year, I wish you'd talked to me about it."

Martha stood still. "Oh, I wasn't expecting that."

This time M.J. stopped too. "My program is teaching me to blend my agriculture knowledge with the principles of economics, business, and management, so I definitely have opinions about how my mom is running the business since my dad died. I happen to agree with her. But whether I liked the direction she was taking the company or not, I could've told you that all her plans align with what my dad wanted. And that could've saved you and our whole family a lot of trouble." He spoke in a straight manner with no emotion, just as before, but the context told Martha that he was not joking.

From childhood, M.J. possessed a professorial demeanor that made him seem wise beyond his years, but Martha struggled at times to take the baby of the family seriously. In a T-shirt and Nike Dunks that he described as being the color of asparagus, he looked as comfortable in Martha's culinary garden as he had in the peanut fields as a small boy. And although he still dressed in the same daily uniform he wore as a teenager—a graphic-less solid-color T-shirt, baggy jeans, and Nikes that he chose based on his mood—his comments were a sobering reminder that he was indeed all grown up.

Martha was used to thinking quickly on her feet with M.J., but not this time. She struggled to pull her thoughts together in light of this new development in their relationship. "I didn't want to pull you into the family turmoil. You didn't deserve to have to deal with all that, especially with school. Plus, you were in Senegal on your exchange program until a couple of weeks ago. I didn't want to bother you with all that."

"I'm not a kid, Martha. And even when I was younger, I was vividly aware of the conflicts in our family. My dad and I had some long talks over the years. I finally decided it was time I let you know I'm not clueless about these things."

"I'm not sure what to say. I want to apologize, but I don't want you to feel like my words are empty."

M.J. folded his arms across his chest and pursed his lips as he scanned Martha's face like he had at the grass lot a few minutes prior. "I've known you my whole life. I can tell when you're being sincere."

She wondered if he realized he was so much like Beau,

not just because of their physical similarities—those had been obvious since M.J. was a baby—but also his mannerisms and the cadence of his voice. *How could I not have noticed this before?* she thought.

"I should've been more respectful to you and your mom," she said. "I've asked for her forgiveness, and now I'm asking for yours. I'm working on being better. I have a lot of years to unpack. I'm sorry."

"Thank you. And I forgive you. I would hug you, but it's too hot out here for all that. Then again, you're probably fine, with that parasol you're wearing on your head."

Martha laughed as she playfully smacked M.J. on the arm. "It's nice having you home." She dabbed at the corners of her eyes, attempting to be discreet.

"Are you crying? I heard that you cry about everything these days. They weren't exaggerating. Oji has really done a number on you, hasn't he?"

She playfully smacked him again, but she gave a little more force.

"Ouch!" M.J. said, wincing.

Martha shook her head. "That didn't hurt."

"No, it didn't. But you aren't the only dramatic person in our family. We've all got a touch of it in our own way."

"No lies told. But hey, since you're a fount of wisdom today, may I ask you a question?"

"Sure. Shoot!"

"You and Oji seem to get along, but you haven't really said what you think of him."

M.J. clasped his hands behind his back and briefly looked up at the sky before he spoke. "I like Oji. He's a sneakerhead like me, so we relate on that level. But he seems . . . uh, how would I describe it . . . strategic. He seems very strategic."

Martha squinted. "What do you mean by that?"

"It's simple. He's strategic just like you are," he said without hesitation.

"And that's a bad thing?" she asked, wrinkling her face.

"Not necessarily. Maybe I'm wrong." He hunched his shoulders. "But it seems to me you're both playing chess. As long as you don't forget that you're not the only one playing, you should be fine."

"We may have some similar qualities . . . *Maybe,*" she said with emphasis on the last word. "But I point out things that he misses all the time."

M.J. looked down at Martha and patted her on the shoulder. "If you say so. Just be careful. That's all I ask."

"Of course I will."

ALTHOUGH MARTHA INITIALLY balked at Naomi's insistence on using place cards for what should've been a casual Sunday afternoon gathering to help welcome Eve into the Gardin women's circle, it was turning out to be a brilliant strategy to address the misalignment between Martha and her future mother-in-law. Sitting at the head of Naomi's dining room table with Naomi to her right and Eve to her left, for the first time since Oji proposed, Martha felt like her wedding was actually going to happen.

Naomi stayed true to form in her methodology for the

seating arrangements. A lover of documentaries, she told Martha about one she watched about how seating arrangements can influence a negotiator's success in corporate and legal settings, and she dug up a YouTube video to give Martha a high-level overview. Then she placed herself across from Eve at the rectangular table and, more important, in her direct line of sight. It was a strategy to help Eve conform to the Gardin women's expectations that afternoon. Ruth, assigned to the chair immediately next to Eve, served as Naomi's reinforcement. Mary, who sat next to Naomi, agreed to serve as a buffer for Martha. When Mary asked for clarification of her role, Martha explained it as emotional support, a natural extension of Mary's job as her maid of honor.

Ever the dutiful host, Naomi served a soothing white tea blend in two matching light-green cast iron tea kettles that maintained the desired temperature over warmers at opposite ends of the table. Notes of mango, hibiscus, and ginger delighted the palate with each sip, a nod to Naomi's fruit-themed menu. Two three-tiered porcelain dessert stands—filled with grilled fruit salad baskets, tea cakes, and assorted macarons—dotted the table. The women consumed the tasty treats while they exchanged pleasantries. Eve began by extolling the beauty of the Gardin family estate and extending her thanks for the invitation to attend Naomi and Nicholas's wedding. Then Eve surprised Martha.

"I've been the only woman in our little family for too long. It's about time I had some company," she said.

"We can team up against Oji anytime you like," Martha said playfully. Eve's words sounded earnest enough, but her tone seemed better placed in the work setting than a family environment. It reminded Martha of when her department chair at the hospital announced that she had been selected as the director of the primary care center. But she felt as though the statement put her on the spot to say something endearing to Eve. A lighthearted reply seemed an appropriate way to manage her inability to respond more emotionally given the way Eve had previously treated her.

"I look forward to it, dear," Eve said. Her voice sounded more cheerful, but her professional demeanor did not waver.

Ruth turned to Eve. "M.J. said the same thing when Nicholas came into our lives."

"Isn't that something how God sends what you need just when you need it?" Naomi remarked.

"And that's certainly true when it comes to Martha and Oji. I've never seen Oji happier," Eve said.

Is this the same woman who hasn't spoken to me since her son asked me to marry him, or did Aunt Naomi drop some medicine in Mrs. Greenwald's cup to get her to behave today? Martha jokingly thought as Eve sang Martha's praises. She pushed herself to come up with a response that would be more acceptable to say aloud, but she couldn't think of anything. Thankfully, Mary bought her some time.

"It's amazing how well they fit together," Mary said, looking lovingly at her sister. "I wasn't sure how it would work out when they started dating, especially with the business dynamic of Oji developing the space for my new restaurant. But it's working out beautifully so far."

Martha blushed. "Thank you both for your sweet words. Since neither Mary nor I work for Gardin Family Enterprises, I never imagined we would ever work together. But we've discovered our own approach to keeping business in the family, and it's not lost on me that Oji brought us together in that way through the new restaurant. It all feels very divinely ordered."

Martha was not convinced that Eve fully believed the warm expressions that seemed to gush so effortlessly from her lips, but her words sounded lovely. They were the exact things a bride-to-be yearned to hear from her future mother-in-law, and from Martha's perspective, that was a good start—one she hoped might eventually lead to a tight bond like the one Naomi and Ruth shared.

The easy conversation had softened the blow of Eve's failure to acknowledge the engagement directly to Martha in the three preceding weeks, and it gave Martha the green light she needed to proceed with wedding planning while she waited on Oji to present her with a ring. And that was sufficient for the time being.

"So, we've reached the part of today's program for us to talk about wedding planning," Martha said with a giggle.

"Program?" Ruth laughed.

"Uh-oh. I feel like we're all going to leave here with homework. Do we need to take notes or anything?" Mary asked, smiling.

Martha laughed. "You do know me well, don't you? But, no, there's nothing for you to do. I'll confess that I considered making a slide deck, but luckily I came to my senses. I just want to take advantage of having all of you here together by sharing what I'm thinking for the wedding. Is that okay?"

Eve looked at Naomi. "She was kidding about the slides, wasn't she?"

"I'm afraid not. You have quite the adventure ahead with Martha," Naomi said, shaking her head.

Laughter spread across the room.

"Consider yourself warned," Ruth said, followed by more laughter.

"I'm not that bad," Martha insisted. She tried to maintain a straight face but immediately cracked, and the women cackled along with her.

The moment of levity brought Martha much-needed relief after weeks of feeling like she was in limbo. As she enjoyed the jovial interaction with her family and Oji's mother, she realized how much she wished her own mother could have lived to be part of the precious moment.

"Are you okay?" Mary asked as Martha grew silent.

"I am. This time together really means a lot to me," Martha said as she looked around the room. "I just needed a minute to absorb it all." She stuffed the feelings about her mother back into the deep crevice of her heart, where she could control them. "All righty, then. Where were we? Oh, yes! We've chosen a date: November 8, in the afternoon. But if either the church or the Edin Inn is booked that day, I'm willing to go with the evening of November 7."

"That gives you plenty of time to plan," Ruth said, nodding approvingly.

"I meant this year," Martha replied. She hunched her shoulders so high that they nearly reached her earlobes as she braced for the women's response.

"Oh," Ruth said.

"Are y'all planning to elope? I thought you wanted a huge wedding. What made you change your mind?" Naomi asked.

Martha shook her head. "I didn't change my mind. And I wouldn't call it a huge wedding. We're not having a big bridal party. Just a maid of honor and best man. But I'm certainly not skimping on anything. We'll have about three hundred guests."

"Now, I support you with whatever you decide to do," Mary said, "but that's a pretty sizable undertaking for four months, especially with the new restaurant opening in less than two months."

Martha nodded. "I promise I'll still carry my weight at the restaurant. Trust me—I don't want you to fire me."

"I sure would. I'm glad you know," Mary said. Then she clenched her teeth.

Martha chuckled. "As I was saying before I was so lovingly supported by my sister, I've been compiling my wedding plans for years. Now that I have the right groom—who also happens to be busy and who doesn't want to get into the weeds of wedding planning—I'll just hand all my ideas over to a wedding planner. Mrs. Jones did a beautiful job with Aunt Naomi's wedding and last year's Gardin Family Enterprises Christmas party." She looked at Ruth and Naomi. "You both trust her, don't you?"

"Absolutely. She has exquisite taste," Naomi said. "But are you sure you can handle not being more involved?"

"I trust Mrs. Jones, but it was challenging for me to turn the reins over to someone else after planning the Christmas party myself for so many years," Ruth said. "Our party is a big reflection on me, but it isn't as personal as a wedding."

"I'll be fine," Martha replied. "I'm going to have to be. As you've said, I'm already pulled in so many directions right now that I don't have the bandwidth for wedding planning. But honestly, I wouldn't want to be much more involved even if I had the time. I want what I want, so as long as Mrs. Jones can execute that, we're good."

"Having worked with her when I catered the Christmas party, I can assure you that she plans events with military-level precision," Mary said. "But she's one of the most sought-after wedding planners. Is she available on such short notice?"

Ruth, usually a stickler for etiquette, even at family gatherings, placed both elbows on the table and held her head in her hands as she exhaled loudly. "Martha, please tell me you've checked with Mrs. Jones already and, by some miracle that none of us deserve, she has an opening."

Martha stared nervously at Ruth. "I wanted to talk with y'all first before I reached out to her."

Ruth gasped, lifting her head from her hands. "Oh dear," she said, shaking her head. "I booked with her two years in advance to get her for the Christmas party. I don't know about this plan."

"Hopefully it'll work out," Naomi said, giving Ruth a look.

It took Ruth a minute, but she finally caught on. She pulled herself together quickly before breaking one last rule of etiquette. She retrieved her phone from her pocket and started typing.

"I hope so. I don't know what I'll do if she's booked," Martha said in a voice laden with angst.

"We'll have an answer soon. We're on it," Naomi said. She glanced at Ruth, prompting Martha to do the same.

Ruth didn't look up from her phone, as she already appeared to be engaged in a dynamic text exchange.

Martha suddenly realized she hadn't heard a peep from Eve. But for her own sanity, she opted not to ask specifically about the wedding date. "Mrs. Greenwald, you've been pretty quiet. Do you have any feedback or special requests when it comes to the wedding?"

"I haven't really given it much thought, dear. I hope that doesn't offend you. We've been fairly busy tending to Adam. But everything sounds good, so far. Notwithstanding the potential wrinkle regarding the wedding planner."

"No, I'm not offended. I can imagine your hands have been full." Although Martha didn't fully buy into Eve's explanation, she pushed herself to extend grace to her because serving as a caregiver for a loved one could be so overwhelming. "Oji says you're a flower lover like I am. Maybe I could use one of your favorites in my bouquet. What do you think?"

Eve didn't flinch. "I wish you wouldn't trouble yourself with that. You should focus on *your* vision," she said nonchalantly.

"All right," Martha said, trying not to sound defeated. "It's no problem at all, but keep me posted if you change your mind. And please let me know if there's anything I can do to help with Mr. Greenwald. I really want to be there for y'all."

"Thank you, dear. We'll be fine. With your busy work schedule and now the wedding, you have enough on your plate."

"I'll always make time for family," Martha said.

Chapter Six

Early July

"Are you listening to me, or are you dreaming about whatever fun you got into this weekend?" Jasmine asked as she placed the dry-erase marker in the holder below the whiteboard in the primary care center's conference room.

Martha was supposed to be helping Jasmine streamline her list of potential community outreach activities, but she struggled to focus. While Ruth's fierce negotiation had secured Mrs. Jones's services, alleviating what should've been the biggest stress of Martha's wedding planning process, Martha now toiled with her uneasiness over Eve's refusing to engage in the wedding-planning discussion the previous afternoon. "I'm sorry. I have a lot on my mind."

"Do you want to talk about it?" Jasmine asked. She pulled out the plastic chair across from Martha and plopped into the seat.

"I'm okay, but thank you," Martha said with a soft smile—kind but one she used to keep people at arm's length. Given the Gardin family's stature in Edin and people's curiosity about them and their successful peanut business, the Gardins were raised to be careful about the company they kept. But unlike her family members, Martha didn't have any close friends. She had decided two decades prior that she didn't need them. And these days, she didn't want them anyway. She had her family.

"You're my boss. I get it," Jasmine said. "But we've known each other since we were kids." She paused pensively, shifting her weight in the chair. "Did you know that my parents credit you with turning me into such a social person?"

Martha looked at Jasmine with narrowed eyes. "Why on earth would they think that? You're a natural," she said with the dismissive confidence of an eyewitness being challenged by a defendant's attorney in court.

Jasmine leaned forward. "Don't tell me you forgot that no one would talk to me until you vouched for me? If we hadn't been forced to sit in alphabetical order sophomore year, I wouldn't have made any friends. I was really shy back then."

Having connected in high school, when Jasmine Gibson's family moved to Edin, the girls became friends when they were seated together for nearly every class. And with Martha growing up in one of the families of the previously enslaved people who founded the town, she took her role as an unofficial diplomat seriously.

Martha shrugged. "I just did what I was supposed to do, and you did the rest. It wasn't a big deal," she said, shedding her characteristic bravado for a more humble tone. Yes, she had shown Jasmine around and taught her to navigate the dynamics in a school where nearly everyone's families had known one another for generations and having new students was a rare occurrence. But once people got to know Jasmine, everyone wanted to be around her, and Jasmine happily obliged. But no one was closer to her than Martha.

They were each other's best friend. When Jasmine's family joined Martha's church, the girls were together nearly every day.

"What you did was a big deal to *me*. You helped me discover a part of myself that I was too afraid to explore, and I want to return . . . Umm . . . What I'm trying to say is I'm here for you if you ever want to talk." The concern in Jasmine's voice sounded just like the tone of the voicemails she had left for Martha twenty years earlier, when they were in high school. Martha didn't remember the words Jasmine had said in the messages, but the emotion they conveyed was etched into Martha's memory.

After Martha's parents died, she had grown distant amid her grief. Jasmine continued to reach out through graduation and even when they attended college in different parts of the state. Martha returned her calls only from time to time, and she kept the conversations superficial. Both women returned to Edin after their studies, but their relationship never advanced beyond a friendly chat whenever they saw each other at church or events around town.

This is what I get for hiring somebody I know from home, Martha thought. Jasmine had fit right in with the staff, and her work was coming along so smoothly that Martha figured they'd moved past the possibility of Jasmine breaching Martha's personal boundaries. Yet here they stood. Martha faulted herself for leaving a crack in a door that Jasmine's empathic personality and their long history wouldn't allow Jasmine to resist trying to push open. Now Martha had to close it.

"I'll keep that in mind. Thank you for always being so

kind and caring." Martha attempted to look Jasmine in the eye, but she shifted, fearing Jasmine would see right into her soul. Her eyes landed on a spot on the wall just over Jasmine's right shoulder.

As if she could read Martha's mind, Jasmine shifted her body to the right and tilted her head to cover the area on the wall in Martha's field of view. "This is an adjustment for me. You know, working for you. You seem happy with my work, but I can't help feeling like I'm picking up on mixed signals sometimes."

"I don't mean to make it confusing. *I'm* trying to figure things out too, but I can assure you that I'm thrilled with your performance. If that ever changes, I'll talk to you about it."

While Martha was impressed with Jasmine's ability to advance the primary care center's community programming, the biggest payoff in hiring her childhood friend was that Martha could trust her. However, that came at the expense of frequent threats of vulnerability, which made her uncomfortable. Martha already had her fill of being forced into openness in her personal life. She didn't have the emotional bandwidth for it to bleed over into the professional setting. She had established firm boundaries when she decided to hire Jasmine, and apparently Jasmine was beginning to notice that Martha wasn't willing to compromise them. Martha wondered if it was worth working with someone who knew her so well. But a certain level of trust was needed to make her working relationship with Jasmine the highest yielding, and she didn't want to jeopardize it.

"That's fair. I'm going to trust you to follow through with that," Jasmine said.

Trust? It's like she can read my mind, Martha thought. But deciding to count her blessings instead of complaining about them, she moved on.

"Let's get back to our work," Martha said, pointing to the whiteboard. "There are three areas on your list that are speaking loudly to me. You thought I wasn't paying attention when you were speaking, didn't you?" she asked with a smile.

Jasmine chuckled. "I stand corrected."

"You mentioned the findings of the hospital's community health needs assessment. It shows that high blood pressure increases the risk of several conditions that affect our patients' neighborhoods more than some other parts of town. The hospital already has several initiatives focused on high blood pressure, but none of them have a component to help people measure their blood pressure at home or guide them in what to do if it's abnormal," Martha said, finally finding her rhythm.

"I attended a webinar about a high blood pressure project where a health system partnered with libraries on educational workshops about high blood pressure," Jasmine said. "They provided blood pressure monitors to the library, and then people borrowed the monitors and practiced using them in the comfort of their own homes. Could we do something like that?"

"The hospital doesn't have any existing partnerships with libraries," Martha said. "So if we can get this off the ground, we would get the innovation nod from the hospital leadership on several levels. Plus, it sounds like fun, and I have some discretionary funding that we can use to support it. Let's think about how we can connect high blood pressure to another condition that was identified as a priority in the community health needs assessment. What about dementia?"

"Ooh! I see where you're going with this!" Jasmine exclaimed.

"We talk a lot with patients about the relationship between high blood pressure and heart disease and stroke, but we don't always connect the dots to vascular dementia. If someone has heart disease or they've had a stroke, they are twice as likely to develop vascular dementia at some point."

"And there's a tremendous amount of caregiver burden associated with vascular dementia in our community," Jasmine said. "That's a pain point that we can help people sort through. People are more likely to attend a community education event if they can relate to the topic."

"I agree. And it gives us a good opportunity to talk about how family members can lower their risk for vascular dementia as well."

"We can also provide resources for people suffering with the condition, as well as for the loved ones involved in their care. If libraries or other community sites are interested in hosting us, would you be able to give a brief talk?" Jasmine asked.

"I'd love to," Martha replied. "And instead of me just talking to people, we can make it an interactive session by teaching them to use a blood pressure monitor. We'll tie everything together."

"We're such a good team!" Jasmine said.

"Yes, we are," Martha said with a soft smile that masked her mounting concern. She could envision promoting Jasmine in the coming months—that's if Jasmine lasted long enough. *If she doesn't feel secure in her current position and our professional relationship, will she stick around?*

THE MIDMORNING SUN cut through the expansive window and lit up the rose-colored tea room at the Stafford-Grant House. Pink flower-shaped pendant lights descended from the ceiling over a sea of bistro tables flanked with purple and green tufted armchairs.

"Doesn't this view make you feel like the room is in the garden?" Martha asked. Worried that her description over the phone may have overplayed the stateliness of the space, Martha held her breath for Eve's reaction. The last thing she wanted to do was disappoint her future mother-in-law.

"It's breathtaking," Eve said. Then she looked out the window at blooms that ranged from pure white to burgundy-red. "And is that a camellia garden? The iridescent pink ones really pop!"

Martha maintained her composure, but she did a happy dance inside.

"It's an *award-winning* camellia garden, in fact," Martha said with pride. A longtime patron of the house and the surrounding twenty-acre property, she had supported its growth from a small family house and garden to becoming a revered jewel in Edin's crown. "We couldn't see this particular garden from the lot where we parked, but guests wouldn't necessarily have to park that far away. There's another lot adjacent to the camellia garden. We may be able to get approval to use it. That'll give guests a shorter walk to get here, and having them come right into the camellia garden will instantly set the mood. Mrs. Jones and her team will work through the specific details."

"Good to know it worked out with Mrs. Jones," Eve said as she stepped back from the window. She turned to Martha, who sat at a circular bistro table near the window. "Now, tell me again, what is it you're planning to have here?"

I explained all that when I called to invite you to visit with me. I had a feeling you weren't listening to me, Martha thought, but to keep the peace, she decided to focus on the question she was asked. "That depends. Mary mentioned this place as a possibility for the bridal shower. But if you'd like to host the rehearsal dinner here, that's also an option. Since y'all live in Macon, you get first preference. But there's no pressure either way."

Eve shifted her body back to the window with the smoothness of a ballet dancer's adagio. "I'll have to talk it over with Oji. We haven't discussed wedding planning yet," she said as she stared through the glass.

"Oji didn't say anything about it when he came over this morning to stay with Mr. Greenwald?" Martha asked as she turned her head toward the window in an attempt to determine what had suddenly drawn Eve's attention. The camellia garden looked still and quiet, just as it had since Martha and Eve entered the tea room.

Continuing to look out the window, Eve shook her head. "Not a word. But you know Oji."

Apparently, I don't know this version of Oji that she knows, Martha thought. Whether there actually was another side of Oji she didn't know or his mother was just being dramatic, Martha's insecurity about looking foolish in front of Eve prevented her from asking any questions to help her distinguish which possibility was more likely. "I'll stay tuned. Either you or Oji can let me know."

"Will do, dear," Eve said. Her nonchalant tone let Martha know she shouldn't expect Eve to follow up with any urgency. Martha would have to check with Oji herself to stay on track with their tight wedding timeline.

Footsteps on the creaky hardwood floors grew louder in the hallway until a woman with smooth pecan-brown-colored skin appeared in the doorway. She clutched two branded folders close to her chest. "Good Saturday morning! I'm sorry to interrupt," she said as she entered the room.

Martha stood up. "Good morning, Tammy," she said, greeting her with a hug. The sweet scent of cocoa butter and vanilla wafted through Martha's nostrils. "Your timing is perfect. No apologies needed. I know my way around, so I played tour guide while we waited for you."

"And you must be Mrs. Greenwald," Tammy said, extending her hand to Eve with a bright smile.

"Yes. Pleased to meet you," Eve said, shaking Tammy's hand.

Martha pushed her shoulders back and straightened her spine before she spoke. "This is Tammy Stafford. The Stafford-Grant House has been in her family for more than a hundred years."

"That's right. Since 1919," Tammy said, nodding. "My paternal great-grandparents owned it, and my parents restored the house and expanded it to be an event space and botanical garden. Then they passed it down to me and my sister."

"It's an exquisite property," Eve said. "I felt right at home walking through the garden on our way in."

"Thank you! That's what we aim for," Tammy said, glowing. "And thank you for being patient with us. Saturdays are our busiest days for tours, and I was just wrapping up our first one of the day. I passed the group off to my sister, who will show them around the garden."

"Tammy doesn't usually take event appointments on Saturdays, but she squeezed us in as a special favor," Martha said.

"The Gardins and the Staffords go way back, so I had to make something work for Martha's busy schedule. And I hear congratulations are in order. The Gardins and the Greenwalds coming together—talk about an influential match made in heaven," Tammy said, her eyes lighting up. "My maternal grandparents are from Macon. I used to hear my grandmother talk about the fancy teas and luncheons your family used to host. She wasn't able to attend, but she said they were the talk of the town."

"Oh my!" Eve said, placing her hand at the center of her chest. "I wasn't expecting to hear that today. Well, dear, it seems you are quite the hostess yourself. I'm sure your grandmother would be very proud of you."

Martha maintained a pleasant smile but smoldered inside. *Why can't she be bothered to get that excited about a rehearsal dinner or the simple fact that her son is marrying me? I just don't understand.*

"Thank you, ma'am," Tammy said, blushing. "We would be honored to host your families here. Martha mentioned that you'll be making decisions in the next week or so. The tea room can be reserved for private daytime events during our regular business hours. We also offer a special selection of dinner menus and full access to the gardens during evening events, although it's closed to the public at that time."

"Who wouldn't love having this charming facility all to themselves?" Eve remarked.

"Right," Martha said curtly. She was taken aback by Eve's sudden enthusiasm about a potential evening event—a rehearsal dinner she hadn't cared enough about to remember as the reason Martha asked her to accompany her to visit the facility. "My wedding planner—I'm sure you know Mrs. Jones—will let you know how we decide to proceed."

"Of course you and Mrs. Greenwald are working with the best planner. I wouldn't expect anything less of you," Tammy said, still clenching the folders.

Me and Mrs. Greenwald? Mrs. Greenwald isn't helping at all. It's me. Just me and my family, Martha thought. "Are the dinner menus included in those folders?" she asked, nudging the meeting to a close.

"Ah yes, the folders!" Tammy exclaimed. She placed the palm of her hand on her forehead, covering the mild widow's peak at the base of her short curly Afro. She turned to Eve. "I was so caught up in having an opportunity to meet you, Mrs. Greenwald, that I forgot all about the folders."

Eve chuckled. "You'll give me a big head if you keep this up."

TIME WOULD TELL if Martha's future mother-in-law would host the rehearsal dinner in the Stafford-Grant House's tea room, and the clock was running out for discussing the heavier issue weighing on the bride-to-be. But Martha didn't feel like talking. She was already bruised from Eve's persistent coolness toward wedding planning, and the woman's warmth toward Tammy added insult to injury. It increasingly seemed that Eve found pleasure interacting with everyone except Martha.

Martha walked alongside Eve through the daffodil garden, the quiet between them punctuated by chirping hummingbirds and the clicking of the large bright-orange butterflies that dipped in and out of the flower bulbs. Martha endeavored to savor her peaceful surroundings, but they only intensified her inner turmoil. The bunches of yellow trumpet-shaped blooms had transitioned to ones with lighter hues and flat petals, and Martha's favorite variety stretched ahead—a double daffodil with pointy white outer petals and a pink center that looked like tissue paper—confirming that Martha and Eve were about to reach the final zone of beauty.

Walking around the tranquil garden usually centered Martha, but instead she grew more anxious with each step that brought her closer to the parking lot, which was the worst place for a potentially stressful conversation with Eve. Martha needed to talk in the garden, where the presence of a few stragglers from the tour would prevent the women from raising their voices but still give them enough privacy to converse without easily being heard.

"Look at these gorgeous flowers," Eve said as she slowed her pace and broke the silence. "It's like two daffodils together, but it's got a bit of pink in the middle."

Martha came to a full stop. "You like those?"

Eve took a few steps backward until she stood next to

Martha. "It kind of looks like a carnation, but it's much prettier."

"I don't like carnations. They look a little cheap," Martha said with an exaggerated wince, which was her best attempt at conveying her personal preference while trying not to sound judgmental.

Eve bent forward, taking a closer look at the blossom. "A little cheap?" she said with a laugh. It was the kind of laugh that a seasoned veteran lets out when a novice starts to think she knows enough to be considered a colleague.

I can admit that I still sounded judgmental, but she didn't even try, Martha thought. Yet the women's shared perspective on the cultivated daffodil presented an opportunity that Martha couldn't resist. "Oji said we're a lot alike," she said, staring at Eve as the older woman admired the flowers.

Eve shrugged as she stood up straight. "I don't see it. Do you?"

"Not so much. But I figure he's entitled to his opinion." Martha shuffled a small rock on the pavement with her foot, working out her nervous energy as she spoke. "I've . . ."

"Is there something on your mind, dear?" Eve asked.

Martha stood still. Beads of sweat accumulated on her forehead as she forced her words out. "I've been wanting to check in with you about Mr. Greenwald. Oji may have passed along some of the thoughts I've shared with him, but that can turn into a game of telephone sometimes. I thought it would be helpful if we talked."

"Oji mentioned that you had some ideas, but go ahead and tell me," Eve said. She sounded like someone who inadvertently answered a phone call from a telemarketer and begrudgingly responded to their questions because it would be too rude to hang up.

"I meant what I said the other day about wanting to help. Whenever I have a patient who's been diagnosed with vascular dementia, I recommend a family meeting where everyone can discuss the plan—both a short-term plan and one for the long term. You know, so everyone can get on the same page."

"Oji and I talk pretty regularly about his father's health. Is there something specific you think we should be discussing?"

"Well, there are resources and programs that might be helpful for Mr. Greenwald, as well as for you and Oji. And I'd like to see y'all take full advantage of them. If Mr. Greenwald's doctor hasn't connected you with a social worker who specializes in geriatrics, I'd be happy to introduce you to one I know. Would you like to talk to her?"

"Dr. Stevenson gave us some information," Eve said dryly.

"Did he also talk to you about day programs?"

"Yes, he mentioned them, but I'm not interested."

"Oh . . . okay," Martha said. She was surprised Eve wouldn't want the opportunity for Adam to spend time in a safe place away from home on weekdays, freeing her up to run errands, rest, or have some time for herself. "Was there something that concerned you about enrolling Mr. Greenwald in a day program?"

"No, I don't have any concerns. Thank you for *your* concern, dear, but we are fine. Okay?"

"I . . . I'm not saying anything is wrong," Martha said.

"It's just that I know how much difference it can make for patients with vascular dementia and their families to have support. It can cut down on emergencies for the patients and even help prevent caregivers from experiencing burn-out. I want to make sure you have access to everything you need."

"Adam made it home safely after your aunt's wedding, as I knew he would. That situation was just a hiccup. He is doing well, and so am I. We don't need anything."

"Since you aren't interested in a day program, would you consider having someone come to the house to work with Mr. Greenwald? Maybe to help him with memory exercises and things like that? Or games?" Martha asked, searching for an open door to gain Eve's interest. "Oji mentioned that Mr. Greenwald used to love board games. That's something commonly used to help with brain health."

"No, dear," Eve said, shaking her head. "We're not ready to do something like that right now. We're fine. Everything's fine."

Sensing Eve's thinning patience, Martha dug deep for a last-ditch offer. "If you'd like, I could even get him started with some activities that could help him. I don't mind. I can stop by on my way home from work to do some memory exercises with him a couple of days a week. I just want to do whatever we can to slow the progression of Mr. Greenwald's dementia. That'll make it easier for everyone," she pleaded.

"I've got an idea," Eve said, waving the folder from the Stafford-Grant House in the air. She sounded excited for the first time since the daffodils grabbed her attention. "Why don't you have your social worker put together a folder of information, and I'll look through it?"

"All right. I'll do that," Martha said, deflated. The star of her high school debate team, Martha would have easily been declared the winner if her exchange with her future mother-in-law had been scored based on strategy, presentational style, quality of argument, and strength of supporting material. But this was real life, and Martha felt defeated. It was clear that Eve just wanted to pacify Martha and find a way out of the conversation.

"Great. Well, I'm going to head home," Eve said. "Thank you for introducing me to the Stafford-Grant House. Enjoy the rest of your day, dear." She raised her hand and wiggled her fingers back and forth as she walked away.

In accord with their pre-movie tradition at the Edin drive-in theater, Martha and Oji sat on a blanket in front of his car, drinking fruit smoothies and munching on popcorn and a giant pretzel. Usually, the hour-long interval between the opening of the drive-in's gates and showtime flew by and the opening credits cut into their chatty conversation. But Martha's morning discourse with Eve hung over the couple like smog, stifling the conversation, until an unexpected encounter ignited it.

"Did that kid just take our picture?" Martha asked.

Oji grabbed a handful of popcorn and lifted it to his mouth. "What?" he asked. His hand froze midair before the snack reached his lips.

Martha pointed a couple of car lengths over to a group of teenagers sitting in the back of a pickup truck in the row of vehicles in front of her and Oji. "See, the young man in the red shirt with the camera in his hand . . . He sees me pointing at him. He's looking over here."

"Are you sure he was taking a picture of us?" Oji asked, sliding his hands against each other to remove the salt residue left over from the popcorn.

"I don't know for sure, but it looked like it . . . Oh! He's coming over."

Oji stood up. "We'll certainly find out," he said as he reached for an antibacterial wipe.

A light-skinned fellow with freckles and sandy-brown hair walked over to the couple. He wore a camera strap around his neck and cradled a camera with a long lens in his hands. "Excuse me, ma'am and sir. I hope I didn't alarm you. My name is Benjamin Thomas Springfield. I'll be a senior at King High School in the fall." He sounded like he was going door-to-door selling candy bars for a fundraiser.

Oji nodded, appearing impressed. He extended his hand and shook Benjamin's. "Nice to meet you, Mr. Springfield. I'm Oji Greenwald, and this is Martha Gardin."

"Hello," Martha said, shaking Benjamin's hand. She instantly felt at ease with his firm handshake and affable demeanor.

"I'm pleased to meet you both," Benjamin said.

"Did you just take our photo?" Oji asked.

"Yes, sir. I should've asked for permission first. Please accept my apology." Benjamin looked back and forth between Martha and Oji. "I was looking through my camera for a bird or something like that for my art class, but then I saw you two, and it was the perfect shot. I was going to come over and talk to you, but you caught me first."

"I appreciate that you accepted responsibility," Oji said.

"I'd like to show y'all the photo, if that's okay," Benjamin said, exposing the screen on the back of the camera.

Martha and Oji leaned in to examine the image displayed.

Her heart leaped as she laid eyes on the image of herself looking out toward the movie screen while Oji gazed lovingly at her. "You're an amazing photographer," she said in a tender voice.

"She's right. You've got a gift," Oji added.

"Thank you," Benjamin responded with a smile so big that Martha noticed he wore clear braces on his top and bottom teeth. "I'm actually more of a painter. I've just been playing around with photography so I can paint the photos I take. Would it be okay if I keep this photo for a project?"

Oji looked at Martha.

"I'm all right with it if *you* are," Martha said to Oji.

"Okay, but one condition," Oji replied. He reached in his pocket and pulled out his wallet. He opened the billfold and handed Benjamin his business card. "Promise me that you'll email the photo to me."

A grateful smile spread across Benjamin's face. "Deal!" he exclaimed. "Thank you so much."

"You've got a bright future ahead, brother. We look forward to seeing where it takes you," Oji said.

Martha smiled, dabbing the corner of her eye.

"Thank you, sir. Have a good night," Benjamin said. He took a couple of steps in the direction of the pickup truck, then turned around quickly and waved. "And good night to you, too, ma'am."

"Good night," Martha and Oji replied, waving back.

"That was odd," Oji said as he and Martha settled on the blanket.

"Yeah, who'd have thought things would've played out that way. Nothing about today has gone as expected," she said, making puppy-dog eyes.

"It's not gonna work, babe," Oji said with a bashful smile.

"What?" Martha dragged out the word and batted her eyelashes.

"You are so sneaky," he said in a flirtatious tone of voice.

"Desperate times call for desperate measures," she said with a coy grin. Then her tone became more serious. "We *do* need to talk about it, Oji. We can't just pretend like this morning didn't happen."

Oji's smile disappeared. "You're right. My mom was pretty heated when she got home from the Stafford-Grant House," he said coolly.

Martha took a deep breath, giving Oji a moment to reconsider his statement, but he didn't speak.

His mom *was heated? And what about his fiancée? I'm sure Mrs. Greenwald didn't mention her disinterest in wedding planning or consider how that might make me feel, and I'm not about to bring that up right now. We'll never get anywhere with this discussion if I do. For better or worse, I've got to pick my battles.* Martha fumed inside but kept her cool when she finally responded aloud, "I assumed as much, but did she say why she was so upset?"

"She feels like you're pushing an agenda."

"An agenda? And what kind of agenda would that be?" She could feel her claws coming out.

Oji's voice stayed cool. "It's about control. You both want control."

Martha inhaled slowly. "Is that what you think? Or is that what she said?"

"Oh, it's what my mom said. I don't necessarily think you want to control her, but I believe that you feel like you know what's best."

She looked at him for a second before she replied. "Because I'm a highly skilled physician who's watching someone she cares about go down a risky path and I'd like for things not to go badly for him or his loved ones." She managed to speak in a matter-of-fact tone. But that was just for emphasis, not because she was managing her emotions all that well. She struggled to understand how Eve, and Oji by default, could ignore sound medical advice from someone with such a deep understanding of Adam's diagnosis and its potential impact on his family—the family she was about to marry into. Adam wouldn't be just Oji's responsibility. He would be hers, too.

"You're accustomed to everyone doing what you say," Oji said. "It's not gonna go that way with my mom. And I probably need to accept that it may take you a while to acclimate to that." It sounded like an attempt at empathy, but it frustrated Martha that the empathy was so misplaced.

"My patients don't all follow my advice. And neither do my family members, though my family does tend to listen when there's a crisis. It hurts my feelings that your mom doesn't want me involved, but the bigger issue is your father's health."

"I understand, Martha," Oji said flatly.

"Do you? Because we are going to be the ones picking up

the pieces if something bad happens to your father. You are not going to turn your back on your parents, not that I would ever ask you to do so. And since you're going to pick up the pieces, that means *we're* picking up the pieces. And I'd much rather be proactive about avoiding the dangers that my professional experience tells me lie ahead for your dad."

"Babe, I respect your professional opinion. But I also have to respect my mother."

"That's fair. But does that mean there's no compromise?"

"Maybe someday, but not right now. My mom needs some time to cool down. Just give her some space. And let me handle her."

Chapter Seven

Mid-July

"Thanks for making the trek over here. Oh—" Martha said as she rushed into the primary care center's conference room only to find one of her staff members looking way too comfortable chatting with Mary. Jasmine was there too, but she was invited.

"What was Dr. Gardin like when she was a kid?" asked Ms. Punchard, the primary care center's longest-serving social worker and a self-admitted social media sleuth. Resting her arm on the table, she leaned toward Mary—close to the point of invading her personal space.

Eager to shut down the conversation, Martha pulled out the chair closest to the door and next to her inquisitive staff member. "Looks like I arrived just in time, huh? But now y'all know why Ms. Punchard is the one I call for reinforcement when I need help getting patients to open up to me about the barriers they face in accessing medical care," she joked, settling into the seat.

"And who I call when I need to know the tea," Jasmine said with wide eyes and a painted smile.

Ms. Punchard laughed hysterically, so hard the table shook. "You're a hoot, Jasmine. You say to my face what everyone else says behind my back. That's why I save all the hot tea for you. And thanks for that compliment, Dr. Gardin. You are an expert at making your team members feel valued."

"You're welcome. It's all about leveraging everyone's individual strengths. Speaking of which, I need your insight on a special assignment. I'll stop by your office after I'm done here." Martha hoped her delivery made it less obvious that she aimed to expedite Ms. Punchard's departure from the room.

"Great! Can't wait! Your little projects are always fun. Y'all have a good meeting, and maybe I'll see you at your new restaurant, Mary. The menu sounds delicious." Ms. Punchard bounced out of the room.

Mary smiled politely.

"Smooth," Jasmine said. "But you don't really have something for her to work on, do you?"

"I actually do. You're my go-to person for community info, and Ms. Punchard keeps me abreast of what's going on in the hospital. She knows about all the hospital plans and job openings before everyone else. She's the one who first told me that Oji had approached the hospital about partnering on the redevelopment initiative across the neighborhood. Ms. Punchard is really good at her job and has taught me so much. But she can be—"

"A lot," Jasmine said, finishing Martha's sentence.

"Exactly," Martha said with a chuckle. "That is why I prefer to meet in my office. It's more private and comfortable. But it would've taken me an additional five minutes to get to that side of the building, and I'm already late."

Martha had contemplated rescheduling the meeting after

having to see patients who were originally scheduled to be seen by a colleague who had an emergency that morning, but she didn't want Mary to think she was flaking on Jasmine's first meeting with them.

"What Ms. Punchard didn't say is that she asks me about you all the time," Jasmine said. "She's always digging. I change the subject, so this was her way of taking another route. Stay ready, Mary. She will strike again."

"As long as she spends some money in the restaurant, it's fine with me," Mary said. "We were raised to handle nosy people with diplomacy."

"It's annoying, but it should settle down after the novelty of having you around wears off." Martha was referring to her sister, but she realized after she said it that the statement applied to Jasmine as well. "But anyway, I'm sorry about Ms. Punchard's intrusion. Let's get started with our meeting. I didn't make an agenda, so—"

"I took the liberty of making one, if that's okay with you," Jasmine said. "I just used the notes you usually share with me after the meeting to guide me through items that require follow-up. Of course, please feel free to add any new items of business."

"Thank you. That's perfect," Martha replied. She could see her sister angling to make eye contact with her, but she avoided her, looking straight ahead at Jasmine instead.

Jasmine handed Mary a copy of the agenda. Then she handed one to Martha. "I know you're environmentally conscious and usually use the whiteboard for this type of thing, but I decided at the last minute to print the agenda since you were coming straight from the exam rooms and probably wouldn't have your notepad."

"What would Martha do without you?" Mary asked, giving Jasmine a knowing glance.

"She would do fine. She'd figure it out," Jasmine replied, blushing as she mirrored Mary's eye movements.

As someone who processed information by writing, Martha appreciated Jasmine's thoughtfulness. But she was less impressed with Mary. Although Martha had secretly appreciated the camaraderie between her best friend and her sister as a teen, Martha was not amused with Mary's less than subtle hint about her relationship with her community outreach manager. But she bit her tongue instead of reprimanding her. The last thing she wanted to do was squabble with Mary at work, especially in front of Jasmine. "As usual, you've considered everything, Jasmine. Thank you."

"I can get used to all this positive reinforcement," Jasmine said with a glow of confidence.

Martha smiled softly. Then she grabbed a pen from the pocket of her white coat, lowered her eyes, and scanned the agenda. "Looks good. I've got nothing to add. Mary, would you like to start with your update on the grand opening?"

"Sure. Let's see . . . We're about a month out, but it's coming together," Mary said as she tapped on her phone. "Okay. Found my notes. Jasmine, thanks for your email confirming that the date and time work for you and Martha. As you know, I'm planning a happy-hour reception for local media, VIPs, social media influencers, and food bloggers. Then hopefully they'll stay for the full dinner service right afterward. We've reached out to Ruth to see which folks from the annual Christmas party should be invited. And thanks, Jasmine, for sending the list of hospital and community contacts."

"That was a mouthful, but a good one! Do you need anything else from us?" Martha asked.

"No, I think we're straight," Mary replied. Then she looked at Jasmine. "So, what's up with the teaching kitchen grand opening? Martha mentioned that you came up with a big idea, but she wouldn't tell me anything about it."

Jasmine's head swung to Martha. "Big idea? Is that what you called it, Martha?"

"Uh, yeah, because it is," Martha said, falling into the comfortable zone that felt so natural with Jasmine.

"Well, could someone clue me in?" Mary said. Her tone told Martha that she was losing patience with being kept out of the loop, just like when they all hung out together as teenagers.

"Since it was Jasmine's idea, I wanted her to be the one to tell you," Martha clarified.

"We're still planning to have an open house," Jasmine said. "We're just calling it a 'Sip, Taste, and See.'" The title was a play on the name of an informal event, originating in the South, in which hosts invite family members and friends to have refreshments and see a new baby.

"I love that!" Mary said.

"We just added in the word *taste* because our refreshment offerings will feature tastings of the recipes we'll use in the teaching kitchen," Jasmine explained.

"Yep, I get it," Mary replied.

"Jasmine has also reviewed Ruth's Christmas party list, and I believe she's inviting the people you selected to the restaurant grand opening as well as a few more. Right, Jasmine?"

"Correct. And I also asked M.J. to help put out feelers for

any culinary garden contacts we may have missed," Jasmine added.

Martha nodded. "Is there anything you'd recommend, Mary?"

"I can't think of anything," Mary said, shaking her head. "Oh, there is one thing. Jasmine, did you know that Martha got sent to the principal's office in first grade because she argued with the teacher about how she thought the word *garden* should be spelled? She delivered a whole soliloquy on the origin of our family name and our legacy of agricultural expertise, tying it back to our ancestors deliberately spelling our name and Edin with an *i* instead of an *e*. So, if Martha is hard to work with sometimes, just think about what her teachers went through. Trust me, you've got it easy compared to them."

Jasmine burst out laughing. "Why are you so silly?" she asked, lowering her head on her arm like she was about to take a nap in detention.

"It's true!" Mary exclaimed.

Jasmine rotated her head toward Mary. "I know. I've heard the story. But you didn't have to bring it up now and add all that commentary. So shady," Jasmine said between laughs.

Mary chuckled.

"Would you two keep your voices down? Or do you need to be reminded again that I work here?" Martha asked, holding in a laugh.

MARTHA PLUCKED HER laptop out of her computer bag and placed it on the white conference table, where a whimsical sphere-shaped art deco chandelier made of porcelain flowers and a gold-leaf-finished frame hung low over the center of the table.

"You won't need that," said Mrs. Jones, who sat across from Martha. Her voice was commanding but not rude. "Would you like some water?"

"No thank you," Martha replied as she returned the laptop to its receptacle.

"Let me know if you change your mind. Brides should stay hydrated," Mrs. Jones said as she opened her laptop and briskly clicked at least fifteen keys before she paused, presumably waiting for her password to be recognized. She kept her head lowered toward the screen, but she lifted her eyes and glanced at Martha.

"Noted," Martha said, straightening her posture in the cream-colored bucket chair.

Tending to a personal obligation in the middle of the workday made Martha uneasy, especially when the appointment required leaving the primary care center on a day she was scheduled to see patients. But the noon meeting with Macon's most in-demand event planner was the only opening that was feasible during a week that had already seen Martha rearranging her calendar and canceling meetings to fill in for a colleague who had an emergency. She didn't have any more flexibility, and she worried her meeting with Mrs. Jones would run past the thirty minutes allotted.

Martha fiddled with her fingernail on her right index finger, freshly chipped from her car door as she hurried inside for the noon appointment. "Does that say West Point?" she asked as she examined the wall of degrees and accolades at Alpha Bravo Events. With a white and beige color palette and gold accents, the studio looked like the lobby of a chic boutique hotel instead of a place where someone with a degree in operations research from an elite military academy would work.

"Yes, it does," Mrs. Jones replied. "I served for twenty years. Turns out the skills I acquired using data science to solve special-operations problems come in pretty handy in event planning, but I get to indulge my love of pretty things in this phase of my career."

When Mary described Mrs. Jones as the Dora Milaje general of party planning, Martha had written off her sister's assessment as a joke. But now that Martha understood that the description extended far beyond the planner's smooth ebony skin and stoic expression, she abandoned her concern about making it back to work in time for her afternoon patients.

But she still felt nervous. She didn't understand why she had to meet Mrs. Jones in person. She hoped the planner didn't bring her to her studio to back out, but she tried to push that out of her mind. Instead, she focused on positive things. *I'm feeling her design aesthetic, and I'll probably make it back to work early. This is going to work out just fine.*

"I'll keep our talk brief, as I understand you have a commitment," Mrs. Jones said. "We can check in virtually in the future if you'd like, but it's helpful to be able to talk face-to-face before we get started with the planning process. I've already reviewed the very thorough document you sent over, as well as your Pinterest boards."

Martha breathed a sigh of relief. *But why do I still feel*

like she's about to use some secret military tactic on me? she thought, quietly caving to her subconscious need to tackle her nervousness with something silly. She smiled so she wouldn't laugh out loud.

"While you're not the first bride I've worked with who's handed me a guide map of sorts and trusted me to deliver, it is a fairly unorthodox request. So I'd like to make sure we understand each other. Are you certain you're comfortable giving me so much latitude to make decisions for your wedding?"

Martha cleared her throat. "Yes, absolutely. I can already tell that we have similar taste, so I'm not worried at all." She spoke slowly, like she was being graded on her diction.

"Let's be clear," Mrs. Jones said, looking at Martha with piercing eyes. "I don't work magic. But I know people. Frequently, I can make things happen that others cannot, but I make no guarantees that it will always work out that way."

"I understand," Martha said.

"Great!" Mrs. Jones replied, with her delivery instantly lightening. "I noticed that you didn't provide a wedding theme. But judging from the requests you made, I would say your style is understated elegance. Would you agree with that?"

Martha nodded quickly. "Yes, that sums it up exactly."

"Perfect."

"May I ask you something?" Martha's vocal pitch raised a level. "How were you able to fit in my wedding and my aunt's this year on such short notice? I would guess that people book you for weddings a year ahead of time."

"Eighteen months, sometimes two years in advance. I

only book eight events per year. Since your family's company is a current client, I extended a courtesy to you and your aunt."

"Thank you so much for accommodating us," Martha said. "And I imagine Ruth also promised you my firstborn."

"Something like that. But seriously, it's my pleasure," Mrs. Jones said matter-of-factly.

Martha laughed, expecting Mrs. Jones to join her, but the woman returned her gaze to her laptop.

"Okay, now for some basic housekeeping. I'll update you each week. What's your preferred method of communication? Would you prefer an email, or do you want to have a conversation?" Mrs. Jones asked, now looking Martha in the eye.

"Email is fine. But I can jump on a call whenever you need me to. I trust that you'll let me know if you feel like you need to discuss something by phone or prefer Zoom to see my reaction to options."

"Sounds good. I'll use the appropriate discretion with requests for calls," Mrs. Jones said. She glimpsed at her laptop screen. "Thank you for sharing the link to your wedding dress. Have you ordered it yet?"

"No. I hope to do that in the next week or so."

"Have you at least tried it on?" Mrs. Jones asked, raising her eyebrows.

"No, not yet."

Mrs. Jones quickly typed on the laptop keyboard. "The dress you want is a very special one. You'll need to go this weekend. I'll make a call and get back to you by the end of the day with the next steps. And I strongly suggest you start looking at other dresses in case this one doesn't work out."

"It may not work out?" Martha asked sheepishly.

"We'll see. I'll do my best."

"THE MOSQUITOES WILL be out soon. We better get ready to head back to my cottage," Martha said as it neared dusk at the lake on the Gardin family estate.

"Awww, do we have to?" Oji playfully whined as he climbed out of the water using the ladder on the side of the pier where Martha sat.

She joined in on the fun. "All right, a few more minutes. But don't let those streetlights come on before you make it home."

He let out a loud laugh. "You sound just like my mom!"

"Don't tell me you think she and I *sound* alike too," Martha protested.

"No, but it's fun to get a little under your skin," Oji said, wearing baggy turquoise-and-white-striped swim trunks that matched the towel placed on the pier next to Martha. He gave her a light pinch on the cheek.

"You're getting water on me!" she playfully yelled. She picked up the towel and stretched her arm toward Oji as she leaned the rest of her body away from him. "Here."

"Thanks, babe. You take such good care of me."

"Next time we have to bring an umbrella or something. I forgot how hot the sun can beat down in the evening. I'm sweating off my sunscreen. But it was a good idea to come here. Before we started dating, it never would've occurred to me to come here on a weeknight."

"Which is so odd to me," Oji said. "You literally have a

serene setting as your backyard. I would come here every night if we stayed here." He casually ran the towel across his legs as he reignited the discussion they had begun on the walk from Martha's house.

"We can keep using my cottage on weekends until I turn it over to M.J. Then we can just shift to staying with Aunt Naomi and Nicholas," Martha said, reading the question on Oji's face before he could ask it. "I'm sure M.J. won't want to stay with Ruth when he goes back to work at Gardin Family Enterprises next year."

"Right. Because you care so much about M.J. having a house to himself. You're such a good big cousin," Oji said sarcastically as he dropped the towel on the pier and sat next to Martha.

"That's me," she said in a melodic voice.

"But I'll humor you. If M.J. isn't moving back until he graduates, why wouldn't we take a year to figure things out? I don't see what's the big rush to move. It's so beautiful here."

"It takes at least a year to build a house, so we need to start now. Of course, you know that better than I do. And think about the time we'll save commuting to work if we live in Macon."

Oji placed the palms of his hands on the pier and leaned back. "We talked about a compromise, babe. Buying a house is not a compromise. Moving to Macon and staying in my place is a compromise. See how that works? We have plenty of time to build our dream home."

"But I don't want to wait," Martha said.

"It won't be that long. Once we live together awhile, we'll

have a better idea of what we need in a home and we can build what you want."

"We barely have enough space for one of us in our current places. It's a no-brainer that we need more space for two people."

"It's not that bad. Either of our homes could work for another year. We're both already pulled in lots of directions with work and now the wedding. We don't have time to look for a house, much less build one. We need to get on the same page about this."

"True," Martha replied. "Our work schedules are taxing. We both used to work late almost every night before things became serious between us. But we promised to prioritize our time together, and we pretty much stick to it, right?"

"Uh-huh." Oji peered at Martha like he sensed he was being set up.

"And maybe once or twice each week, when one of us has something important that requires us to work at night, we work together in the same room, right?"

Oji sighed. "Yes, babe."

Martha could tell from Oji's abbreviated responses that she was losing him, but that only made her try harder. "We both have strong work ethics. Neither of us spends our money foolishly. And we deserve to use it on the life we want. That's why I'm not sparing a penny when it comes to the wedding. I want us to start our life together off right, and I feel the same way about our future home."

Oji's furrowed brows told Martha that he'd finally reached his limit. She'd be better off picking up the conversation again later.

"We can keep thinking about it," Martha said. She couldn't blame Oji. After more than an hour of talking about where they would live, she, too, would have tired of the conversation going around and around in circles without any progress if she felt the way Oji did about the issue. She expected him to reengage if they moved on to a more fun topic. "Okay, let's talk wedding updates. Did you finish your homework, or do you want me to share my updates?" She hoped the levity would lighten the tension that thickened the air.

"Why is yours called *updates* and mine called *homework*?" Oji asked.

"You wanted more time to play outdoors earlier, so I was just sticking with the metaphor we had going," Martha kidded.

"You're so quick," he said with a playful smirk that told her his attitude was softening. "Okay, I'll go first. I called both of our pastors, and neither has an opening for premarital counseling. My pastor mentioned a couples counselor who happens to have a premarital couples retreat next weekend. Apparently, it's supposed to revolutionize your relationship, according to one of the reviews I read."

"Perfect timing! It's meant to be," Martha said.

"I thought so too. I went ahead and signed us up," Oji said proudly.

"Great. Who's the person leading it?"

"Her name is Shari something. I don't remember her last name. Her bio said she conducts premarital counseling sessions out of an office here in Edin. I figured that would make it convenient for us to continue seeing her after the workshop."

"Oh, no," Martha said, hanging her head.

"What? Do you know her?"

"We're not friends or anything, but she's the therapist Ruth and Mary go to. Remember I told you about her?"

Oji put his arm around Martha. "I remember that y'all butted heads a little. Honestly, she sounded like she had good suggestions. But I understand if you'd rather not see her."

"It's fine," Martha mumbled. "Time is getting tight. I'll make it work. Besides, I'm sure it'll be an entirely different experience going to counseling with you than it was attending one of Mary's sessions."

Oji kissed her on the forehead. "Good, because I already paid for it, and I would hate to lose my money."

She playfully hit him on the arm. "You are so cheap sometimes."

"I'm frugal, thank you very much. One day you will appreciate it," he replied with a laugh.

"And the rehearsal dinner? Has your mom said anything about it yet?"

"No, but let's go ahead and move forward. Maybe Mrs. Jones could just take over all of the planning."

Martha considered asking for details about Eve's decision, but she didn't want to ruin the evening. Although she and Oji had not come to an agreement about their housing situation, they had found a way to table the discussion and reset. Martha finally understood why everyone says wedding planning is so stressful. Although she had initially assumed that delegating everything to Mrs. Jones would alleviate all the stress, the chaos concerning Eve's single wedding responsibility had clarified everything for Martha—

that much of the stress around weddings was caused by people and their unnecessary drama.

"Okay, I'll let Mrs. Jones know, and I'll ask her to reach out to you with the next steps. Is that okay?" Martha asked as a mosquito buzzed around her ear. She waved it away.

"Works for me. Thanks for your patience with this, babe," Oji said sweetly.

"No problem. I've got to follow up with her anyway. She's calling in a favor to help me get my dress. I have to go to New York on Saturday."

"Seriously? You can't get a dress here?"

Martha looked at Oji with raised eyebrows as the early-evening sky lit up in shades of red, orange, and pink.

"Got it. I'll stay in my lane," he said, bowing his head as he raised the palms of his hands toward Martha in deference.

"That would be a very wise decision, Mr. Greenwald," Martha said. "Ouch! Okay, let's go. The mosquitoes are getting me."

MARTHA READ THE questions on her sister's face as she parked her car in front of a large French provincial home surrounded by magnolia trees. "Bear with me. It's just a little detour."

Mary squeezed her eyelids tight and then quickly stretched them open wide. "Where are we?" she asked. Exhausted from catering a birthday party the previous evening that had stretched late into the night and then waking up early to attend Sunday service, Mary had dozed off in the passenger seat during the car ride.

"Just outside of Macon. It's not as close to the hospital as I'd like, but it might work."

"I can't believe you still brought me here, after I said I didn't want to go with you. I don't like being used in whatever scheme you're cooking up to trick Oji into buying a house," Mary said with growing irritation in her voice.

"Just come inside for a minute. I need your opinion," Martha pleaded. She raised the pitch of her voice to sound like a child.

"Does that work on Oji?"

"Sometimes," Martha said, continuing the vocal adaptation.

Mary flung the car door open. "Let's go. The sooner we get this over with, the sooner I can go home and get back to bed," she barked.

"Thank you!" Martha exclaimed. "I promise we'll be quick."

Martha hopped out of the front seat and followed her sister up the steep driveway, sharing the details of the house as they rushed past the manicured flower bed composed of lush green bushes interspersed with the bright-orange blossoms of the butterfly weed and the shiny iridescent purple leaves of Persian shields. "The house has five bedrooms and five and a half bathrooms. It's on four and a half acres, and the river runs through the backyard," she said, her voice filled with anticipation.

Mary didn't respond. As they reached the black double

front doors, Mary placed her hand on the lever-style handle at the left door and pushed it open.

"And I'm not trying to trick Oji into anything, but I needed to see the house before I talked to him about it," Martha continued.

Mary jerked the door closed and spun around to look at her sister, who walked a couple of footsteps behind her. "But you thought it was okay to trick *me* into coming instead? You should be ashamed of yourself." The women faced each other.

"I was desperate. You wouldn't have come otherwise. But I should've been honest. I'm sorry," Martha said.

The front door slowly crept open.

"Welcome to our open house!" said a bubbly woman with long platinum-blond hair. "I'm Terah."

"Hello," the sisters said in unison as they entered the grand foyer, where a rustic wooden chandelier hung from a vaulted ceiling, giving the room a slightly casual look. Martha sounded jovial and eager, but hints of annoyance still peppered Mary's tone.

Martha was delighted by the winding staircase in the middle of the foyer. Made of wood and wrought iron, its white risers matched the walls in the hallway as well as those in the office located just off the entrance. "This is beautiful."

"The owners made some substantial updates before listing the home. It's very luxurious. It won't be on the market long," Terah said. "May I give you a tour, or would you prefer to look around on your own?"

"We'd love to just wander around, if you don't mind,"

Martha replied. She'd have preferred the tour, but she doubted that Mary would keep quiet.

"Sure thing. Just holler if I can be helpful," Terah replied.

"Thank you," Martha said. She walked toward the open living area but retraced her steps when she noticed that Mary lagged behind.

Martha grabbed her sister's hand as she met her halfway down the hall. "Let's go!"

"Just go ahead. I'll catch up," Mary said.

"It's quicker and more fun if we walk together," Martha said as she walked alongside Mary.

Mary shook her head.

Martha returned to the living area with her sister. As Martha admired its architectural ceiling and built-in bookcases that flanked the gas fireplace, Mary folded her arms across her chest and leaned on the wall next to the L-shaped sofa.

"Are you going to pout like that the whole time?" Martha asked as she made her way to the chef's kitchen.

"How easily you revert to your old games to get your way. I was starting to get used to the new and improved Martha, but it's two steps forward and one step back with you."

Martha was too busy imagining herself preparing meals at the enormous kitchen island to say anything. With white custom cabinets that stretched to the ceiling, there was ample space for all her pots, though she'd likely display the copper ones on a rack that hung from the ceiling. She had always wanted one of those. Martha slid her hand along the brown veins of the white marble countertop on her way to get a closer look at the eight-burner ZLINE range.

"I don't like the way you maneuvered your way into getting me here," Mary griped. "You said we were going to look at maid-of-honor dresses."

"That's not exactly what I said. I asked if you wanted to look at dresses." Martha's eyes leaped to the adjacent dining room, where she envisioned hosting birthday parties and holiday gatherings.

"Martha, that's the same thing. You are not a child. You know better. I specifically told you I didn't want to be your accomplice. This is between you and Oji." The frustration in Mary's voice was increasing.

"I figured you understood and were playing along with me. Why would I need to look at more dresses? You already ordered your dress, and so did Ruth."

"I assumed you saw a dress that you liked better when you went to New York yesterday."

"Nope," Martha said nonchalantly as she turned her back to the dining area and faced her sister. "I stuck to sorting out everything with my dress, so I was in and out of the store in a heartbeat. Since I had to give that health highlight on hypertension at church this morning, I had to make sure I didn't miss my plane to come back last night."

"Well, I'm glad everything worked out for you. But you'd better hope it doesn't all come crashing down," Mary said with pity in her eyes.

"Don't be like that," Martha said in a dismissive tone as she noticed a door just outside the kitchen. "Ooh! How did I miss this? A butler's pantry in addition to all those cabinets!" Her eyes widened as she peered through the glass arch-top door at rows and rows of shelves. "And here I was wondering if this kitchen would allow us enough space to grow. Where do I sign?"

"I don't have time for this," Mary snapped. "Far be it for me to distract you from your dream. I'll be waiting in the car. Enjoy."

"Come on. We haven't even made it to the river running through the backyard."

"Suit yourself. We have a lake at home. That's good enough for me."

Chapter Eight

The room exploded in applause as couple number nine wrapped up a stellar display during the icebreaker at the Before We Jump the Broom premarital counseling retreat. The couple—childhood sweethearts and recent college graduates dressed in jeans and T-shirts that read *Future Wifey* and *Future Hubby*—were the only duo so far to match all their answers correctly in a game called In the Love Seat. Although the exercise was not intended to be a competition, Martha was keeping score, and she and Oji were up next.

A riff on *The Newlywed Game,* the ten couples were separated and placed on opposite sides of Edin library's community room—an open space with dark stamped-concrete floors, white walls, and colorful artwork celebrating African American Southern artists. Each attendee received a list of questions to answer independently, and then the couples were called to sit on the two-seater couch at the front of the room to discover how many of their answers matched.

As Martha and Oji approached the love seat, she raised her hand in the air. "We got this," she said confidently as their palms made contact in a high five.

Oji chuckled. "Babe, I like your enthusiasm, but it's not really a contest. Let's just have fun," he said as they sat down on the yellow and green sofa.

The colors, combined with the furniture's midcentury modern design, produced a playful look that reminded Martha that the activity should be fun. Not that she took that to heart. *We'd better at least get second place,* she thought while giving a half smile. She was willing to lose the game to a couple who had spent most of their lives getting to know everything about each other, but she wouldn't easily be outdone by the other couples.

"Last but certainly not least, we've got couple number ten," announced Shari, the therapist hosting the retreat. She wore a short pixie cut with natural curls and bronze highlights that perfectly matched her skin. But instead of being in the wheelchair she used when Martha last saw her, she sat atop a mobility scooter in the same bright-blue color as her round retro eyeglasses.

A chatty woman from Macon, who sat next to Martha during the opening remarks and whose name Martha had already forgotten, began to clap. Her partner joined in, and soon a brief but rowdy round of applause broke out among the attendees.

When the clapping died down, Martha spoke. "Thank you, but you're obviously just anxious to get on with the morning snack break," she said with a giggle.

Nodding and soft laughter spread across the room.

"Please introduce yourselves," Shari said with a smile, picking up where she left off.

"Good morning. I'm Oji, and this is Martha, the love of my life," Oji said.

Martha blushed. "Hi, everybody. I didn't expect him to say that last part." She sneaked a loving glance at Oji as she addressed the group.

"Great! Thank you, Martha and Oji," Shari said. "You're our last couple, but I'll give you the same reminder I gave the others. Please try not to say what you think your partner will say just to get matching answers. Speak from your heart. Ready?"

Oji nodded.

"Yes!" Martha announced. Then she nudged Oji.

"Got it," Oji said.

"The first question is a fill-in-the-blank for Oji. The thing I love most about my fiancée is . . ." Shari said.

"This is easy," Oji bragged. "The thing I love most about my fiancée is that we're so much alike. She is essentially the female version of me."

Martha's eyes widened in surprise.

"And now, Martha, what is the thing that Oji loves most about you?" asked Shari.

"I said that I'm so supportive," Martha replied.

"Awww. *That's* true too," Oji said. Then he put his left arm around Martha and gave her a tight squeeze.

She leaned into his side hug, but apprehension replaced the burst of comfort she usually felt being close to him. *We do fit together rather nicely, but I've never thought about describing us quite the way he did. I wonder what he meant by it?*

"Okay, next question," Shari said as she adjusted her glasses. "It's another fill-in-the-blank for Oji. My fiancée hates my . . ."

"I have no doubt that we'll both get this one," Oji replied.

Martha chuckled, relaxing a bit.

"My fiancée hates my home office," he said.

"Yes! I said junky office," Martha said, waving her arms in the air.

"Now it's time for a high five," Oji said with a laugh. "Good job, babe!"

"We asked Oji, 'If your fiancée could have a new car or new clothes, which would she choose?' But let's switch it up and have Martha respond first," Shari said.

"Oh, okay. This one was hard, but I said clothes," Martha replied with a hint of hesitation in her voice. Then she hunched her shoulders as if she were waiting for a loud alarm to sound.

"Awww, man," Oji said, dragging out each word. "I said neither, because all you can talk about lately is a new house."

Martha playfully sulked. "But that wasn't an option. Can we get a do-over?"

Oji laughed.

"Unfortunately, there are no do-overs," Shari said a smile. "But you and Oji are learning about each other. That's what this game is really about."

"Good point, and who knew learning could be so much fun? Are we done yet?" Martha said sarcastically.

Oji shook his head.

Shari looked amused. "Not quite yet, but we're getting there. Oji, when is the last time you gave Martha flowers?"

Oji looked at Shari. "I promise you, we will get this one right. If we don't, we'll head straight to the car."

Martha laughed, and several people in the group joined in.

"Martha got flowers yesterday," said Oji, beaming.

"That's right!" Martha said. "Oji gets me flowers every Friday. It's a wonderful way to end the week."

A bright smile stretched across Oji's face. He lowered his head and tilted his neck so that his face was close to Martha's, and he tapped on his left cheek.

Martha laughed. "All right. You may have earned this," she said before kissing it.

"See, Martha, everyone wins in their own way," Shari said.

Martha and Oji chuckled.

"Here's your last question," Shari continued. "Who was interested in marriage first—you or your significant other? Oji, would you like to go first?"

"Gladly, because I know we'll get this one. Definitely me."

Martha pivoted in her seat. "Really? I said me," she announced as she looked at Oji with confusion on her face.

Oji put his arm around her. "I must say that I'm flattered," he boasted playfully, prompting a slew of laughs from the couples in the audience.

We may have failed that game, but at least he knows me well enough to understand how much I needed a moment to reset. I'll give him an extra point for that, Martha thought. She inhaled and imagined she just saw a cute puppy. A soft smile slowly appeared on her face as she exhaled.

The laughter began to die down. "You *should* be flattered. You found me, and I'm a good thing," she said, lightly pinching Oji's cheek. Then the laughter kicked up again.

"A *great* thing!" Oji added.

"Thank you, Martha and Oji. You can return to your seats with the other couples," Shari said.

Martha and Oji rose from the love seat as Shari explained how the couples could play the game at home on their own, but Martha didn't pay attention. And neither did Oji. He grasped her hand. Then he leaned down and whispered in her ear.

"Babe, don't sweat it. This is just a game. And we'll keep getting to know each other better day by day."

"Yes, of course," Martha responded, but her words didn't come out as light and airy as she intended. She felt weighed down.

She followed him to a pair of vacant chairs on the left side of the room, pretending to listen as Shari moved on to announcements about the snack options and restroom locations. She had more pressing matters on her mind.

Shari was right, Martha thought. Martha had indeed learned a few things in the game. Now she had to figure out what to do with them. She no longer cared that she and Oji hadn't won. Her focus shifted as she pondered their mismatched answers. And they all added up to one big question: If she and Oji were so much alike, did that mean he also came into the relationship with ulterior motives? Of course she loved him, and she didn't doubt his love for her any more than she doubted her love for him. But now she had questions about how they had arrived at this point, and she wondered what it meant for their future.

IN A MOVE that would surprise no one who knew her well, Martha ignored the instructions for the vision board activity—the last exercise of the retreat—and made up her own. She wasn't interested in working with Oji to build a visual representation of their goals around one of the suggested themes: wedding and honeymoon, family, material possessions, or finances. It wasn't so much that she had a problem with the approach per se. It just didn't align with the questions burning in her mind. And Oji had all the answers.

"What do you think of switching it up a little and making a vision board that reflects our long-term goals and overall relationship aspirations instead of drilling down on a particular area?" Martha asked as she rifled through the dozen magazines spread out on the rectangular folding table.

"I could tell something was on your mind as Shari explained the activity. I like where you're going with this. So, would the board kind of function as a vision statement for our relationship?"

Martha handed him an *Architectural Digest* magazine. "Exactly. It'll help us to determine if we prioritize working toward the same things."

"Or, as I like to say, to see if we're on—"

"The same page," they said simultaneously. They laughed together at his frequent use of the phrase. And for the first time, Martha realized she'd begun to use the phrase in conversation with people other than Oji, which made her laugh harder.

"Okay, let's choose some photos and then compare notes," she said.

"Sounds good. I already know what I'm looking for," he said as he rested the magazine on the table and opened it.

Martha grabbed an issue of *Essence* magazine for herself. She flipped the pages, cutting out several images along the way, but she felt like she was being watched. She lifted her eyes and found the source in the woman seated opposite her.

"Sorry, I didn't mean to stare," said Jessica, a woman who looked to be in her early thirties. She wore a Kool-Aid–red twist-out bob and a tight bodycon dress. "It's sweet that you two finish each other's sentences."

"Oh, that's kinda become a thing because Oji says 'on the same page' all the time," Martha replied as she flipped the magazine page and picked up a pair of scissors to cut an image. "At this point, I can almost sense when he's going to say it."

"Can I ask you something personal?" Jessica said. But she didn't wait for Martha to answer. She glanced at her fiancé, a conservatively dressed man with salt-and-pepper hair who looked old enough to be her father. Then she scooted her chair close to Martha and lowered her voice to a whisper. "You two seem a lot alike. Does it ever cause any problems? My ex-boyfriend and I were similar, so much so that we used to fight all the time. So for my next relationship, I found someone totally different," she said. She nodded her head quickly in her fiancé's direction to indicate that the next relationship she referenced was with him. "I couldn't see me and my ex lasting long term, but maybe you've discovered a secret to making it work that I wasn't able to figure out."

Martha froze. Already nervous about the issue of being similar to Oji, Jessica had spoken Martha's emerging fear— that their shared cunning nature would destroy the love they'd built despite starting their relationship for the wrong reasons. "What makes you say we're a lot alike?" she asked softly, still holding a page from the magazine in her left hand and with the fingers of her right hand inside the scissors' handles.

Jessica pressed her lips together and raised her eyebrows. "You don't think y'all are alike?" she asked, her voice still in a hushed volume.

"Not really," Martha replied. She rested the scissors on top of the open magazine.

"You both seem confident and comfortable in your skin and also with each other. And I noticed during the game this morning, Oji ignored the multiple-choice options in one of the questions and gave his own answer, just like you made your own rules with the vision board activity. But, girl, maybe I'm reading too much into it because of my history with my ex."

"That's interesting," Martha said, nervously tapping her foot.

"Just my two cents. But now I'll go back to minding my own business," Jessica said with her voice at a normal volume as she inched her chair back to its original spot.

Martha stared into space as Jessica's comments pingponged in her mind. In a vacuum, they would be meaningless, but she started connecting dots that she hadn't noticed before. *Was this what M.J. warned me about in the garden the other day? He said Oji and I are both strategic and that we're both playing chess.*

Martha vaguely heard Oji call her name, but she was too deep in her thoughts to respond.

I brushed off what M.J. said because I thought I had the upper hand. Then what does it mean that Oji said during the game that he loves that we're so much alike? Is he up to something? And he said he was thinking of marriage first, which adds a different context to his sudden proposal with no ring . . . and hiding the severity of his father's illness . . . and the secrecy about his parents. What is going on? What if all my maneuvering to get here is going to cause me to lose him now that I'm in love with him? And what if our relationship is one-sided and I've just ended up tricking my-self about us?

Rattled, Martha shifted her gaze to sneak a peek at Oji, but he stared back at her.

"What were you two whispering about over there?" he asked as the women continued to search the magazine pages.

"Just a little girl talk," Martha replied, acting unfazed.

Jessica flashed a melancholic smile.

"As long as y'all weren't talking about us," Oji said with a charming grin. He made eye contact with Jessica's fiancé, who smiled politely.

"This is your ten-minute warning to wrap up your vision boards," Shari said from the front of the room. "If you don't finish here, you can always complete them at home. We'll do brief closing remarks, and then that will be it for today's group activities. If you also sched-uled a private couples counseling session with me or one of the other counselors who joined us today, please check your confirmation emails for details about where to meet."

Martha turned to Oji. "That's our cue to discuss our photos. Are you all set?"

"I suppose that means I'm going first," he replied, with three images laid in front of him. He lifted one of the photos as he described it and placed it on the table between him and Martha. "For my first suggestion, I chose a photo of a couple sitting on a pier in the sunlight. It represents us having a bright future."

Martha picked up the half-page sized image. "They're looking at water. Is this your way of saying we're staying on my family's property for a while?"

"I didn't choose it for that reason. But that tracks with my preference, so I'll happily go along with that," Oji said with a smirk.

Martha shook her head.

"My next image is a photo of people stacking their hands together. This represents our families coming together."

Martha nodded. "That's thoughtful. I like it."

"And finally," Oji said, his eyes dancing with excitement, "this one is so perfect that I had to save it for last. I can't believe I found it: an image of two trees that have grown together so much that they look like they're hugging each other."

"And they just happen to look alike. What a coincidence," Martha said, straining to camouflage the uneasiness in her voice. She glanced at Jessica, who met Martha's gaze for a second before returning her attention to her fiancé as he spoke to Jessica about their vision board.

"That's true. Somehow I hadn't noticed that," Oji responded pensively.

"Do you mind if we finish at home? I need to run to the restroom, and I don't want to miss Shari's closing remarks," Martha said.

"No problem, babe. I'll be here."

PER THE DIRECTIONS in their confirmation email, Martha and Oji followed the back hallway outside the library's community room to the administrative suite, where each of the office doors was painted a different primary color. Oji seemed his usual self as they reached the green door, but Martha didn't say much. She was saving her words for whatever awaited them on the other side of the entryway. During Mary's counseling session, Martha had been put off by Shari's evenhanded approach and lack of deference to Martha's position at the hospital where they both worked. On one hand, since Shari hadn't been fooled by Martha's antics during Mary's counseling session, Martha wondered if today was the day she would have to pay for it. But on the other hand, who better to help Martha figure out if she was about to marry a man who, like her, had come to the relationship for the wrong reasons?

Before Shari asked some basic questions about Martha and Oji's relationship, she confirmed that they were both comfortable working with her even with Martha's previous experience attending Mary's counseling session. To the average person, Shari's gesture might have come across as an expected demonstration of professionalism, but it moved Martha. Of course she and Oji had no objections to having

Shari as their premarital counselor. They wouldn't have shown up if they felt otherwise. But the therapist's checking reassured Martha that Shari was indeed fair and unbiased.

"Are there specific things you want to cover in our sessions?" Shari asked as she looked back and forth between the couple. "Please keep in mind that we'll cover the usual topics, like spirituality and faith, money, interacting with each other's loved ones, sex, and kids. But it would help me get an idea of where we should start."

Oji glanced at Martha. "I would say communication is a priority."

"I agree," Martha replied. "I'd also add making decisions about where we'll live and navigating in-laws, but those problems may also be connected to communication."

Shari pushed her eyeglasses up on her nose. "Oji, do you agree with Martha that the issues around in-laws and where you'll live are tied to communication?"

"To some extent, but the housing issue really just comes down to different opinions about where we should live."

"Clearly, we value different things, but I don't understand the disconnect between us," Martha said. She looked at Oji when she spoke, but then she shifted her gaze to Shari. "Oji wants to move into my cottage on my family's property, but I want to move to Macon. His condo doesn't have enough space, so I'd like us to buy something together."

He shifted in his seat.

"Oji, you seem uncomfortable. What bubbled up for you as you listened to Martha's summary?" Shari asked.

"I'm dealing with a lot of stress because of my business and looking after my parents. It would be so much easier if Martha would just let this rest awhile," he said with a sigh.

"I don't understand what's the big deal," Martha said. "Neither of us is getting any younger. We need to hit the ground running if we want to grow our family and our careers."

Oji's voice grew tense as he doubled down. "But we don't need to move urgently, Martha. I'm telling you I can't handle it right now."

"Martha, before you respond, tell me what you understood Oji to say," Shari said.

"He says he can't handle it and that we have time. But it feels like the decision is all about what *he* wants. We both want kids, and I'm thirty-eight. Time isn't on my side, but Oji's not considering my perspective at all."

"I understand that this situation can feel overwhelming," Shari said. "It sounds like there's more than one issue here, and it's important not to lump everything together. I understand Oji to say that he can't handle buying a house right now. That's not exactly the same issue as family planning. Would it be the worst thing if you had a baby while you were living in your cottage or Oji's condo?"

Oji didn't look at Shari or Martha. With closed eyes, he placed his palms together and held his pointer fingers against his lips and nose.

"But why would I want to live in a smaller space or move while I'm pregnant if we don't have to do that?" Although Martha was responding to a question that Shari asked, she looked at Oji. "Why wouldn't we use our resources to make life more convenient and less stressful? Isn't that the whole point of working hard and saving? If the money is there, why not use it?" she continued, exasperation growing in her voice.

Oji hung his head and let out a loud sigh. "There's something I need to tell you, Martha."

Martha twisted her body in her seat to face Oji. *This sounds scary,* she thought.

After a second of silence, he lifted his head, faced Martha, and looked her in the eyes. "I can't afford a house. I didn't know how to tell you."

"That doesn't make sense," Martha said as she shook her head. "I get that you need more investors for the company, but the company is not failing, is it? No, it can't be. I've seen the income statement."

"My business is fine. It's my personal expenses. I'm supporting two households," Oji replied with big, gloomy eyes.

"What? Have you been keeping a secret love child from me? Or a whole family in another country?" Martha asked, raising her voice.

"No. But, babe, please keep your voice down. Someone might—"

"*Babe?* Don't *babe* me! And don't tell me to keep my voice down! *Now* you care about what people think? You weren't worried about that when you asked me to marry you in front of a hundred people with no ring? Oh! That's why there was no ring. You couldn't afford *that,* either, huh? *You* were trying to marry *me* for my money?" Tears streamed down her face.

Oji extended his arm to put it around her, but she wiggled away.

"Martha, I know this is really difficult and you're processing," Shari said. "But we want to make sure we talk to each other in ways and with tones that are still respectful."

"Please let me explain," Oji said.

Martha stared at him without uttering a word.

"My parents' finances are in shambles. It's a long story . . . The short version is they filed for bankruptcy after my dad had a stroke several years ago. My parents always lived above their means because my dad just never made the money my mom was accustomed to having with her family before she and my dad got married. So money was always tight, and my dad didn't prioritize taking his blood pressure medication. He didn't have health insurance when he had the stroke. And like for lots of people, the hospital costs took my parents under. So I support them financially."

"Wow. I'd never have guessed that," Martha said, with her feelings swinging like a pendulum after Oji's confession. "I'm so sorry. Why didn't you tell me? I would've understood."

"At what point would you have understood, Martha?" Oji asked. His voice cracked with emotion. "If I had told you when we first got together, I'm sure you'd have lost interest. Am I wrong?"

Martha shook her head as another round of tears formed in her eyes. "Probably not," she mumbled. "But I don't feel that way now."

"It's different for *me* now too, because I actually fell in love with you and you became my best friend. We aren't just a convenient match anymore," he said as he took Martha's hand. "I thought I would make more money on my last deal, which would've given me a cushion to get your ring and then everything else would've fallen into place sufficiently."

"You thought you could pull this all off without me noticing?" Martha asked through her tears.

"I figured we were enough alike that you would understand when it all worked out and we both got what we wanted."

Tears poured down Martha's face. "I can't do this," she said as she pulled her hand away from Oji. "I can't marry you."

MINUTES AFTER Oji's confession, Martha and Shari sat in silence across from each other. With Oji having left the counseling session to give her an opportunity to decompress and sort out her feelings with Shari, Martha rocked from side to side with her hands covering her face. The movements didn't soothe her as much as she'd hoped, but they provided a channel for the nervous energy in her body as, over and over, she ran through the words exchanged during the session. No matter which angle she used to assess the situation, she felt played—by Oji and by herself.

"Do you feel ready to talk, or would you prefer some additional time?" Shari asked after the five minutes of cooldown time Martha had requested.

Martha snuffled as she lowered her hands to her lap. "I'm probably as ready as I'll ever be."

"As you know, I can't serve as your individual therapist since I'm seeing you and Oji for couples counseling. But given what you've just learned, I want to check in with you to make sure you're okay. I'm happy to refer you to another counselor for individual counseling if you're interested."

"I would welcome your recommendation. You must think I'm a piece of work after the way I behaved with Mary and

now seeing this situation I've gotten myself into with Oji."
She fiddled with the three large freshwater pearls on the
gold bracelet she wore on her left wrist.

"No, I don't judge you. Most people have some sort of
emotional baggage or unprocessed trauma that can affect
their lives and their relationships. And that baggage can
play out differently for each person."

Martha cracked her knuckles. "So I need to work on this
with my own therapist?"

"Yes, you should explore it with your new therapist. And
if you and Oji decide to continue your relationship, I would
strongly suggest you both continue couples counseling. I
told him the same thing when I stepped out to check in with
him before he left."

"You did? What did he say about that recommendation?"

"He agreed. And he said he hoped you'd also be willing
to do so," Shari said with a soft smile.

"That's a relief," Martha replied. "If I may ask, how was
Oji when you spoke to him?"

Shari nodded. "It seems the session was challenging for
both of you, and I encourage you guys to discuss it. How
are you feeling now?"

"I'm devastated that Oji wasn't honest," Martha said as
she grabbed a tissue from the box on the desk and dabbed
her eyes. "But as hard as that is to deal with, I'm having a
tougher time dealing with myself. How was I attracted to
someone so much like myself? And how did I miss it?"

"What do you mean by so much like yourself?"

"It's embarrassing, but I was also initially interested in
Oji because of superficial things."

Shari pushed her glasses up on her nose. "Like what? Are you saying you were attracted to Oji because you thought he had money?"

"Yes. And his family is well-connected in the community. I've always wanted to marry well."

"So, are you upset with yourself because you were superficial or because it backfired?"

"Both. I should've known better."

Chapter Nine

The members of the Gardin family chatted on Naomi's back porch after their weekly Sunday dinner, still reeling from the news of Martha's canceled wedding. But Martha didn't join in the conversation. She swung back and forth in the egg-shaped basket swing with closed eyes, quietly contemplating the preceding day and what would happen next. After nearly eighteen hours of ignoring Oji's calls and texts, Martha had finally relented when her phone rang with an entry request from the front gate of the Gardin family estate. She kept her split-minute decision close to her chest and opted not to keep watch for Oji's arrival, choosing instead to let her family respond to him first.

A moment of silence fell across the back porch, signaling to Martha that the time had come. She opened her eyes to bewildered looks on her family members' faces as Oji stood on the stretch of well-manicured St. Augustine grass adjacent to the porch, holding a double bouquet of pink peonies, hydrangeas, and queen proteas.

"You didn't think you were still invited to Sunday dinner, did you?" Mary snidely asked. She sat in a chair next to Ruth, who placed her head in her hands after Mary finished speaking.

Nicholas jumped to his feet. "How did you get through the gate?"

Oji's eyes widened as he whipped his head toward Martha.

"Y'all, it's okay. I let him in through my cellphone," Martha said coolly.

"Oh, all right," Nicholas said.

Naomi rose from her seat next to Nicholas on the sofa and grabbed his hand. "We're going to head inside and give you two some privacy," she announced as she looked to Martha.

Ruth stared at Oji with cold eyes. "Pretty flowers," she said as she rose to her feet.

"We'll be just inside if you need us, Martha," Nicholas said.

"That's right," Mary added.

"May I say something before you leave?" Oji asked with apprehension in his voice. He paused for a moment until he had everyone's attention. "I understand that not only did I hurt Martha, but I hurt you too. And I'm very sorry. I was selfish, and my initial intentions were not pure. But I did not intend to dishonor your family or Martha."

Oji shifted his gaze to Martha, who wiped her eyes with the palms of her hands. "I love Martha very much. We have some things to work through. I understand that I have to earn her trust again."

Then he again looked back toward the Gardin family members, making eye contact with each of them briefly as he spoke. "And I have to earn *yours,* too. I hope you can find it in your hearts to forgive me."

"Thank you, Oji. That was very moving," Naomi said as

she dabbed her eyes with her free hand. The other hand still clutched Nicholas's. "We can extend forgiveness to you because that is the right thing to do. As far as rebuilding our relationship with you, first we'll see what Martha decides. Then we'll go from there."

"That means a lot to me," Oji said. He clutched the flowers in his left arm and wiped his eyes with his right hand.

"Yes, we'll see," Ruth replied with a stern face.

Mary looked down at her feet.

Nicholas looked Oji in the eye and nodded his head a single time. Then Naomi pulled her husband away to go into the house with Ruth and Mary.

Martha slid out of the swing and walked to the edge of the porch without making eye contact with Oji. She extended her arms to accept the flowers, but she still didn't look directly at him when he transferred them to her arms. Then she pivoted toward the doorway. "Aunt Naomi, would you put these in water for me?"

After a swift handoff, Martha made her way to the sitting area.

Oji stepped up from the thick carpet-like lawn onto Naomi's back porch and followed Martha to the sofa. "I can fix this. Please don't cancel the wedding."

"It's done. I've already talked with the wedding planner," Martha said in a monotonous voice as she plopped onto the sofa and crossed her arms. She looked away from Oji as she spoke, fighting to hold in her emotion.

He sat down next to her, turning his body to face her. "We can always call and tell her the wedding is back on. I'm sure we wouldn't be the first couple she's had to do that for."

Martha shook her head and looked away. "No, I meant

that we're not in any position to get married. We're not ready. Do we really even know each other? And is our relationship even salvageable?" Tears fell from her eyes.

"Oh, babe, please don't cry. I can't take it," Oji said as he placed his hands on the sides of her face and wiped away her tears. "We can get through this. Please don't give up on us. We actually know each other well. That's part of why we fit together so easily."

"Well, how did we end up here?" Martha asked.

"We probably know each other *so well* that we tricked ourselves."

"Huh? I was with you for a minute, but then you lost me."

"I suspect we recognized similarities in each other and took it for granted that the other person had similar unspoken expectations. Does that make sense?"

"I think so. You mean like when you referred to us as a 'convenient match' yesterday in counseling?" Martha asked.

"Yes, exactly. And then when we really fell for each other, the rules we were playing by changed. But we never talked about that part. We just went along with the relationship. So when I wasn't honest with you about my finances, you felt betrayed." He looked so confident that Martha imagined he explained complicated real-estate projections to potential investors with the same conviction.

"That's why I'm kicking myself," he continued. "First of all, I shouldn't have begun our relationship under what I knew to be false pretenses. But I should've believed in you . . . No, in *us*. I should've believed in us enough to realize that our relationship would survive if I came clean about my financial situation and the extent of my father's illness."

Martha looked down as she cracked her knuckles. *But how can we really survive this if I can't say the part that I've been holding back?*

"Did I lose you again?" Oji asked.

Martha lifted her head and stared into his pleading eyes. *The love I feel for him hasn't changed, and I can't bear the thought of ruining it by not being honest,* she thought, finally finding the strength to say what needed to be said. "No, that was almost right."

He leaned forward. "Almost?"

"I mostly felt betrayed because I thought I was fooling you about my initial interest in you. But it turns out you saw me for what I was . . . and you were the one fooling me," Martha said with downcast eyes.

"Oh, I see," Oji said. He sounded relieved. "I'm accustomed to women being interested in me for those reasons." He put his arm against the top of the sofa and rested the side of his head in his hand.

Martha's head spun toward Oji. "But I'm not the other women you dated before me," she said with wide eyes and a voice laden with hurt. "And I certainly don't want to be treated like them. I hate that you thought of me that way. But, regardless, I owe you an apology too. I'm sorry."

"No, you're not like the women before you. I've never let anyone into the spaces of my life that I've shared with you. Or my heart, for that matter," he said, his voice cracking a little. "And I didn't expect an apology from you, either, but I appreciate it. I guess we both have some things to work on. And we need to get on the same page about the state of my finances."

Martha slowly closed her eyes and reopened them, bracing herself. "What is it?" she asked.

"My parents have been reluctant to downsize to a less stately home, as my mother put it," Oji said. "So they took out a second mortgage. But I make the monthly payments. I also cover the costs of landscaping and exterior upkeep, but the inside of the house could use some TLC."

Martha dropped her arms into her lap. "That's why you leave me in the car whenever we have to stop by your parents' house and why your mom hasn't invited me over for dinner?"

"That's one of the reasons." He ran his hand across his forehead.

Martha leaned closer to him. "What else is there?"

"My mother and I have had some discussions about how she and my dad will manage financially after we get married."

"She's threatened by *me*?" Martha asked.

Oji smiled softly. "Those probably aren't the words she would choose, but I think you can understand that she feels a bit insecure in her future since another woman will become my priority."

"So how do you see us working through this?" She felt exhausted just thinking about the drudgery of a financial tug-of-war with Eve. But given the way Martha had treated Ruth after she married Beau, she could admit that it would be fair to reap what she had sown.

"Before I answer that, I want to make sure we're clear on one thing: It never crossed my mind to use your money to take care of my parents."

"That's a relief," Martha said with a sigh. "We both came to this relationship for superficial reasons, but it would've ventured into a different territory if you were expecting me to subsidize your parents."

Oji hung his head. "I'm sorry I've made you doubt me so much."

"I just didn't know what to think anymore, and that's no way to start a marriage. I want to be confident about who we both are as individuals as well as a couple before we move forward with the wedding."

He lifted his head. "I can't argue with that. I've put us in the situation, and I'll get us out of it," he said. "The best solution is to sell my company. I'll have enough money to provide for my parents for a good while and make a plan for their long-term care. I can also buy your ring and be on solid financial footing when you're ready to get married. And in the meantime, we can work on ourselves and our relationship."

"But you said you weren't ready to sell. Are you sure that's the right thing to do?"

Oji picked up Martha's hand and interlaced his fingers in hers. "Sometimes we have to make sacrifices for the people who are most important to us."

"You arranged these so nicely," Martha said as she entered Naomi's living room.

Naomi was cuddled with Nicholas on the sofa. "Thanks, but I just trimmed the stems and dropped the flowers in water. That's it."

Martha lifted the five-pound hand-cut vase a couple of

inches off the black grand piano, admiring its pointed arches and elegant curves. "Why didn't you put them in one of those vases that come from the florist instead of such a nice crystal one? You've got to have some of those around here somewhere."

"Nicholas moved them to the garage for the thrift-store drop-off. I know where you live. I'll just come to your house to get my good vase if you don't bring it back quickly enough. But you can enjoy it for now," Naomi teased as she craned her neck to get a glimpse at Martha. "Now, stop stalling and tell us whatever update you planned to share."

Nicholas twisted toward the piano. "Yes, please," he chimed in. "This is a very new experience for me. My nieces and nephews lived far away. I didn't have this kind of access to what happened in their daily lives, so I've been pestering your aunt with my thoughts. She's not as excitable as I am."

"Honey, I wasn't going to tell on you. You can't hold water, as my mother used to say," Naomi said with a laugh. She placed her feet on the floor and straightened up on the couch.

Nicholas blushed. "I can keep a secret when it's necessary, but I don't care if Martha knows that I'm interested in her well-being."

Martha smiled and sat down on the piano bench. "I love that you each have your own ways of showing how much you care for me. I really treasure that. It seems Oji and I are on the same page now."

Nicholas's mouth fell open. "So the wedding is back on? Are you sure you want to do that, Martha?"

Naomi placed her hand on his knee and rubbed it gently.

"Oh, no," Martha said, waving her hands. "Hopefully,

we'll get there eventually. But for now we're going to work on our relationship. Time will tell about the wedding."

Nicholas looked at Naomi. His tense facial muscles had relaxed, but Martha could tell he wasn't sure what to say.

"And how do you feel about that?" Naomi asked her.

Nicholas nodded.

"Better than I did before Oji and I talked. Things between us didn't feel bad before, but it's amazing how much freer and lighter I feel. And the path seems clearer, though we'll likely still have some bumps ahead . . . I feel more positive than I sound. I'm actually quite optimistic," Martha said with the analytical tone and cadence she usually reserved for discussing patient cases with her clinical colleagues.

"I don't know. It sounds like there's a *but* in there somewhere. Am I wrong?" Nicholas said.

Martha flashed a soft, endearing smile. "No, you're right. There's still the issue of Oji's mom. That still weighs on me. I'm not saying I need her approval to marry Oji, but I'd prefer to have it. It'll make everything so much smoother, don't you think?"

"We can relate to that," Naomi said. "We wouldn't have married until Ruth was comfortable with it, but it's very much a personal decision. You and Oji need to be in one accord about it, whether y'all decide you want her approval first or not. That's the most important thing."

"And how do the two of you feel about Oji?" Martha asked.

Nicholas tilted his head. "Well, I'm disappointed in the way he handled things, but I appreciate his accountability. I stand by what your aunt said to him on the porch. We had talked about it beforehand, and we feel similarly."

Martha looked at Naomi.

"I really don't have much to add to what Nicholas said. You know my general rule: As long as y'all feel safe in your relationships, I'll continue to be supportive. Of course, I'm cautious about anyone trying to take advantage of our family. We welcomed Oji with open arms, so that's the part I'm still a little sensitive about."

"That's understandable. Oji and I are working through that, and I admitted to him that I initially had similar motives in regard to his family. I needed to be honest with him about that because I don't want to play any more games going forward," Martha said with her voice becoming shaky. "And it's important to me to share all that with the two of you, too." Tears fell from her eyes as she blinked.

Nicholas cleared his throat and caught Martha's gaze. "I'm pleased to hear that you're learning and taking the opportunity to grow through all this. I feel like we're getting to see you become the best version of yourself."

Naomi sniffled.

Without turning away from Martha, Nicholas lifted Naomi's hand from the couch cushion. He sandwiched her hand in his and rested their hands on his leg. "I'm reminded of when you asked me about my intentions with your aunt. Remember that protectiveness you expressed for her? That's how I feel about you and the rest of this family, so I'm watching Oji closely. I hope to regain the sense that I can trust him with you . . . With all of you."

"I'm proud of you, Martha," Naomi said as she dabbed her eyes with her free hand. Then she leaned her head on Nicholas's shoulder. "Thank you for that," she whispered.

"I believe Oji will regain your trust," Martha replied.

"So do I," Nicholas said. "It's an honor to earn the love of a Gardin woman. It's truly been a transformative experience in my life. I hope Oji realizes what's at stake."

"This may not be the best time to bring it up, but I have a favor to ask of you," Martha said.

Nicholas raised a single eyebrow. "Okay," he said, exaggerating the second syllable. "What is it?"

"Please hear me out before you respond." Martha cleared her throat. "Oji is thinking about selling his company. I'm not sure that's the best thing for him to do, but it's his decision. I'm not going to try to change his mind. I would like him to make an informed decision and not do anything hasty."

Unsure of what to make of the blank expression on Nicholas's face, Martha kept talking. "Since I happen to know one of the most sought-after merger-acquisition-divestiture consultants in the world, I'm wondering if you would consider talking with him." She ended with a nervous smile.

"Martha, I'm retired from consulting. I stopped opening the dozen or so emails I get each week asking me to take on projects. My hands are full at Gardin Family Enterprises."

"I'm not asking for you to take him on as a client. I'm just asking for a conversation. Even thirty minutes would be helpful."

Nicholas shook his head. "I don't know about this."

Martha peered at her aunt, with her big eyes begging for help.

"No, ma'am," Naomi said without flinching. "You couldn't pay me enough to add my two cents to this conversation. This is strictly between the two of you."

Martha cracked her knuckles as she pondered the situation. Nicholas frequently said he'd happily failed at his first attempt at retirement because his version of working part-time as the chief operating officer of Gardin Family Enterprises involved as many hours per week as most people spent on a full-time job. He had been vocal about the responsibility he felt to share his insight with interested family members and friends. He enjoyed the interaction with them and saw his efforts as a way to contribute to building generational wealth. So Nicholas's lack of enthusiasm didn't add up by Martha's calculation.

Martha let out a big sigh. "Tell me the real reason you're reluctant. I can take it," she said, digging into the vulnerability she felt was needed for a productive dialogue.

Naomi swung her head in Nicholas's direction.

"Did Oji ask you for this?" Nicholas asked plainly.

The look on Naomi's face told Martha she wondered the same thing.

"No, it's my idea. I didn't share it with him at all. I wanted to bring it up with you first," Martha said with the punchiness of someone who sensed she was making progress.

"Martha, and I say this with love, if I find out you're trying to manipulate me in any way, we're going to have a serious problem," Nicholas said.

Martha winced. "I can't blame you for that. I've more than earned it with my behavior over the years. But I promise you, this is an earnest request. I will not betray your trust."

Chapter Ten

Late July

Jasmine whisked Martha into the corridor next to the circulation desk as soon as Martha crossed the threshold of the Minnie Lee Smith Public Library.

"Great! You made it. Traffic must've been brutal. Let me give you a quick briefing before you get started." The words came out of her community outreach manager's mouth fast and forcefully, like water from a fire hydrant. Martha could tell Jasmine didn't want her to say anything.

Martha leaned against the light-blue wall, attempting to look unfazed. But in a pair of tailored navy slacks, a simple white button-down shirt, and sensible black flats, she felt like a schoolgirl caught by her favorite teacher in the hallway. "Do I have a minute to stop in the restroom to check my hair?" she asked, caving to the shift in the usual power dynamic between her and Jasmine.

Jasmine shook her head. "No, but your hair looks nice. It's stylish but unpretentious, which is perfect for a community talk."

"Thank you," Martha replied, shrugging away her self-consciousness about her appearance with an anxious grin. After an emotionally exhausting weekend, she had overslept. With no time to curl her hair, she wet it during her shower, applied some gel, and brushed it away from her face before putting on a pair of medium-sized silver hoop earrings.

"I sent a flyer to some local senior groups, so we've got a nice turnout—way more than I expected," Jasmine said. "The blood pressure monitors are on the tables. I'll introduce you briefly. Then I'll follow your lead when it's time for the demonstration."

"I suppose that's good news, but I'd actually hoped for a small group this morning," Martha replied in a bashful tone.

Jasmine's face looked as though someone in the passenger seat had suddenly slammed on the brakes in a car she was driving. "Why would you want that?"

"I had a busy weekend and didn't prepare my notes. I expected to get here a few minutes early to gather myself, but traffic was horrible."

Jasmine put her hands on Martha's shoulders. "I'm not worried at all." Then her words finally slowed to a regular pace. "You've got all the information you need in your head. Just talk to them like you would talk to your patients or one of your family members."

"That's really helpful," Martha said, taken aback by how much Jasmine's words soothed her self-doubt.

Martha rarely let on how much she struggled with insecurity. As a college student, she'd learned that she performed better on assignments if she dedicated herself to intensive planning and preparation. This carried over into medical school, where she began to struggle with performance anxiety during rounds and worsened whenever she had to speak in front of a crowd. She easily spent two evenings writing and rewriting her notes for an informal fifteen-minute presentation like the one at the library. She was okay once she got started, but getting to that point was frequently an uphill battle. Standing before Jasmine, Martha wondered how different things might play out if she shared more with people she trusted instead of keeping her challenges bottled up.

Now that the door to her emotions was pried open, Martha walked through it to process her thoughts out loud. "And since we have quite a few people this morning, I should probably keep my talk to about ten minutes so there's adequate time for a robust question-and-answer period as well as the demonstration and practice session with the monitors, right?"

"Precisely," Jasmine said.

"Great," Martha said, buoyed by the validation. Ordinarily, she would've wondered whether sharing her apprehension caused Jasmine's faith in her to falter. However, Jasmine's voice exuded firm reassurance, and her word choice signaled to Martha that there was no cause for concern.

Martha followed Jasmine halfway down the hall to a meeting room with a placard that read *Storytime* next to the doorframe. A new idea for her talk popped into her head the second she read the sign. Jasmine commenced her ninety-second introduction as soon as she entered the room, providing just enough time for Martha's idea to take root before she talked herself out of it.

"I'm here to tell you a story. This story is not based on a particular person. It's based on my overall experience studying medicine and seeing patients for the past nine years,"

Martha said as she paced back and forth across the front of the room. "If any parts of the story seem familiar, it's a coincidence. But coincidences are entirely possible, because this is a story that happens to many people across the country, including people in our community, our family members, and our friends. If you have questions at any point during the story, please let me know. I'd like this to feel like a conversation, so jump in at any time." She spoke calmly and confidently, capturing the attention of the nearly fifty people seated at circular tables.

"Ms. W. is a sixty-five-year-old woman. She has had high blood pressure for thirty years. She hasn't been diagnosed with any other medical problems. She was prescribed medicine for her blood pressure, but she doesn't like taking it. She says it makes her go to the bathroom a lot. Can anyone here relate to that?"

"Mm-hmm." said several people in the audience. And multiple attendees raised their hands.

"I see that Ms. W. has some friends who've joined us here today," Martha said.

"Doc," yelled a man at the back of the room. "I used to have that problem. Would you suggest Ms. W. talk to her doctor about switching to another medicine? Seems to me she could get into trouble because she doesn't take it."

"Yes, you're absolutely right. I should have you attend all my talks from now on," Martha replied with a bright smile.

"Always happy to help, Doc," the man replied, poking out his chest with pride.

"So, Ms. W. came into the office to see me because she has begun to experience difficulty with making decisions. It takes her longer to decide what to do. She doesn't feel confused, but she has trouble solving everyday problems such as how to rearrange her schedule after a former neighbor asked to change the time they would meet up at the movie theater. Does anyone have questions so far?"

Martha scanned the room. None of the attendees raised their hands. But since their eyes were glued on her, she kept talking. "So I ran some tests and I diagnosed Ms. W. with vascular dementia. Has anyone heard of that?"

A young woman sitting in the rear of the room raised her hand. "Is that like Alzheimer's?" she asked as she bounced a toddler on her knee.

"That's what *I* was about to say," said a man seated at an adjacent table. He hastily typed into his cellphone and barely looked up.

"Good question!" Martha declared, feeding off the energy in the room. "There are many types of dementia. Alzheimer's is the most common. Vascular dementia is another. It can happen when the blood vessels supplying the brain narrow or become blocked. People with these two conditions can have similar symptoms, but I'll tell you a difference that we've noticed between them. Do you want to know?"

No one uttered a peep, but eyes across the room stared back at Martha. She cupped her right hand, held her hand to her ear, and tilted her head toward the audience. "I can't hear you," she said.

"Yes," mumbled a handful of voices among the audience.

"What was that?" Martha replied, again repeating the gesture with her hand and ear.

This time nearly the entire crowd joined in with a resounding response. "Yes!" they exclaimed.

"Shhhhh," Martha replied, holding her index finger to her lips. "This is a library."

Laughter broke out across the room.

"Okay, back to business," she said with a grin. "People with Alzheimer's dementia may have similar symptoms as people who have vascular dementia. People diagnosed with Alzheimer's *usually* have memory loss. People with vascular dementia *may* have memory loss, but they more frequently notice difficulty with their speed of thinking and problem solving, especially in the early stages of the disease. They can also have short periods of sudden confusion. Those are general things we've noticed, but symptoms can vary based on the individual."

She stepped up to the round table in front of her. "May I have your help?" she asked a woman wearing a red baseball cap and denim dress.

"It depends," the woman replied timidly.

"That's a wise answer," Martha replied with a smile. "There's a device close to you on the table. Would you mind handing it to me?"

"Easy enough," the woman responded as she lifted the monitor from the table and extended her arms toward Martha.

"Thank you," Martha said, balancing the monitor in both hands. "This is a blood pressure monitor. Uncontrolled blood pressure is one of the biggest risk factors for developing vascular dementia. Other risk factors include diabetes, high cholesterol, smoking, and a history of heart disease or stroke. Today we're focusing on blood pressure, so we'll show you how you can use a blood pressure monitor. You may have seen similar monitors in a store or online.

But now you can also borrow one from the library to use at home, or you can come here and use one."

FUELED BY THE remnants of adrenaline that had rushed through her body during her talk, Martha stuffed the last monitor into its box and gathered the leftover educational handouts from the table.

"If you keep doing my job, you won't need me anymore," Jasmine said jovially.

"No need to worry about that. What would I ever do without you?" Martha asked, rotating a hundred eighty degrees on her heels to find Jasmine and a woman who had observed quietly from the corner of the room during her presentation and the early part of the blood pressure monitor exercise.

"Hello, Dr. Gardin. I'm Samantha Stamos, the adult services librarian. But everyone calls me Sam," said the woman, who wore curly auburn Sisterlocks.

Martha shook her hand. "Thanks so much for inviting us, Sam. I hope you're pleased with the way everything turned out today."

"I couldn't be happier," Sam said with a twinkle in her almond-shaped eyes. "I've never seen one of our groups so engaged in a health discussion. I hated to leave early, but I had to step away to prepare for another event. Would you be willing to work with us on activities related to the other vascular dementia risk factors you mentioned?"

"Yes, we would love—" Jasmine stopped. "I'm sorry. I got carried away. But I'll calm down and let Dr. Gardin answer for herself." She made a playful, exaggerated exhale gesture.

"No worries, Jasmine," Martha said with a chuckle. "We're a package deal. I wouldn't dream of coming back without you."

"Thank you!" Sam exclaimed. "And I don't mean to ask too much from you, but one of our seniors made me promise to invite you to the kickoff of our new walking program. It's in September."

"Too much? It touches my heart that one of your seniors would make the request," Martha said, overlapping her hands at the center of her chest. "Plus, physical activity helps with blood pressure control and blood flow to the brain, so your walk is a fantastic tie-in to today's discussion topic. I need to check my calendar, but I would be honored to attend."

"Wonderful! I hope you can make it. Either way, I'd love to talk with you and Jasmine about other ideas for the walking club and also the possibility of partnering on other programming. And the two of you may have some ideas too. That's why partnerships are so powerful. We can feed off each other."

"Agreed!" Jasmine declared. Her face glowed like a proud coach after her team won a championship game. "I'll follow up with you when I get to the office. This sounds like the start of a rewarding partnership."

"Sounds good," Sam said. "Please forgive me, but I've got to finish preparing for the event we're having this afternoon. I'm filling in for our teen librarian."

"No problem," Martha replied. "We're just about done

here gathering our materials, so we can see ourselves out. I'm looking forward to following up with you."

As soon as Sam left the room, Jasmine covered her mouth with her hand and pretended to scream as she jumped up and down.

Martha let out a belly laugh, which felt appropriate both as a celebration of her advancing work with the library and as a response to Jasmine's excitement.

Jasmine jumped a few times more before suddenly stopping. "You are the bomb diggity."

Martha froze. "Are you serious right now? You remember that?"

A huge grin spread across Jasmine's face. "You are the bomb diggity," she repeated.

Martha stood silently, staring at Jasmine. Suddenly she wasn't a doctor standing in a library meeting room with a member of her staff. She was a teenager again, studying with her best friend and celebrating when one of them got the answer right as they quizzed each other on historical facts for Mrs. Osborne's midterm exam.

"Come on, Martha. Don't leave me hanging," Jasmine cheered.

"No doubt," Martha said softly. She couldn't muster the vigor required for the celebratory call-and-response affirmation she and Jasmine had used daily to encourage each other as adolescents. Although it was as fitting in this setting as it was when they were kids, it was also a bittersweet reminder of the close friendship Martha had missed for many years.

"I would give you a hug, but that might be too much, huh?" Jasmine said, still sounding giddy.

"Yeah, let's hold off on the hug," Martha replied. She smiled nervously.

Jasmine stood up straight and held her head high. "Got it," she replied, transitioning to a less excited and more professional tone. "We don't need much time for a debrief. Since we've got the room, do you want to go over things here or when we get back to the office?"

Martha quickly weighed the pros and cons. As the day went on, more and more vulnerability was seemingly required. It was beginning to weigh on her, and she needed some time alone to recover. But in the moment, she desired Jasmine's objective assessment of her performance more than she craved emotional distance. "Let's talk now. I'm going to work from home the rest of the day."

"Is everything okay? Since when do you work from home?" Jasmine said.

Martha nodded. "Yeah, I could do with a little change of scenery, that's all," she said, hoping to squelch any further inquiry from Jasmine.

"All right." Jasmine moved her eyes to look at Martha without turning her face. "Just checking. Today was a different vibe for us, so I want to make sure we're good."

Martha looked away from her. "Absolutely," she said, instantly wishing she'd have opted to have the discussion another time. "You did the job you were hired to do, and you excelled at it."

"That wasn't just the job, Martha. Last time I checked, giving my boss a pep talk is not part of my job description. And don't tell me it falls under 'other duties as assigned.'"

"I see you've got jokes today," Martha said, softening up.

"See what I mean. You wouldn't say that to anyone else

you supervise. You're the one who's supposed to motivate and encourage me to excel at my job, not the other way around."

"I didn't see it that way, but you've raised a good point," Martha said. "It speaks to your leadership skills. Perhaps I could recommend you for the hospital's leadership-development program."

Jasmine shot her boss a knowing look. "Thank you, but giving me a compliment is not going to distract me from the issue, Martha," she said firmly.

Why do I feel like I'm about to be sent to detention for being smart-alecky with my teacher? Martha thought as she stared blankly at Jasmine.

"I'm constantly flip-flopping back and forth from interacting with you in a professional manner to acting like we're buddies who hang out on the weekend," Jasmine said. "You're my boss, yet we work together so seamlessly because I still know you so well."

Martha blinked slowly, still staring at Jasmine. *She's not wrong. She pulled me together just like she used to.*

"Please stop looking at me like that. You're making me feel like I'm asking my friend with benefits for a real relationship, and that's not cool," Jasmine said with one of those laughs people let out when they've had their fill of someone's foolishness.

"You're right . . . I'm sorry I came off that way. I'll work on that . . . I value your insight, and I don't want to lose it."

Jasmine scoffed. "That still sounds like something you read in a management book."

"I'm doing the best I can right now, but I promise I hear you," Martha said with frayed nerves.

"Thank you. I just don't know how to take you some-times. I keep feeling like I'm going to step on a land mine one of these days and you're going to cut me off again. But then I'm like, 'She's your boss. She can't just dip out. She has to show up to work.'"

Martha leaned against the table. "I hate that I make you feel that way. I don't know how to do this either," she con-fessed, making eye contact with Jasmine. "It's not like I usually let people tell me what to do, but it's different with you. I trust you. You didn't lead me wrong today. Actually, you never have. I feel like you're about to leave me. We have a good thing going, and it's just starting, so please don't quit," she said, her voice wavering under the weighty con-versation.

Jasmine leaned on the table next to Martha with her arms still folded. "I just don't want it to get to the point where it gets messy between us. My career is important to me. I don't want our history to become a professional liabil-ity."

"It won't. I'll make sure of it," Martha resolved. With the chaos in her personal life, she couldn't bear to lose the sta-bility she'd gained at work through Jasmine.

THE STIFLING SUMMER heat couldn't smother the freedom Martha savored as she turned her car out of the library parking lot onto the tree-lined street. It wasn't so much that her discussion with Jasmine itself had stressed her out, but the emotional fluctuations she had experienced over the previous hour and a half left her feeling boxed in. She still hadn't decided if she would work from home or take the rest of the day off. That would depend on her state of mind when she got home. For now, she looked forward to decompressing on the drive, but she would have to do a little work before she got on the interstate so she wouldn't feel like she was cutting corners by being away from the office.

Although Martha knew a fair amount about Macon and the surrounding towns by virtue of having grown up in Edin, she'd learned the hard way that she still had a lot to learn about the attributes of the various neighborhoods and villages in the vicinity, as well as the people who lived in them. A patient or two had put her in her place about the assumptions she'd made.

"There's more to our communities than what you see on the news," a woman had told Martha at a church's health festival when Martha had assumed that people in the neighborhood didn't walk for exercise because of the crime in their area. The woman told Martha that while recent incidents deterred residents from utilizing certain spots after dark, a number of new initiatives had popped up, including a slew of walking clubs, group bicycling events, and advocacy activities to formalize a trail that had developed along a path people frequently used in a wooded patch of land near the playground.

In addition to hiring Jasmine, Martha integrated an approach her new outreach manager suggested to help her address her blind spots: performing windshield surveys on a regular basis. Jasmine described them as a fancy way of saying Martha would drive around and see what's happening in the communities she served. And Jasmine shared a strategy with Martha that she borrowed from people looking for housing in an area in which they're not familiar. "A neighborhood can take on an entirely different personality in the daytime compared to the evenings and weekends that you're usually available to visit them. If we're going to work in communities, we need to know what happens there around the clock," Jasmine had said.

Did the insurance company move, or did it go out of business? Martha thought as she drove by a green shotgun house that looked like it was built in the early 1900s. More and more, houses in the area had become commercial properties, and Martha worried that the people who used to live in them were displaced to areas farther away from the primary care center, where many of them received health services and medications at a reduced cost. She made a mental note to stop in to meet the new bakery's owner and also talk to Jasmine about ways to partner with the library and other community partner organizations to support residents dealing with housing issues.

Martha found herself so immersed in her windshield survey that she made a wrong turn, which took her in the opposite direction of the interstate. She spotted a gas station up ahead where she could turn around, but as she approached it, she recognized that she'd ventured into the rear portion of the neighborhood where Oji's parents lived.

Well, this is the perfect opportunity to do a windshield survey for my personal life, she thought. The notion amused Martha so intensely that she laughed out loud.

As Martha turned onto a quiet residential street, she abandoned her usual tendency to rush. Driving at the posted twenty-miles-per-hour speed limit hardly gave her enough time to absorb the architectural details of the historic homes, so she crept along at a relaxing fifteen miles per hour. The few times Martha had ridden through the neighborhood with Oji, her head whipped back and forth endeavoring to take in the assortment of beautiful late nineteenth- and twentieth-century Revival-style mansions. At the four-way stop, Martha recognized the large white late Victorian home with a wraparound porch—the landmark designating the Greenwalds' street. She turned right, admiring the steeply pitched gable roof of a brown Tudor home across the street with a tennis court visible through the fence.

Martha felt like a private investigator on a top-secret mission, only her covert adventure lacked an important objective, unless nosiness somehow counted. Although she hoped to evade Eve's field of view, she certainly wanted to catch a glimpse of the Greenwald matriarch in her natural surroundings. Martha didn't have a plan, except that she needed to drive by quickly to decrease the likelihood that she would be caught.

Although Oji had explained why Martha had not been invited inside his parents' abode, the reason remained a bit far-fetched to her. Of course she believed Oji, but she couldn't conceive of the inside of the home being in such significant disrepair that he would be embarrassed for her to see it. *But maybe I'll pick up some clues by taking a careful look from the street.*

Martha slowed to ten miles per hour to ensure she didn't miss the Greenwald residence, but she needn't have worried, for as much as the Neoclassical Revival–style home's beige-brick exterior and ornate wrought iron railings across both the small front porch and the second-floor Juliet balcony stood out to her, seeing Adam Greenwald in his pajamas, tussling with a sizable bush in the flower bed, was even more of an indication that she had indeed reached the correct home. Eve usually parked her car in the semicircular driveway during the daytime, but the driveway was empty.

Alarmed by the sighting and resisting the urge to lower her window and scream for Adam to go inside, Martha eased into the driveway. She had to stay calm, especially because she was unsure if Adam would recognize her. She prayed he wouldn't cause a commotion or draw unnecessary attention from the neighbors or, worse, any law enforcement officers who might be patrolling the area. She always carried with her the worry that a misunderstanding could lead to a fatal mistake.

Adam released the bush, which stood at least five feet tall and four feet wide, and looked intently at Martha as she parked the car and walked toward him. "Hey, Martha! Did Eve send you here to help me transplant my camellia bush? She said it would be too hard to do it myself, but it just takes a little time. And I've got plenty of that. I wish I could find my tools, but I don't know where they are." Sweat dripped from his face like water from a freshly dipped sponge.

"No, I was just in the neighborhood, so I thought I'd stop by and see how you're doing. Where's Mrs. Greenwald?" Martha asked. Judging from the lack of gardening tools and the sprinkle of leathery serrated leaves strewn on the ground near Adam's feet, he had been fighting with the bush for only a few minutes.

"That's a good question. Wherever she is, she couldn't have gone too far without me."

"I see," Martha said. She was certain Adam wouldn't easily comply with a directive to go inside, so she had to think quickly on her feet. "I sure am thirsty. Could I please have a glass of water?"

"Well, what kind of host would I be if I denied a guest a glass of cold water?"

"Thank you. I'll follow you," Martha said, hoping Adam's usual gentlemanly manners would divert his attention.

He shrugged his shoulders. "If you insist," he said.

Good. That went easier than expected, Martha thought. She followed him up the three pristine white-brick steps to the front door in case he stumbled and fell backward in the backless slider slippers he wore. *Those are a fall risk on a regular day, but even more so with him trying to remove that bush.*

Adam turned the knob back and forth. "It's locked. Do you have a key?"

"Oh, no. I'll have to call Oji," Martha replied.

A NARROW WINDOW filled with frosted glass flanked both sides of the big black front door at the entry of the Green-wald home, so Martha couldn't get a glimpse inside as Oji unlocked the door. Although the paint on the exterior was intact with no chips or other signs of wear, she suspected the door was original to the residence. And Martha could tell the creaky door was as heavy as it looked by the way Oji leaned into it to hold it open while she and his father crossed the threshold ahead of him.

Oji let go of the door. "I'm going to try my mom again," he said as he reached in the pocket of the dark-gray chinos he wore and pulled out his phone.

The door slammed with a loud thump, confirming Martha's guess about its heft.

"How many times have I told you not to slam the door, Oji?" Adam asked. He sounded like an exhausted parent chastising his teenager.

Oji unlocked his phone and tapped on the screen a few times. "Sorry, Dad," he replied without looking up from the phone.

Seconds later, a marimba ringtone rang out in the distance.

"I figured she left it here," Oji said, shaking his head.

"Is there anything I can do?" Martha asked. Despite the internal pressure she felt to worry about Eve's whereabouts, she resolved to follow Oji's lead. When Martha had called Oji to alert him that his dad was locked outside, Oji sounded irritated that his father was home alone and relieved that he was okay but not so worried that his mother was in danger. Martha had expected an even mixture of the two.

"My mom will probably walk in any minute, but would you mind staying here with me until everything gets figured out?" Oji asked. "Just to be sure . . . I mean, you know . . . unless you need to go."

"Of course," Martha replied. She grabbed Oji's hand and tried not to seem so obvious as she took in her surroundings.

Still standing near the front door at the periphery of the living room, Martha was so jarred by the electric-blue and silver foil paisley-print wallpaper covering the entire room that she almost didn't notice a magnificent staircase along the wall that stretched to the second floor and across the top of the front entry. The visible scratches on the hardwood treads matched those on the floors, and the white paint on the risers had seen better days. But she could imagine how grand it must've looked for someone to stand in the hallway above the living room and wave down to guests who had just entered when the home was at its glory.

To prevent herself from inadvertently commenting on the home's interior, Martha shifted her attention to the smell of freshly baked goods wafting through the air. She inhaled deeply through her nostrils, drawing in the aroma. It reminded her of when she bought cranberry-orange muffins and reheated them in her air fryer for a treat on weekend mornings.

"I never pegged your mom as a baker," she said.

"Really? She cooks and bakes just like you do," Oji said, making eye contact with her. His voice perked up, a drastic departure from the gruff mumbling and averted eyes he displayed on his arrival. He seemed relieved not to have to talk about the dilapidated surroundings.

"Interesting that you've never mentioned that before."

He lowered his eyes. "I can see that I need to get better about sharing some things."

"Eve grew up with cooking staff in her home, but I couldn't afford that, so she had to learn on her own. She was terrible at first, but she eventually got better. By the time Nile was born, her food was fairly edible," Adam said with a laugh. Then he turned to Martha. "Do you know Nile? He's Oji's big brother."

"Yes. I mean, no . . . I haven't met him yet. I've only heard about him," Martha said, flustered. She wondered how Oji felt hearing Mr. Greenwald mention Nile's name so casually and if Oji did the same when he spent time alone with his parents. Although Nile had come up a few times in Oji and Martha's couples counseling sessions, Oji didn't mention him much otherwise. The brothers' communication was usually limited to the occasional text exchange.

Adam nodded in the way people do when they only wanted a yes-or-no answer instead of the longer response you gave them. "Well, like I was saying, by the time Oji came along, I actually liked Eve's cooking. Speaking of which, I don't know why I'm still standing around here with y'all. I'm hungry. I'm going to see what she left for me in the kitchen."

As he shuffled toward the arched doorway opposite the front door, with his slippered feet dragging against the hardwood floors, Martha's eyes darted to Oji. Since he had tried for years to broker peace between his parents and brother, Martha expected more of a reaction from him when Adam mentioned his other son's name.

"Let's sit," Oji said, stepping toward the sofa, a rectangle-shaped monstrosity in a shade of blue darker than the hue of the wallpaper. There were three square cushions along the seat and three block cushions along the back. She'd seen a similar sofa only on television. If anyone in her family had one when she was a child, too many years had passed to recall the memory.

The fabric on the sofa looked stretched and worn. As Martha settled on the couch, she rested her elbow on the strip of brown wood that ran along the armrest. A spring pushed through the seat cushion, but it didn't hurt. It was a tolerable nuisance, which seemed like an apt metaphor for the setting. And she was thankful she could deal with the spring, because she was afraid she would embarrass Oji if she moved or mentioned it.

"Should we check on your dad? I mean, is it okay for him to be in the kitchen alone?" Martha asked.

"I think he's okay. He's never cooked, so the chances that he would try now are pretty slim. And my mom usually leaves muffins, plates, napkins, and whatever else he needs on the countertop so he can grab it. You know, to allow him to be as independent as possible."

"That's good," Martha said. "But does your mom leave him alone all the time?"

Oji shook his head. "She's done it a few times . . . well, that I know of. I do wonder what happens when I'm not here. Whenever I bring up the day programs you mentioned, she shoots down the idea."

"She's worried about paying for it?" Martha asked. Now that Oji was being transparent about the state of his parents' affairs, it was easier for her to figure out the potential barriers Eve faced and suggest potential solutions.

"That's *my* guess too," he replied.

"There could be other mechanisms to pay for it. She doesn't have to talk to me about it if she's not comfortable doing so. That's why I wanted to connect her with a social worker. They help our patients navigate through all sorts of challenges, including financial ones," Martha explained.

"If we're not careful, pride can stand in the way of the breakthroughs we need."

She sighed. "Tell me about it. But maybe what happened with your dad today might help her see it's time to do things differently."

"Something's got to—" Oji said before he was interrupted by the creaking front door.

"Oji! Martha! Is Adam okay?" Eve yelled from the doorway. She had that wild look in her eyes that people get when they fear the worst but the adrenaline rush won't allow them to cry.

Oji sprang to his feet. "Dad's fine, Mom. Are you all right?"

Before she spoke, Eve looked back and forth between Oji and Martha as if she were looking at their faces for answers to another question. "Yes, I ran to the store for what should've been a quick trip, but I got a flat tire. Thankfully, I noticed it in the parking lot and one of the grocery store staff changed it for me." She paused briefly, again scanning Oji and Martha's faces before she continued. "But why are you two here?"

"We can talk more about that later. I'm just glad you're safe and you got help," Oji said while his head moved quickly like a bobblehead doll. His voice carried elements of empathy, but it shifted to sounding like a courtroom reporter as he then answered his mother's question. "Dad's in the kitchen now, but Martha happened to find him outside in the front yard. He was in his pajamas and slippers, trying to pull a big bush out of the ground. Martha tried to get him inside, but he'd locked himself out, so she called me."

Martha sat quietly. She mostly looked at Oji but stole a couple of glances at Eve when she couldn't resist the urge.

"Oh, thank you, heavenly Father!" Eve wailed, throwing

her hands in the air. Then she closed her eyes and breathed heavily out her mouth as she brought her steepled hands to her lips. "I'm so glad he's okay."

"I should head home so you two can talk," Martha said, popping up from the sofa.

Eve opened her eyes and stopped her in her tracks. "Martha, thank you so much for helping Adam. I don't know how I could've lived with myself if something had happened to him. Please stay a while longer if you can."

Before Martha could respond, Adam appeared in the arched doorway opposite the front door. "What's all this commotion?" he asked, holding a bread plate with a half-eaten muffin on top.

Eve dashed across the foyer to Adam and threw her arms around him. "I'm so sorry you got stuck outside. Are you sure you're okay?" she asked feverishly.

"Yes, of course. Don't get yourself worked up. I was just trying to get some yard work done before it got too hot." He put one arm around Eve and clutched the plate with his free hand.

Eve let out a boisterous laugh that Martha could only interpret as relief after a stressful moment. "Yes, I can tell you've been out in the heat, Adam. Your pajamas are still damp." She released her husband from a visibly tight embrace. "Why don't you finish your raspberry-streusel muffin and then you can jump in the shower, okay?"

"Sounds good," Adam replied with a laugh.

Even Mr. Greenwald is tickled by her behavior. I guess it is kind of cute that Mrs. Greenwald has her own little quirks that come out when she's in a sensitive situation,

Martha thought. She made a mental note to keep that in mind, as it would likely come in handy in the future.

"And please don't sneak another muffin," Eve said, placing her hands on her hips. "I baked a dozen, and I'll count them when I make my way to the kitchen. But you should have some fruit with what's left on your plate. I cut up some mangoes and peaches for you. They're in the fridge."

Adam's face lit up. "My favorite! You love to spoil me, don't you?"

"Well, that's my job, isn't it? But you still can't have an extra muffin," Eve replied sweetly.

"Okay," Adam said with a chuckle before heading back to the kitchen.

I see where Oji gets his easygoing attitude, Martha thought.

Eve sighed. Then she pivoted toward Martha and Oji, who had watched her interaction with Adam as though they were on one of their dates at the Edin drive-in theater. "Now, where were we? Oh, yes. Martha," Eve said as she headed to the living area.

Eve made a beeline to Martha and extended her arms. "I hope you don't mind. But since I'm giving out hugs, I owe *you* one too," she said with the authenticity usually reserved for everyone except Martha.

"I don't mind at all," Martha replied as Oji looked on. But she stayed cautious, unsure how much she could trust the shift she'd just witnessed.

Eve placed her arms around Martha like a claw-machine arcade game tightly grabbing a stuffed toy. "Thank you, dear," Eve said as she awkwardly patted Martha on the back twice before letting go.

Baby steps, Martha thought as she smiled. She held in a laugh, amused by the contrast between the nearly robotic way that Eve hugged her compared to the more natural way she had hugged her husband. While the exchange didn't give Martha the warm fuzzies she expected, she could tell Eve's intentions were genuine. And that's what mattered most. She silently hoped she and Eve would work out the kinks between them over time.

"Please sit, Martha, so we can chat," Eve said. "And, Oji, where are your manners? Why haven't you gotten Martha some water? Or would you prefer some sweet tea, dear?" She sounded like a delightful hostess welcoming an honored guest, instead of a woman who had just found out she left her husband who had dementia outside in the summer sun.

"No thank you, ma'am," Martha said as she took her seat on the sofa. She discreetly tapped Oji's leg to signal to him that he should sit with her. Although her throat was a little parched, she didn't want to be left alone with Eve.

Oji settled beside Martha. Without looking, he found her hand on top of the sofa cushion and gently squeezed it reassuringly.

"Where is my mind?" Eve asked. "I forgot my purse and the oranges in the car. That's why I ran to the grocery store. I was planning to serve the navel oranges with your father's breakfast. Would you get them for me, Oji?"

"Oranges . . . Sure, Mom. But Martha can't stay long. It's a workday. So I'll get the fruit when I walk her out."

"Work! Oh dear, I'd forgotten it's not the weekend," Eve said, looking at Martha. There was something in her eyes. Not kindness, but something Martha couldn't put her finger on. "Just because I can dillydally all morning doesn't mean I should keep you from your duties."

Martha felt like she was wading across a river with a deep end and that treading carefully was the only way to stay safe. "It's okay. I had some flexibility with my schedule this morning," she replied slowly.

It never had seemed like Eve actually wanted to talk to Martha in the past, so her interest in doing so was new territory. But there was something familiar about the way Eve carried herself this morning. When Adam went missing at Naomi and Nicholas's wedding, Eve didn't act like it was a big deal. Martha had interpreted Eve's reaction as denial. But now that Adam was safe after being locked outside alone while his wife was at the grocery store, Eve's light-hearted and jovial banter made Martha wonder if Eve's tendency to minimize the seriousness of Adam's health condition might be a coping mechanism. And just as Martha had shared resources with the group gathered at the library earlier that morning, she was ready to help.

"I gave a community talk nearby, at the—"

"So, that's how you came to save the day? You were driving by?" Eve asked in a sugary sweet voice as she sat on the settee positioned across from the sofa. Although its blue brocade fabric looked a tad faded, the furniture's curved silhouette and carved wooden sides conveyed an elegance befitting a royal ruler on whose turf Martha had apparently trespassed.

Martha could hardly believe her ears, but she maintained a straight face. She hadn't quite figured out what to say until she remembered that during her and Oji's last couples counseling session, Shari had encouraged him to step in when his mother needed to be reoriented. At the time, Martha had doubted her own ability to stay quiet, but she proved herself wrong by being at a loss for words.

"Mom, you can't keep doing this," Oji said. The heaviness in his voice made him sound like a parent pleading for relief after toiling all night with a colicky newborn.

"Keep doing what?" Eve asked. The baffled look on her face matched the intonation of her voice.

Oji leaned back, folding his arms. "Mother, come on. You know what you're doing." His tone was staid but respectful.

"I apologize," Eve said, lowering her chin to her chest. "I don't mean to be brash. I remain grateful for your intervention today, Martha."

Instead of lashing out, Martha extended the grace that had been offered to her so many times when she behaved badly with her family members. "I understand. You've been through a lot today too. I hope both you and Mr. Greenwald will take it easy for the rest of the day. Doctor's orders."

"I'll see to that, babe. I'm going to work here for a while," Oji said.

Martha stood up. "That's a good idea. And I'll only be a phone call away if I can help with anything." She made eye contact with Eve and walked toward her. "I hope you don't mind if I give you another hug. I think we both could use it," she said with an earnest smile.

Martha didn't wait for Eve to respond. She leaned down over the Greenwald matriarch, who was still seated on her regal settee. Martha wrapped her arms around Eve and pulled her close. Eve placed her arms around Martha—a little less clawlike than before—and Martha leaned her head on Eve's shoulder for an instant before releasing her.

As the women separated, Oji reached for Martha's hand, gently interlocking his fingers with hers. "I'll walk you out," he said with a bold grin.

Chapter Eleven

Mid-August

Nearly one hundred fifty guests had come and gone over the three-hour Sip, Taste, and See event that Martha hosted at the teaching kitchen in The Alabaster Plate. The gathering attracted a venerable list of Macon's who's who in the medical, culinary, and community services, and philanthropic sectors.

A few dozen people still lingered, and they couldn't get enough of the tasty hors d'oeuvres that highlighted the recipes Martha planned to use in the kitchen. The attendees oohed and aahed at the flexible design and capabilities of the space, which included a teaching island at the front of the room with a large induction range and smaller versions of the appliance at cooking stations across the way. Martha showed them off during the scheduled small-group tours she led, where she never tired of explaining that the cooking stations would allow community members to learn to make healthy food via the stovetop as well as by using the baking, griddle, and air-frying functions.

With Mary having had her moment in the spotlight during the restaurant's grand opening the previous week, all eyes were on Martha. And she loved it.

"You did great," Jasmine said, nudging Martha as they walked away from a chat with the president of the local medical society. "Quick update—the TV crew said they got some great clips. It should run on the six o'clock news, but I'll reach out to the hospital publicist after we wrap up to see if she can confirm the airtime. The reporter from the *Macon Tribune* will get quotes from a few attendees to go along with your interview, and she said she'll follow up with you if she has any questions."

"There's only one correction, but I can't believe you missed something so significant," Martha said with a demanding voice.

Jasmine slowed her pace. "What's that?" she asked, squinting her eyes.

"*We* did great," Martha responded in a delighted tone. "I couldn't have done all this without you. You're the one holding it all together, and it's going perfectly."

"Thank you," Jasmine said, blushing. "But this is your baby. Enjoy your moment."

A broad grin spread across Martha's face. "Oh, you know I'm loving every second of it, but I still give credit where it's due."

"And I don't take that lightly," Jasmine replied.

"Excuse me, Dr. Gardin?" said a voice from behind.

Martha pivoted to find Daisy Miller, her former boss and self-proclaimed mentor—though Martha had never agreed to the designation. She wore a starched white coat, despite the fact that she had retired three years previously and no longer took care of patients.

"Dr. Miller. Good afternoon. Thanks so much for joining us. Let me introduce you to Jasmine Gibson, the primary care center's community outreach manager. Jasmine, Dr. Miller is—"

"I'm the founder of the primary care center. I recruited Dr. Gardin and sent her to her first culinary medicine conference," Dr. Miller said brusquely.

"Pleased to meet you," Jasmine replied with a fixed and sober expression.

"Congratulations on the teaching kitchen, Dr. Gardin," Dr. Miller said in the dry tone that was characteristic of her personality. "I tried many years to convince the hospital administration to do something like this, but they didn't prioritize the community before the human resources department helped them get rid of me. But I'm sure you'll do some amazing work here."

Martha was surprised by the compliment, but she couldn't say the same about its backhanded qualities. Not known for her charming demeanor, Dr. Daisy Miller was one of the first female physicians in a leadership position at Macon General Hospital. Martha had often wondered how anyone in an executive position had tolerated the frequent interruptions and disrespectful questions for which Dr. Miller was known for employing as power moves during conversations as well as meetings.

"Thank you, Dr. Miller," Martha said with a pained smile. "Times are changing at the hospital. The new chief medical officer is quite forward-thinking. I'm sure he has a lot to do with the open-minded approach to community we're seeing these days."

Dr. Miller shrugged. "Either that or you made some inroads through your relationship with the real-estate developer who headed up the redevelopment project."

"Well, that perspective certainly doesn't account for my accomplishments since taking over your position or prior to my doing so. I'd recount my achievements for you, but I seriously doubt you've forgotten them." Martha feigned a pleasant smile. "Enjoy the rest of the Sip, Taste, and See."

Martha and Jasmine walked away, leaving Dr. Miller with a pretentious smirk on her face. Out of the corner of her eye, Martha spotted Oji talking with her family across the room. She and Jasmine made a slight turn to head their way. When the childhood friends came upon a perky young lady carrying a tray of alabaster punch—a sangria-inspired mocktail made with hibiscus tea, apples, and oranges, Martha got an idea.

"See that woman standing there?" Martha asked, gesturing toward Dr. Miller.

The server nodded attentively.

"She's thirsty," Martha said, her tone further conveying her frustration with her former mentor's desperate need for attention.

"More like totally dehydrated," Jasmine chimed in.

Martha barely held in her laugh. Then she pointed at a drink on the tray as she continued. "Please take one of these to her and say, 'Dr. Gardin thought you might like this. She adapted it from a recipe she learned at the conference you sent her to.'" Then she remembered the cash she'd stuck in the pocket of her lilac linen wrap dress to give to servers who did something particularly helpful, a hostess trick her grandmother had taught her years ago. She slipped the server a folded twenty-dollar bill. "Thanks so much," she said, adding a melodic quality to her words.

The server's face lit up as she chuckled. "Yes, ma'am,"

she said before darting over to Dr. Miller, who still stood alone in the same place as before.

Jasmine cackled as she and Martha resumed their walk across the room. "Nobody reads like Martha Gardin. But you were so professional and smooth with it that I almost don't want to consider it a read. *Almost.* Then you promptly found an opportunity to put some sugar on top."

"That woman exhausts me, but I will not let her ruin my day," Martha replied with the poise of a seasoned politician.

"As you should not. Negativity has no place in this blessed day," Jasmine said emphatically.

Martha exhaled. Daisy Miller had hit a nerve, one that went deeper than Martha was willing to acknowledge during a celebration that meant so much to her both professionally and personally. The bruise inside her ached, and she yearned for a balm. Jasmine's support was a start, but she couldn't get to her family and Oji fast enough.

"Was that Dr. Miller?" Naomi asked as soon as Martha and Jasmine reached the spot where the Gardin family and Oji huddled.

Martha's eyes lit up with amazement. "You remember her?"

"I don't forget anyone who causes any of my loved ones pain," Naomi replied.

Oji's face grew tense.

"You all right, Oji?" Jasmine asked with no trace of emotion in her voice.

Martha hoped she was the only one who noticed the change in his countenance, which she interpreted as his being sensitive to the fact that he'd caused Martha and her family a great deal of pain when they found out the reason Martha called off the wedding. But Jasmine's pointed question let her know that the entire group likely picked up on it too.

"It's okay, Oji. She has a heart of forgiveness," Ruth said. She turned to Naomi. "Right?"

Naomi smiled innocently. "Certainly. And I also keep track of what Dr. Miller's up to since she retired."

"What do you mean?" Oji asked. He spoke slowly, as if prolonging the sentence would lessen the blow of her answer.

"I have my ways. I just like to know what's going on, that's all," Naomi said in a calm, straightforward tone.

Oji's head spun toward Nicholas.

"Don't look at *me*," Nicholas said with a chuckle. "I know enough to stay in Naomi's good graces."

Mary shot Nicholas a playfully dismissive smile and waved him and Oji off. Then she looked at Martha. "Don't keep us in the dark. What did your old boss have to say?"

"If y'all don't mind, I'd rather not give it any more energy right now. But I'll tell you all the details later."

"Suffice it to say, y'all would've been proud," Jasmine said. "Dr. Martha Gardin was the epitome of grace under fire."

AFTER WRAPPING UP what the hospital CEO had called "only the first of many brilliant initiatives that this promising young physician leader has in store for our community," Martha prepared to leave her office. The Sip, Taste, and See event had gone extraordinarily well, except for one thing: Dr. Miller's words reverberated in Martha's head. They were like a sharp pebble in her shoe that nagged her on an otherwise smooth walk.

A soft rap at the door interrupted Martha as she stood at her desk packing her briefcase. "Come in," she said.

The door opened slowly and Jasmine peeked her head through. "You want to walk out together?"

"Actually, could you step in?" Martha asked. She grabbed a box of facial tissues from her desk.

"Sure," Jasmine replied, slipping inside and closing the door.

"Let's chat on the sofa," Martha said, clutching the box with one hand and pointing to the couch with the other as she walked in that direction.

"What's up?" Jasmine asked as she sat down.

Martha exhaled deeply.

"You're scaring me," Jasmine blurted.

Martha shook her head. "No, it's not anything life-threatening. It's just hard for me, because I've only told two other people: my therapist and Oji. And I only told them in the past couple of weeks. They both think it's important for my healing that I share it with *you*, too."

"Me?" Surprise reflected on Jasmine's face as well as in her voice.

"Uh-huh," Martha said with a nod. She exhaled again through her mouth, long and slow. "You probably can guess that things changed a lot for me after my parents died in that horrible car crash. It was hard losing them . . . and going through all that." Her voice cracked, and she snatched a tissue from the box and held it in her hand.

"But you didn't deserve the way I treated you," Martha continued. "You were a good friend to me. You reached out and I barely responded, yet you were so patient and understanding. I'm sorry I put you through all that rejection. I don't know anyone else who'd have kept trying for so long, and that really means a lot to me."

"Martha, are you sure you want to do this here at work?" Jasmine asked.

Martha nodded as her eyes filled with tears. "I'm afraid I'll lose the nerve to do it if I don't do it now. It looked like I did a good job handling Dr. Miller, but her words really tore at me."

"She's not important in your life, Martha. Who cares what she thinks? Please don't let her get to you," Jasmine pleaded.

"It's not her. She was just a trigger for me today. I rarely let on how much I struggle with insecurity. I've found ways to manage it for years, but with the unexpected challenges that have been thrown at me over the past several weeks, it's been harder. You really came through for me at the library talk, but I can't risk being on the verge of falling apart at work again."

Regret consumed Jasmine's face. "So, did I go too far in that discussion we had after the blood pressure monitor demonstration? I didn't mean to—"

"No, you were very appropriate. Just let me finish, okay?"

"I'm sorry," Jasmine said, lowering her head.

"Don't worry about that. I just need to get this out."

Jasmine nodded.

"What I mean is that I haven't been dealing with the words I hear in my head all the time . . . telling me that . . .

I'm not good enough. The night before my mom died, I . . ."
Tears streamed down Martha's cheeks as she tried to speak.

She wiped her face with the tissue she clutched and
grabbed another. "I overheard my mom talking to a couple
of friends she had over. They were in our kitchen discussing
the ups and downs of parenting, and my mom said she
wasn't worried about Mary. She said she thought Mary
would be fine. But 'Martha isn't so smart,' she said. She
said she was afraid I would lead a life of . . . of mediocrity
unless I married well . . . And she wasn't sure I could pull
that off because I was weird with social stuff . . . sometimes."

Jasmine began to cry too. "I'm so sorry, Martha. That
must've been devastating to hear. I . . . I don't know what
else to say." She pulled Martha into a hug.

"She didn't mean for me to hear it, but it broke my heart.
And my dad . . . I don't know if . . . if he agreed with her. He
always followed . . . followed her lead, but . . . I . . . I just
don't know," Martha sobbed, taking breaks to catch her
breath.

Jasmine squeezed Martha tightly. "And you've just been
walking around for more than twenty years with all this inside. Carrying all that pain by yourself. Oh, my friend, I'm
so sorry."

Friend, Martha thought. She pulled away and looked at
Jasmine, whose mascara had started to run. "How can you
still call me your friend after the way I rejected you and put
so much distance between us?"

"I didn't even think about it before I said it. And I can see
that you felt dismissed by your mother, and you had to deal
with that plus grief. You were a kid—a hurt kid. I couldn't

have guessed what you were going through, but deep down I always knew that it didn't have anything to do with me."

Martha pulled two tissues from the box and handed one to Jasmine. She dabbed her eyes with the other one. "Thank you. I felt like I didn't deserve you as my friend . . . That's really hard for me to say, but I needed to say it out loud."

"You were a good friend to me, too, Martha. It might help if you try to remember that."

Martha squeezed her eyes closed and took another breath. "I'll work on that. Part of me feels like it's come alive again through hearing you say I was a good friend, because I've never thought of myself that way. If it's okay with you, I'd like for us to try to build a real friendship. I mean, as adults," she added quickly.

"I would love that."

Martha smiled. "Thank you. I really missed you." Her eyes filled again.

Jasmine handed her a tissue. "I got you."

Martha laughed.

Jasmine squinted at Martha. "That was funny?"

"No, but it was funny—in an awkward way—when you called Oji out in front of my family this afternoon. That's what I thought about just now when I laughed. You have my back even with him."

"That's what I figured you wanted to talk about when you asked me to come in," Jasmine said. "I felt so bad after I said it, but I still meant it. God is working on my heart. I may need to spend some time with your aunt Naomi." She sighed. "I don't know what went down between you and Oji, but one of my sources confirmed that he proposed. Then I heard that you called off the wedding. I could only hold in my frustration with him for so long. You don't know what I went through every time I saw you or Oji . . . especially Oji. Are you okay?"

Martha's mouth fell open. "I can't believe you knew about that and didn't say anything."

"What could I say? But that's why this job has been so hard for me. The workload is perfectly manageable, but balancing it while reporting to someone who used to be my best friend—that almost took me under."

"I'm actually good," Martha said. "We can talk about me and Oji later, but I'm sorry you were in such a tough position. I can see now that this was torture for you as an empath."

"Yes! The worst! Girl, I was stressed. I joked that I was gonna send Oji my therapist's bills," Jasmine said with a laugh.

"Sounds like I owe you even more than I realized. But there's something I found out about today that might start to make up for it."

"What did you do?" Jasmine asked with a grin.

"Not much, really. I heard about a new position that's opening up, and I think you'd be perfect for it. The hospital is revamping its community health improvement services. You know—community screenings, outreach, and stuff like that. The position hasn't been posted yet, but it should go live next week. Everything has to be aboveboard, so you'll still have to apply and interview. But I have a feeling they'd love to hire quickly from within. And I've already put in a good word for you. I hope that's okay."

"That is more than okay! Thank you!"

Chapter Twelve

Late September

Walking and chatting—that's all you have to do, Martha thought as she stretched along with the thirty or so people gathered on the grass near the park shelter at the Minnie Lee Smith Public Library's inaugural walking club meetup. She recalled the one-liner Jasmine had included in the calendar invitation she used to place the library walk on Martha's schedule. But it was more than just a summary statement. It was a motivational nugget for Martha at her first community event without her outreach manager since they began working together.

With Jasmine's upcoming transition to her new role at the hospital on Monday, Martha decided it would be selfish to require her to work on a Saturday morning. Although Jasmine likely would have happily obliged if asked, Martha realized that she had grown so accustomed to having her around that she worried Jasmine might have become a crutch. Doing the walk without Jasmine would best position Martha to use the tools she had learned in her individual therapy sessions to address the negative self-talk in her head. Although the women's paths would still cross at work, they promised to talk by phone and hang out regularly, and Martha looked forward to upholding her end of the deal.

"Let's go!" said Sam, the adult services librarian. The phrase signaled Martha and the library staff members in attendance to implement the plan Sam had laid out for the walk around the park adjacent to the library. Martha and Sam took off with the crowd, and the other staff members stayed behind to orient anyone who arrived later.

Sam stepped onto the paved trail between the grass and the parking lot ahead of Martha, and she instantly began talking with a long-standing library volunteer who had welcomed Martha when she arrived.

Martha found herself next to a trio of silver-haired women in colorful athletic attire. They walked faster than the other attendees and lightly pumped their arms. The one closest to Martha made eye contact. "We'll talk to you at the end," she said. "We're having a little contest between the three of us."

"Have fun," Martha said with a wave. *That went well. I can do this. I do well with natural conversation. Just let things flow naturally from here,* Martha thought.

In keeping with the plan for the walk, Martha decreased her pace to allow the group of people behind her to walk beside her. As she did so, she turned around to assess her placement in the group. Her face lit up as she recognized the woman wearing a T-shirt that said *World's Best Grandma,* who walked alongside a teen who looked to be in middle school. The duo and Martha were soon walking side by side.

"Good morning. I remember you from my talk!" Martha exclaimed without a trace of apprehension.

"It's good to see you, Doc. My name is Paula. Yes, I was the one who suggested that the library staff invite you to the walk. This is my granddaughter, Charlotte."

"Hello, Dr. Gardin," the girl said. "Grandma learned a lot during your talk. She told me all about it, and I learned some things too."

Paula grinned proudly.

"It's nice to meet you, Charlotte. Thank you for the amazing feedback. I bet your grandma loves having you in her corner." Martha tugged down on the brim of the baseball cap the teen wore.

"Yes, she helps me out all the time," Paula said.

"That's a gift. Thanks so much for suggesting that I join the walk," Martha said.

"You're welcome," Paula said. "You seemed like someone I could relate to, and I didn't want to ask my question in front of the whole room of people. I don't mind Charlotte being here though. I was wondering if all blood pressure medicines are supposed to make you go to the bathroom. The lady in the story you told the other day took a medicine that made her urinate frequently, but my medicine doesn't do that."

"I'm glad you felt comfortable asking me that now," Martha said. "We didn't have enough time to go into the different types of blood pressure medicines, but they don't all work the same."

"Charlotte told me I was worried for nothing."

"I did," Charlotte said with confidence. She sounded precocious but not rude.

Martha smiled. "The woman in the story took a diuretic, which we sometimes call a water pill. You might be on a different kind of medicine. You can always talk to your doctor or pharmacist to find out more about the medicines you take."

"That's a good idea. I'll do that," Paula said.

"The other seniors need to know this information too. Would the library ever put on a talk about that topic?" Charlotte asked.

"Of course they would! Why didn't I think of that? Thanks, baby," Paula said.

"Every senior needs someone like you in their life, Charlotte," Martha responded. "I'll share your idea with the library staff and see if we can schedule something. And maybe we'll have it at a time when you both can attend. I hope you won't hold it against me that I need to talk to some of the other attendees, but I'll hang around at the end of the walk in case you have other questions."

Martha chatted with the next group of attendees and then the next. When she came to a bend in the trail, she noticed a couple lagging behind at the end of the group. Martha inquired with the library assistant hosting the walk, who told her the couple preferred it that way and they'd mentioned they understood if the doctor ran out of time to talk to them.

As Martha worked her way to the back of the walking group, she got a closer look at the lingering couple. *Mr. and Mrs. Greenwald?* She broke out into a light jog to hasten her chat with them.

Martha slowed to a walking pace when she got within several feet of the couple.

Adam Greenwald came to a complete stop and burst out laughing as Martha drew nearer. "Look who it is."

Eve, who appeared to be preoccupied with something on her shoe, lifted her head. Then she brought her hand to her parted lips.

"I didn't mean to surprise you," Martha said.

"So, *you're* the doctor they were talking about?" Eve asked, blinking rapidly.

Martha chuckled. "I suppose so. I take it you didn't know I'd be here?"

"No, dear," Eve said. "We overheard some men at the grocery store talking about a doctor who gave a talk about blood pressure and vascular dementia, and one of them said that doctor would be at the walk. He went on and on about how great you were, and Adam wouldn't let me rest until I promised to bring him."

"What a lovely compliment! Would you like to keep walking while we talk?" Martha asked.

"Yes, we would," Adam said.

Eve looked aghast. "All right, then."

"Mr. Greenwald, what would you like to talk about?" Martha asked.

"What do you recommend to help me with my blood pressure?"

"I can think of several things, but let's talk about two important ones today. We're almost to the end of the walk, so we can talk about the other ones later, if you'd like."

"Sounds good. You know where we live," Adam said with a laugh.

Martha chuckled again. "That's true." She glanced at Eve, who held in her laugh. "Do you use a pillbox?"

Adam shook his head. "No. Eve puts my medicine out for me in the morning. She's good about helping me remember to take it. But do you recommend that I use a pill-box?"

"I think it's a good idea, but it's up to y'all. I suggest a pillbox because it allows you to be in charge of taking your own medicine. Mrs. Greenwald would still be able to keep an eye on it."

"But I get forgetful sometimes. How would we manage that?" Adam asked.

Eve's eyes widened as she slowly nodded her head.

"They make these really cool ones now that come with an alarm to remind you to take your medicine," Martha said.

Adam tilted his head and looked at her from the corner of his eye. "I don't bother with fancy technology. I'd have to get Oji to set that up."

"It's pretty easy, but he wouldn't mind. He would probably enjoy having your help to pick one out," Martha said.

"And what's the second thing you were going to tell me?" Adam asked.

Eve's mouth fell open. "Martha has captured your attention, hasn't she? I'm impressed."

Martha grinned from ear to ear. "You can check your blood pressure at home with a monitor. I'll show you how to do it. We can even ask Mrs. Greenwald and Oji if they'd like to join us."

"I would like that," Eve replied.

"Me too!" Adam said.

"And perhaps you might stay awhile to discuss your other recommendations—the ones you have for blood pressure control and also anything else that might be a good fit for Adam and our family," Eve said. "I will—or shall I say,

Adam and I will—think them over, but we're open to hearing your suggestions."

MARTHA SLURPED THE last of the strawberry-banana smoothie and placed the glass on Ruth's white marble kitchen counter. The stainless steel straw clanked against the glass. "Believe it or not, I was raised with home training. I was famished, but that hit the spot. It's hard work growing your career while trying to forge a way forward with your fiancé's parents."

Ruth smiled knowingly. "I'm sorry I don't have anything cooked. I usually keep breakfast light on Saturdays." She picked up the glass and placed it in the sink.

"No problem," Martha replied. "I'm grateful for your smoothie leftovers. It's just enough to hold me until I get home. Besides, that's what happens when you drop in unannounced. I'd have gone to Aunt Naomi's to eat if I was counting on a hot meal on a Saturday morning."

"That would be the right place to go," Ruth said as she sat on the barstool next to Martha. "She doesn't miss, but I'm glad you stopped by. I'm thrilled you and the Greenwalds have turned a corner."

"Thank you. I considered calling, but I needed to see you in person," Martha said. Over the preceding weeks, Martha had talked with each of the Gardin women about her experience overhearing her mother's statements about her, but she still had some unfinished business with Ruth. "You were right when you said months ago that I needed to have the right intentions and let my actions speak for themselves with Mrs. Greenwald. I just had to get myself all the way together first instead of doing just enough to get by."

Ruth blushed. "I said that?" she teased, leaning her elbow on the countertop.

"Fortunately for me, you've said lots of wise things over the years. I've just finally started listening. I'm blessed to have you in my life, and you deserve to have a real apology. I'm truly sorry for all the pain I've caused you. Yes, I've apologized before, but not with my whole heart."

Ruth sat up straight on the stool. "You don't have to say all this. I can see the change."

"No, I need to say it. You've felt my pain and acted on my behalf, often from the background. Not because that's where you wanted to be, but because I pushed you there. You didn't deserve that," Martha said, dabbing the corner of her eyes. "But you still always looked out for me. You'd never have told me that the tea with Mrs. Greenwald was your idea and that you positioned Aunt Naomi to take the lead on it. You're the one Oji really needed to be worried about if he didn't get it together. You're even more covert than Aunt Naomi is. You just don't announce it."

Ruth wiped her eyes. "That's true," she said with a laugh. "And don't forget about his mother. *She's* on my radar too."

Martha chuckled. "I suspect she's figured that out." She paused briefly. "Now that I think about it, you're also part of the reason I struggled so much with Mrs. Greenwald's coolness toward me. You opened your heart and your house to me from the moment I met you. That's why you're apologizing for not having more than a smoothie to offer me. I'm grown and I can walk to my house from here. I've dropped in and out whenever I felt like it, without as much as a second thought. You don't need to worry about feeding me, but you still do . . . after everything I've done." Tears jetted down her face.

"Here," Ruth said tearfully, handing Martha a paper towel.

"Thank you," Martha said with a sniffle. She pointed to Ruth's collection of red-enameled cast-iron pots. "I've learned so much by watching you. Aunt Naomi taught me how to cook, but *you* taught me about nice cookware. I could name lots of other examples based on the way you run the business, or more fun things like your fashion sense, your interior design tastes, and other things that make life more enjoyable. But most of all, you were a model of resilience when I most needed it after my parents died. So, what I'm trying to say is, with all the pain I've been working through with my mom and what she said, I've realized that I projected so much of that hurt onto you—from falsely accusing you of embodying the ugly traits I carried inside to resenting you for being here instead of the loved ones I lost. Let me correct that—the loved ones *we* lost."

Martha paused to take a deep breath and wipe her face. "That was the most unfair thing I could do to you, because you love and miss them too. I wish I could get back all the years I've wasted, but I promise to do better going forward. I'm not making any more excuses. Please forgive me."

Ruth grabbed Martha's hand. "Without question. I'm thankful to have you in my life, and I'm proud of the woman you've become. It hasn't always been easy, but it's worth it." She squeezed Martha's hand lovingly.

"That means the world to me," Martha replied. "It's so

healing to finally be able to say something like that to you."
As she spoke, the doorbell rang.

"That must be my dad," Ruth said. "He's coming over to change a recessed lightbulb in the living room for me."

As Ruth darted to the door, Martha dabbed her eyes and checked in her phone's camera to make sure she didn't have lint from the paper towel on her face.

"You look fine. Don't tell me you're on the way to a date or something," Nicholas said as he and Ruth entered the kitchen.

Martha startled. "Good morning. I think I've had enough excitement for the morning. I'll see Oji this evening, but I'm going to relax a bit first."

"Nothing bad, I hope. What's going on?" Nicholas asked with trepidation in his voice. He stood at the island while Ruth returned to her stool.

"Actually, it's great news," Martha replied. "Mr. and Mrs. Greenwald and I happened to attend the same community walk this morning, and I think we're going to be okay."

"What a powerful breakthrough on a Saturday morning! It's barely eleven, and you've squeezed a whole day's worth of work in already," Nicholas said with a laugh. "I like seeing things come together for you and Oji."

"Thank you," Martha said. "Since you mentioned work, that reminds me to thank you again for agreeing to advise Oji on selling his company. We want to take you and Aunt Naomi out to dinner to express our gratitude."

"Oji and I aren't quite done figuring things out yet, but is that your way of trying to maneuver your way out of that fat invoice I was planning to send him?" Nicholas teased with a serious tone and facial expression.

Martha looked at Nicholas out of the corner of her eye. "You would never!"

"Your aunt has expensive taste. I have to stack my coins," Nicholas replied. He didn't crack a smile.

"You two are hilarious," Ruth replied with a friendly eye roll.

Martha let out a loud laugh, tickled that Ruth picked up on Nicholas's joke too. "We've all come a long way. Thankfully," she said, alluding to the conversation she had with her aunt and Nicholas months prior when she insinuated that Nicholas might be after her aunt's money, lacking the knowledge that his net worth far surpassed Naomi's. And now she was counting on his sage advice to help Oji sell his company to dig himself out of a financial hole.

"Indeed we have," Nicholas replied with a wink.

Chapter Thirteen

Mid-October

We've completed fourteen sessions already? Martha thought as Shari raised the topic of the next steps in couples counseling. For someone who'd scoffed at the idea that she needed therapy, Martha had become a willing worker— both in her individual therapy and the sessions with Oji. She looked forward to the visits, so Shari's recommendation that Martha and Oji decrease the frequency of their meetings to every other week took Martha by surprise. But it's not like she hadn't been warned. After their first six weekly visits, Shari had then provided the option of semi-monthly sessions. But Martha and Oji wanted to continue to power forward on a weekly basis.

"What if we have an issue during our off week?" Martha asked. She glanced at the lavender and gray striped accent wall behind Shari, remembering her ill-placed intentions the first time she'd come to the office for a family visit with Mary. Now she could hardly get enough of the place.

Shari pushed her round copper eyeglasses up on her nose. "I feel confident that you've both got the tools to effectively navigate any challenges that might arise. But if you need an urgent session to talk through something that pops up, don't hesitate to reach out for a time to talk."

"That's good to know," Oji replied. He turned to Martha and made eye contact. "I feel like we'll be okay, but I like having a backup plan so—"

"We're on the same page," Martha said simultaneously with Oji. Then she giggled. "But seriously, that plan works for me."

Shari smiled. "Great. Any other questions before we move ahead?"

"I have one more," Oji said with urgency in his voice. He looked at Martha again quickly, then back at Shari. "When do you think we'll be ready to get married?"

Martha's eyes widened.

"That was the next thing I was going to bring up," Shari said. "But I'd like to know what Martha is thinking right now."

Martha softly dug her nails into the plump seat cushion of the purple tufted love seat. "Oji and I have started talking about the wedding again. And, obviously, we've discussed it here, too. But I can't help being worried that you're going to give us a failing grade."

"There's no end-of-quarter report card in therapy," Shari explained. "It just doesn't work that way. The two of you are consenting adults, so you don't need my approval. *But* if you'd like my opinion on what I need to see from a couple in your position to feel like they're in a healthy place for marriage, I'll tell you."

Oji lifted Martha's hand from the sofa cushion and interlaced his fingers with hers. "Please do. We can handle it," he replied, looking back at Martha and smiling reassuringly.

"I typically need to see recognition of the need for change

and the commitment to continue to progress toward your healing. In other words, you both see what you need to do for your relationship to improve, and you should be actively moving toward it."

Martha wrinkled her nose. "That's it? We've done all that. But there's got to be more to it. Nothing is that simple."

"Well, I wouldn't call it simple. It takes a great deal of effort. But those are the two things I would need to see as a couples therapist. And if you're saying you and Oji have accomplished that already, I would agree with you."

A broad smile spread across Oji's face, but Martha didn't look convinced.

"You get to decide who you want to partner with. My job is to support you in doing so in a healthy way," Shari continued. "And let's not forget that you've both made substantial strides in working on yourselves individually. You've recognized the issues you've each brought to the relationship and sought help for them with your own therapists. Over the past fourteen weeks, I've heard various examples of you both having aha moments, identifying your previous traumas, and recognizing how they show up in your lives now."

"That makes sense, but I'm going to need some time to sit with this a little longer," Martha said. "You know, just to think through it."

"That's understandable. But just to make sure I'm clear, do you have reservations about marrying Oji?" Shari asked.

"None at all," Martha said emphatically. "Our love has grown stronger and clearer through this process. It feels . . .

more real now. Sometimes I wish I hadn't pushed pause on our wedding planning. It's just my personality to take time for things to settle in."

Shari nodded. "Okay, I see."

"I accept responsibility for my role in causing you to feel that way, and I will keep my promise to make it up to you," Oji said, sandwiching Martha's hand in his. "In the meantime, I appreciate the vote of confidence, Shari. I realize we still have work to do to keep growing, but I'm proud of us. You've been very patient with me, Martha. You didn't sign up for all my baggage."

Martha dabbed the corner of her eye with her free hand. "Thanks, babe. You didn't sign up for mine, either. I can see the progress we're making. It means a lot to me that you're setting boundaries with your mom and working on a plan for how to financially support your parents and rebuild your finances by selling your business. I want to acknowledge that because you shouldn't let my response to Shari's assessment cause you to think you're not doing enough. I just need some time to sit with this, that's all."

"I get it," Oji said. "I know how your brain works. We're a lot alike, but we have some differences, too. All this therapy has helped me see that."

"All this therapy," she repeated, mimicking him.

He released her hand and lifted his hands with his palms facing their counselor. "Oh, no offense, Shari."

"None taken," Shari said with a chuckle. She picked up her notebook and thumbed through it. "And since it can help to be reminded of how far you've come in such a short time period, would you like to add to the highlights of your progress that Martha just mentioned? If it helps, you might think about the list of premarital counseling topics I shared at the retreat, since we've extensively covered all of them in our work together."

"That sounds like useful reinforcement. I need to remember that kind of stuff when things get overwhelming," Martha said.

Oji nodded. "It all feels like a blur for *me* at times too."

"Thanks for saying that," Martha said. "It's comforting to know that you don't think I'm making a big deal out of all this."

"Not at all, babe," Oji responded. "But okay, I'll start with the list. Our relationship is grounded in friendship. I actually like being around you. That's important to me."

Martha blushed. "Me too. We have similar spiritual and moral perspectives."

"And alignment in our goals," Oji added. "And our values and principles, too."

"You stole my answer," Martha teased. "Let me think . . . We communicate well. I'd have said that before we started counseling, but it's actually true now."

"I agree," Oji said. "We also have a healthy support system. I'm thankful for your family. They provide support without being intrusive. My mom is . . . shall we say . . . getting there."

"I agree, but your dad is my secret cheerleader," Martha said with a smile. "He knows how to come through, and I have a feeling that won't change."

"Those are all solid examples," Shari said. "I'd suggest that you write them down when you get home. That could be a good exercise to complete together. And we can check in again in two weeks."

⚘

"WHEN ARE WE going to do therapy?" Adam asked Martha. "Eve said you and Oji were coming over on Saturday afternoon to show me how to use my new blood pressure monitor and so I could have some therapy. The monitor is straightforward, but all we've done is play games."

Leaning back in his office chair, Adam reminded Martha of a long-suffering supervisor who was losing patience with an uncooperative employee.

Martha sat in one of the two antique mahogany porter's hall chairs on the other side of Adam's desk in his office, which was tucked next to the primary bedroom on the first floor of the Greenwald home. The two chairs, desk, and built-ins reminded her of the decor in the fancy offices she saw on the soap operas when she used to sneak and watch them when she was a kid. Dozens of real-estate plaques and awards peppered the shelves and walls, with occasional family photos sprinkled in.

"I can see how Mrs. Greenwald might've explained it that way, but I'm not a therapist. I'm a—"

"You're a doctor. I know. But she said you were coming to do therapy. So when are we doing therapy?" Adam persisted.

Martha smiled. "Some therapists play games with patients. Games can help keep your brain active, and they can help with memory, too. I heard that you used to enjoy board games, so I thought they would be a fun thing for us to do together."

"You were right. They were fun," Adam said with a grin. "Will we play again the next time you come over?"

Always so charming, even when he's being a grouch. Just like Oji, Martha thought. "Is that your way of asking me to come back?"

Adam laughed as though he'd just heard a funny joke. "You caught me. You're sharp."

Martha got up from her chair. She moved it and its counterpart away from the desk to create standing room. Then she picked up a brown shopping bag from the mahogany-stained parquet de Versailles floor and placed it on the middle of the heavy desk separating her and Adam.

"I'll come back. And I brought something you might enjoy in the meantime," she said as she stood next to Adam's chair in case she needed to assist.

"What is it?" he asked, stretching his neck.

"Hmm, let's see if you can guess. It's something you used to do with Oji and Nile when they were boys." She'd intentionally placed the bag on the desk to see how Adam would interact with it. She hoped to get some clues about what questions she should ask Eve and Oji, as well as any additional testing and resources she might suggest for him.

"A football?" he asked.

"That's all I'm at liberty to say. No more clues," Martha said with a sly grin.

Adam pulled the bag toward him, moving it only minimally. "Huh. That doesn't feel like a football. I can't wait to see what it is."

Martha discreetly inched closer to Adam, standing close by in case she needed to react quickly to help him.

Adam placed the palms of his hands on the heavy traditional-style executive desk and attempted to stand, but his chair slid backward. He quickly recovered, grabbing the desk and planting his feet on the floor. "Whoa. I must be more careful."

When Martha had arrived and discovered that Adam's office chair was a modern version with wheels, she suggested that they switch seats. But he put up a big fuss. As far as she knew, he had never fallen, but she didn't like him sitting in a chair with wheels. It increased the risk. *At least there's no rug under the desk, but we've got to get rid of this chair today.* She would have to convince him it was his idea, but she had come up with a plan.

She helped him to his feet. Then she slid the bag to the side of the desk where she previously sat. "I have an idea. How about you stand over there and see what's in the bag while I check out your chair?"

Adam shrugged. "Okay."

Martha stayed close while Adam moved to the other side of the desk. He looked inside the bag. "A present!" He reached in and removed a two-tone storage box with a woven chevron design and a bright-red bow tied around it.

Martha gave Adam's office chair the once-over and slid it to the corner near the built-in bookcase. *I've seen enough of that thing,* she thought.

Adam pulled the bow loose and lifted the top from the box. "Word-search books! I used to do them with Oji!" he exclaimed, still holding the lid in his hands.

"A little bird told me that," Martha said.

Adam laughed. "That bird would be Oji," he said, setting the lid on the desk.

"There's something else," Martha said. She folded her arms and leaned on the built-in bookcase.

Adam thumbed through the books inside the box. "There are six books in here. I don't see anything more."

"Hmm, there might be something different about the books," Martha said coyly.

Adam lifted each book out of the box one by one, comparing their covers. He made two stacks. "Three word-search and three crossword puzzle books. I like variety. They will be fun. Thank you, Martha."

"You're welcome. Oji told me you're particular about your writing instruments, so I didn't buy any pens."

"That's right. I keep them in my desk. I began collecting pens during my real-estate days. I can never get enough of them."

"You were one of the top agents in Macon?"

"Voted agent of the year twice," Adam said. Then he paused briefly, appearing to savor the memory. "I had my own firm. I ran circles around those other agents until I got sick. I bought a fancy pen for each house I sold. That's why I have so many pens now. I knew about this house before it was put on the market. They call that a pocket listing," he said with a scholarly tone.

"I bet you used to get the scoop on all the good properties."

He nodded. "That's what happens when you're the best."

"I can tell that's the case. Are you the reason Oji is so good at real estate?"

Adam blushed. "I don't know about that. But he and

Nile hung out in here all the time when they were boys. He might've picked up a thing or two." He laughed. "I spent a lot of hours working back then. Oji would bring his word-search books, and Nile liked to do crossword puzzles. They would do their work—that's what they called it—while I did mine. Then I would help each of them with their puzzles when I took a break. Those were the good old days. I started completing the newspaper's word-search and crossword puzzles in here when they went off to college."

"It sounds like there was a lot of love in this office."

"You could say that." His mood shifted to a melancholic one.

"We should show Mrs. Greenwald your gift," Martha said.

"Eve will be surprised," he said with smile.

"Yes," Martha said as she reached for Adam's office chair, which she'd pushed away earlier. "You said you wanted to be careful, so how about we get rid of this old thing? We can pick out a new one together that's sturdier."

"Let's do that." He put four of the books back in the box and carried the remaining two out of the room.

Martha followed his lead, pulling his old office chair along with her.

"How in the world?" Eve said with shock on her face as Adam and Martha strode into the den like championship professional athletes parading through their city's streets.

Oji, who sat on the opposite end of the ivory sectional

sofa as his mother, clapped silently after Adam walked past and could no longer see him.

Martha chuckled. Eve's response made up for the cool treatment Martha had received from her in the past, and the applause from Oji was an unexpected bonus. *Nice touch, babe,* she thought, reveling in the triumphant celebration after being underestimated by Eve.

"Martha reminded me about doing crossword and word-search puzzles, and we're going to pick out a new chair," Adam announced. "You can help too if you want." Then he pivoted to Martha, who stopped with the chair near the entry to the den. "That's okay with you, right?"

"It's your show, sir. I serve at your pleasure."

"That's a good one. I like that," Adam replied with a smile so bright that it lit up the room.

"Mr. Greenwald can use one of the other chairs in his office until the new one arrives. We talked about it on the walk from his office, and he's in full agreement," Martha said, aiming to reinforce their negotiation so the next step of her plan would go smoothly. She hadn't discussed it with Adam, but she needed a fail-safe to make sure he didn't renege later.

Adam nodded as he sat on the sofa between his wife and son.

Eve still looked aghast at the afternoon's biggest development. She had discouraged Martha from broaching the topic of his chair. It was a sensitive subject that Eve and Oji had brought up with Adam numerous times, always prompting him to shut them down expeditiously and without discussion.

"So, Oji, would you throw this one out?" Martha asked, making eye contact with him. Since the chair was just a few years old and in relatively good condition, she and Oji had already decided to donate it. But Adam didn't need to know those details.

Oji popped up from the sofa. "Sure. Let me take it now."

"Thanks, son," Adam said. He handed the books to Eve while Oji and Martha swapped places.

Eve browsed the pages of the books. "You and Martha have completed your fair share of progress this afternoon," she said with disbelief still plastered on her face.

"We're just getting started," Adam said. "Imagine what we'll do next. I'll fill those books up in no time. Do you play tennis, Martha? Or garden?"

Martha smiled. "I can buy more books, but I'll get back to you about the tennis and gardening."

"I'll hold you to that," Adam said as he stood up. "I'm heading to the kitchen for a glass of water. Anybody want anything?"

"No thank you," Martha replied. Like a toddler exploring one of those board books designed to stimulate a child's senses, she subtly ran her fingers across the nubby bouclé fabric covering the plush couch.

"I'm still working on mine, thanks," Eve said sweetly, looking at Adam with hope in her eyes.

"Okay, I'll be right back," Adam said.

"One of the most important things you can do for Mr. Greenwald is keep him busy," Martha said once he was out of earshot.

"We stay on the go," Eve replied.

"I know," Martha said. "You do a great job with that, but

I'm not sure he's getting the stimulation he needs. Given the amount of time he worked and the things he loved to do for fun before he got sick, I wonder if he looks for opportunities to be more high functioning."

"Would trying to replant a bush and getting locked outside count?" Eve asked. Martha could hear the irritation in her voice.

Martha nodded. "Yes. There may have been lots of factors at play in that instance, but Mr. Greenwald is still pretty sharp. I wonder if he noticed that he had an opportunity to try replanting his bush—which was something he told me that day was important to him—while you were out, and he just went for it."

"Could be," Eve said pensively. "He's adamant about using the pillbox and slippers that you recommended. He even took it upon himself to throw the flip-flop slippers out. He's also taken quite well to having a schedule and daily tasks to complete. His personality is much more regimented than mine, so I suppose that shouldn't surprise me."

"I'm pleased to hear the process is working. Structure can help most people if there's someone to help with checking in and providing reminders," Martha said. "Did you have any problem setting up the appointment with Mr. Greenwald's doctor for a fall-risk assessment?"

"I had no problem setting it up, but what should I ask during that appointment?"

"Since Mr. Greenwald is specifically interested in tennis and gardening, I'd suggest that you talk to his doctor about whether he can safely participate in those activities or what, if any, restrictions or accommodations might be needed. If Mr. Greenwald could benefit from physical therapy first, his doctor can order it. And as far as his safety at home, getting rid of the office chair is just the first step. Please talk to his doctor about ordering a home-safety assessment. It's a wonderful way to learn about steps you can take to decrease Mr. Greenwald's risk of falls at home. We also want to make sure he has any support he might need for getting into and out of bed, using the bathroom, and other activities he does each day."

"That's helpful," Eve said. "We'd like to keep him home as long as possible. And if we have to get creative about convincing him, like you clearly did, that's okay too." She chuckled.

Martha laughed. "I don't know what you're referring to," she said, drawing her hands to her chin.

"And you mentioned previously that you had someone who could talk to us about navigating through the programs and resources," Eve said. "What exactly did you mean by that?"

"I know only a sliver about the resources available when someone gets sick, so I work very closely with a medical social worker. We have multiple in our primary care center to help our patients work through all the emotional, social, and financial needs that may come up during illness and treatment. It's something that's just part of dealing with illness. It can be a heavy lift to manage, so medical social workers can help patients sort through the programs and resources that are available, from insurance options to day programs and support for caregivers. If you'd like, you could talk with one who specializes in geriatrics."

"Yes, we could use that guidance," Eve said with a solemn look.

"That's great. I'll help you get an appointment with her in the coming week," Martha said.

"I thought I knew how to work through this, but you've helped me see that we all need help," Eve said, simultaneously tapping the corners of her eyes with her fingers.

"No one can do it by themselves. I sure couldn't."

"That's kind of you to say." Eve sniffled as she stood.

Martha remembered the box of tissues on the end table next to her, but she couldn't quite reach it. She rose to her feet and pivoted toward the box.

"I'll get it," Eve said.

"Oh, okay." As Martha turned to go back to her seat, Eve suddenly threw her arms around her.

"Thank you for being patient with us and not giving up. We're so blessed to have you," Eve said, weeping as she squeezed Martha warmly.

ROARS OF LAUGHTER filled Ruth's dining room as the Gardin family chatted after Sunday dinner. The women cackled as Nicholas explained his persistent confusion over M.J.'s texting lingo despite having read numerous articles and blog posts to learn to communicate with his grandson, and the women finally confessed they'd conspired with M.J. to make up texting acronyms that didn't exist. The gag had been running for months.

Nicholas took it in good humor. "You just wait until he texts me again. He has it coming . . . Wait, I have an idea! Let's not tell him that I found out. Then I can pull a fast one on *him*."

"This is going to be good," Martha said. She nudged her sister, who sat next to her at the table.

"I'm in too," Mary said.

"I'm staying out of it this time," Naomi said soberly, though she had laughed so hard at Nicholas's confusion minutes earlier that she almost choked on the water she drank.

"M.J. has always had you wrapped around his finger," Ruth said with a chuckle from the head of the table.

Naomi playfully rolled her eyes. "Whatever. We haven't shared our highlights from the week yet."

Martha welcomed this part of the family's weekly meetup for Sunday dinner, especially when it was Ruth's turn to host. Her dining room's sophisticated monochromatic design—with a bold bluish-gray hue on the tray ceiling, walls, drapes, and chairs—lent itself to solemn conversations as well as lighthearted ones. "Smooth way to change the subject, Aunt Naomi."

"Please stop encouraging her. She only gets worse when you do," Ruth said with a chuckle.

"I'll help you out, honey. Let's see," Nicholas said, clapping his hands together one time. "By way of work updates, I'm making good headway on several of my projects. I won't bore you with the details since you'll hear them at the board meeting next week. On a somewhat personal note, I'm on track with my plans to scale back my time at the office."

"Boo!" Ruth said with a mischievous grin.

Nicholas laughed while shaking his head. "You live next door, and I'm training my replacement, who will also happen to live in your house. I doubt neither you nor M.J. will let me get too far out of your reach."

"That is correct," Ruth teased.

"I wouldn't have it any other way," Nicholas continued. "So, as I was saying before my very spoiled daughter interrupted me . . . Well, first let me add that I enjoy spoiling all of you by sharing my wisdom whenever I can help . . . Anyhow, after I cut my hours at the office, I plan to work on some pet projects. I'm just figuring out what those will be."

"So, your retirement hobby is going to be work? Did I understand that correctly?" Mary asked. Her questions largely came off as a mixture of concern and curiosity, but Martha picked up on a sprinkle of reprimand in there too.

"It's not work if I can do it when I feel like doing it," Nicholas replied. "Plus, it keeps my brain young."

"Whatever works for you, honey. I will be gardening. And that's my whole update," Naomi said, slapping the table with her hand.

Giggles spread around the table.

"But seriously. My highlight is about my garden. I'm planting cabbage, collards, onions, radishes, spinach, carrots, and maybe some beets," Naomi said, counting each vegetable on her fingers as she spoke. "Per usual, I'm happy to share, so feel free to place any special requests for weekly delivery."

"M.J. mentioned that he'll take whatever you have when he comes home," Ruth said. "It seems we may see him a few times this fall, if everything goes according to plan."

"As if he had to ask. You know I'm gonna take care of my baby," Naomi declared.

Ruth looked amused. "Of course. Who else sends a freshman to college with a chest freezer?"

"He's a picky eater. I needed to make sure he stayed well nourished," Naomi said with defensive coolness.

"But you still keep his freezer stocked with home-cooked meals, although now he's in grad school and his passport has more stamps than both of ours combined," Mary said. "What do you think he eats on those trips?"

"That's M.J.'s business, not mine," Naomi said with a smile.

"How convenient," Ruth said over laughs across the table.

"Okay, so let's shift the conversation to what we can actually do something about," Mary said as the laughter died down. "I have an accountability request. I'm struggling to leave work at work. I suppose that's par for the course when you open a new restaurant while your first restaurant is still in its infancy, but I'm nervous about slipping back into my workaholic tendencies. I'm thankful for having strong teams at both restaurants, but I need to trust them to do their jobs."

"I can relate to that," Martha said.

"Me too," said Ruth. "We can check in with you about it from time to time."

"Yep. I'm down for that," Martha said.

Naomi and Nicholas also agreed.

"I'll be counting on it. Thanks, y'all," Mary responded.

"Since we're talking about work-life balance, I'll share that I've met my goal to stick with yoga classes," Ruth said. "As you know, we've embraced succession planning at Gardin Family Enterprises, and I want to have a solid plan in place for when M.J. is ready to take over the company. That's a long while away, but I'm committed to practicing my yoga in the meantime. And maybe one day I'll get certified to teach so I'll have something meaningful to do when I retire."

"That's wonderful, Ruth!" Naomi said.

"You didn't have to show me up like that," Nicholas replied. "I'm just kidding. I'm proud of you."

Ruth met eyes with Mary across the table. "You challenged me to stick with it, so thanks a bunch for the push."

"No problem," Mary replied. "I'll be looking forward to cashing in your thanks for some free classes once you get your certification."

"Happy to oblige!" Ruth responded.

"Is it just me, or does everybody want something for free around here?" Nicholas teased.

Then the table broke out in another round of laughter.

Martha blushed. "I appreciate the advice you're giving Oji about his company without charging him, but I'll head off any further jokes about it by sharing my update."

"Don't worry, Martha. He never complains when I bring him free treats from the restaurant," Mary said.

"Touché," Nicholas replied over more laughter.

"I'm on the edge of my seat, Martha. What's your update?" Ruth asked.

Martha shifted in her chair. "You already know my big news about the breakthrough I've had with Oji's parents. But there's another development this week that I've been tight-lipped about . . . Shari told us that she's supportive of me and Oji moving ahead with the wedding whenever we'd like." She clenched her teeth, bracing herself for her family's reaction.

"Why does your face look like that?" Mary asked.

"I racked my brain but haven't been able to decide what y'all will think about it," Martha huffed.

Naomi leaned forward. "What do *you* think about it? That's what's most important."

"I couldn't agree more," Nicholas said.

Ruth watched intently but didn't chime in.

"I've been really quiet and prayerful about it the past couple of days. That's why I haven't said anything to you individually before now," Martha said.

"And?" Mary pushed.

"Mary, shush!" Ruth said.

Sorry, Mary mouthed.

"I'm good with it now," Martha said confidently. "Oji agreed with her on the spot. I started to see the light during the session. I even said that I wish I hadn't paused the wedding planning, but I needed a little more time to be sure."

"So, you're going to restart the wedding-planning process with Mrs. Jones?" Ruth asked.

Martha put her elbow on the table and rested her chin in the palm of her hand. "I considered it, but she's deep in preparation for the company Christmas party. We're already missing the date I really wanted, so—"

"Mom and dad's anniversary," Mary said with a melancholic sigh.

Martha shrugged her shoulders. "Yeah, so I'll just follow up with Mrs. Jones after the party. I'm not even giving her a chance to catch her breath," she said with a forced smile.

"Makes sense," Naomi said.

Nicholas wiped his brow and sighed loudly. "As long as you aren't thinking of eloping. We don't tell y'all what to do, but my heart has already been through too much with you and Oji. I want to see you two get married with my own eyes."

Naomi put her arm around Nicholas, rubbing his back. But she kept her eyes locked on Martha. "Baby, you can elope if you want to. We'll be okay. We wholeheartedly support you *and* Oji. We are here for y'all." Mary and Ruth nodded in agreement. Nicholas was a little late, but he joined in the nodding too.

Chapter Fourteen

November 6

"We were so busy poring over the health awareness month calendar that I didn't get to follow up with you about the text I sent you last night," Martha said as she and Jasmine exited the elevator in the hospital lobby. With the primary care center backing up Jasmine's office for important community events, the women still worked so closely that they met each Thursday morning. They were headed to the teaching kitchen to review the menu for an upcoming event with Mary.

"Girl, I fell asleep," Jasmine said. "I glanced at my phone when I woke up, but it was three A.M. I didn't want to disturb Tony by replying. Then I forgot to do it this morning. Anyway, I'd love to go to the mountains this weekend. The kids won't even miss me. They love when their dad cooks. He comes up with all sorts of concoctions for them. But are you sure Oji won't mind you going out of town with me? With . . . you know."

Martha scurried behind Jasmine so they could keep talking, barely making it inside the divider of the revolving door at the hospital's main entrance. "You can say it. I'm okay about it being . . . well, what was supposed to be our wedding weekend."

"Where is Oji going?" Jasmine asked. "Don't tell me I'm gonna have to hem him up already. I at least need to get y'all down the aisle before I start butting into your relationship."

"Start?" Martha said with a grin. "You and Tony are always all up in our business."

Jasmine playfully nudged Martha. "Umm, if I recall correctly, it was *your* idea that we join y'all for date night last month. But since Tony and Oji started playing golf together and Tony just happens to drop some pearls of wisdom every now and then, we're all up in your business?" she joked.

"For some reason, we like hanging around old married couples, and additional opinions seem to come along with the territory," Martha quipped. "But we love y'all."

"Good one," Jasmine said as they dashed across the plaza to the building that housed The Alabaster Plate.

"But to answer your other question, Oji has to fly to Austin for a last-minute meeting with the investor who's buying his business. I'm not thrilled that he has to do the meeting on a Saturday, but how can I complain when we need the deal to go through so badly?"

"Marriage is about compromise, and the deal will make both of your lives better in the long run," Jasmine said reassuringly.

"I agree," Martha said with a long sigh. "You may need to tell me that a few times this weekend. I hope you don't mind."

Jasmine opened the side door to The Alabaster Plate and held the door ajar for Martha. "Not at all. That's what friends do."

Mary leaned against the wall, surrounded by framed artwork done by the kids in her Potato Bud-ding Chef culinary camp. She tapped her wrist with her index finger even though she didn't wear a watch.

"Sorry we're late," Martha said as she approached the door. She shot Jasmine a look that said, *Why didn't you warn me?*

Jasmine grinned and looked away as she followed Martha into the building.

Martha then led the trio down the hallway.

"Did y'all forget *I* have a demanding schedule too?" Mary asked.

"Our other meeting ran over," Martha said. "We'll be efficient so we don't delay you for the lunch rush. Come to think of it, you can leave once we're done with the questions Jasmine has for you. I can stay behind and show her the new promotional items we bought."

Mary and Jasmine slowed their speed as Martha neared the door to the teaching kitchen.

"*I'd* like to see the items too," said Oji, who appeared at the threshold of the learning space, which was cloaked in darkness, other than the light coming in from the hallway.

"What are you doing here?" Martha asked with confusion in her voice.

Oji bent down to greet Martha with a kiss on the cheek, but she backed away. "Oji! We're at work!" She looked down both sides of the hallway to make sure no staff members were around. There were none, but Mary and Jasmine had also disappeared.

"Babe, you're right. What was I thinking?" He grabbed her by the hand and led her into the teaching kitchen.

"What are you doing?" she asked as he closed the door and turned on the lights.

Martha let out a loud gasp as her eyes fell upon a sea of easels displaying poster-sized photos of the couple spread across the room. Her eyes welled with tears as she scanned the photographic inventory of their relationship: the photo she begrudgingly agreed to on their first dinner together, Oji's first Easter brunch with the Gardin family, the two of them holding Martha's dull and discolored copper pot, pre- and post-engagement photos at Naomi and Nicholas's wedding, and an array of photos taken on their dates. But one of the date night images stood out.

Tears dripped down Martha's face as she made her way to an easel near the large teaching island, slightly set away from the others. Oji slowly released her hand as she got close enough to notice that the appearance of the image differed from the others. He reached into the pocket of his navy linen pants, removed a handkerchief, and slipped it into Martha's trembling hand.

Martha's heart leaped as she recognized the image of herself looking out in the distance while Oji gazed lovingly at her at the drive-in theater. "An oil painting of the photo the teenager took of us," she said through her tears. "Benjamin . . . Benjamin Thomas Springfield. I said the day he took the photo that I would remember his name because he'd be famous one day. But I will always remember him because he helped me see the strength in our relationship on a day when I felt so defeated.

"This is gorgeous," she said. She stood alone, taking in the bright colors and brushstrokes that told the story of her and Oji's love. "Thank you, babe. What a special thing to do for me."

Hearing no response, she tried again. "Babe?" she said,

clutching the handkerchief's soft bamboo fabric as though her life depended on it as she spun around.

And there was Oji on bended knee for the second time. But in this instance, his left hand rested on his knee while his right hand gently trembled in the air, holding the ring Martha had dreamed of for nearly five months.

"I brought you here today because this teaching kitchen pulled us together. It's a beautiful symbol of growth in our individual professional lives, but it reflects our relationship too. It brought you to me and to my family. You've saved us, Martha," Oji said, his voice cracking. He wiped his eyes before taking her right hand into his left one and starting to speak again.

"Cadence Martha Gardin—my love, my guiding star. You make me a better man. A better son. A better friend. You are the answer to my heart's prayer. I wake up every morning thankful that you chose me. And it would be my greatest privilege to spend the rest of my life showing you my gratitude. Will you marry me?"

"Yes!" Martha exclaimed, jumping up and down. She threw her arms around Oji as she bawled.

"I love you with all my heart. Thank you so much for loving me back," he whispered in her ear.

"I love you, too," Martha replied breathlessly.

As they separated, Oji leaned toward Martha and slowly and gently touched her lips with his.

"Let me put the ring on your finger," he said, swiping his eyes.

"The ring! I forgot all about it!"

As Oji slid the vintage sapphire and diamond engagement ring on the ring finger of Martha's left hand, she awed at the sparkles in the large cushion-cut-sapphire center stone and twelve cushion-cut diamonds flanking it on a platinum band.

"A perfect fit. Just like us," she said.

"I COULDN'T HAVE dreamed of a more perfect proposal. I just hate that you have to go to Austin this weekend," Martha said with wistful eyes.

"I'd like to talk to you about that." He guided Martha through the sea of photos to the tasting table, a long rectangular one lined with teal and lime-green chairs that looked like the grown-up version of the ones she used in elementary school. "Have a seat," he said, pulling a chair away from the table.

She dropped down into the chair and nervously wrapped her legs around the chair's wooden ones. "Please don't tell me the sale fell through."

"No, babe. I'm sorry to alarm you. The deal is still on. I'm actually ready to sign the contract. I just didn't want to move forward before we could have an honest discussion about it."

"Okay," Martha said, dragging out the word. She readjusted herself in her chair, remembering to sit like a lady.

"Nicholas is the one who made the offer. He is the investor."

She looked puzzled. "Why didn't either of you mention that to me?"

"I'll explain. But first I want to make sure you understand that I will not go through with the sale if you have any reservations at all. For now, please try not to hold it against me, okay? Can you just try that for me?"

"Sure. Keep going," Martha blurted, flicking her opened hand at her wrist.

Oji exhaled loudly. "Nicholas is giving me the opportunity to sell forty-five percent of my business to him. He would be my partner, but he would also serve as my mentor. Though he's never invested in the development side, he owns multiple real-estate properties. His overall business acumen and specialized skill set in mergers and acquisitions could help me grow the company in ways I didn't expect to be able to for years. Plus, obviously, he has access to lots of capital."

"I see," she said, weighing the pros in her head.

"And I could buy the company back anytime I wanted, so there's always a way out if things go south for some reason. That's in the contract."

Martha stared Oji in the eyes, trying to read his face. "What are the potential downsides?"

Oji sat up straight in his chair. "To put it bluntly, there's only one: that he's the new husband of the aunt who raised you and the current father figure in your life."

"I'm not worried about that," she said without hesitation.

"Not at all?" he asked, leaning forward.

"Nope. Aside from Beau, he's the most fair businessman I've met. Of course, not counting *you*, babe," Martha said, clenching her teeth at her oversight.

"I'm not insulted. I've got big shoes to fill when it comes

to those two. I'm sorry I never got to meet Beau, but I'll learn everything I can from Nicholas."

She smiled pensively for a moment before she spoke. "I still don't understand why Nicholas's offer had to stay a secret. What am I missing?"

"It's so lucrative that it allows me to provide for my parents and keep them in their house. *And* I can also do something special for you," Oji said with a cautious smile.

"On top of the ring?" Martha asked. She sounded like a game show contestant eager to see what was behind door number two. "Are we going on a trip or something?"

He shifted his weight to his right side. "Eventually. But how about we get married on Saturday?"

"*I* thought about eloping too, but you have that trip to Austin, and I want at least our families there. Wait a minute. If Nicholas is buying part of your company, then the trip to Austin isn't real, right?" Martha asked as she began to rethink the trip details Oji had shared leading up to the morning.

"I have another secret," he said with a grin. "Although you asked Mrs. Jones to pause the wedding planning, I convinced her to restart it, but I didn't do it alone. It took some serious reinforcement from your family. She would barely talk to me at first. Then Ruth got in touch with her. The three of us had a short conference call, where Mrs. Jones agreed to proceed. From my perspective, the rest of the wedding planning happened in a flash because Ruth ran point with Mrs. Jones."

Martha shook her head in disbelief. "Are you serious?" she asked with wide eyes.

Oji took both of her hands in his. "Yes, babe. I want to

spend the rest of our lives making your dreams come true. And I mean that."

"But how are you paying for all this if the deal hasn't gone through yet?" she asked, squinting her eyes.

"I finally received a delayed payment from a real-estate project. That took care of Mrs. Jones for a while. I'll get the first installment from Nicholas when I sign the papers this afternoon, and that'll take care of the rest. That's why I wanted your approval of Nicholas's offer first. I needed to be sure you felt no pressure to give your okay." Oji squeezed Martha's hands. "This is something I want to do for you. Don't worry about the money. We're good."

She pulled her hands back from his and rubbed her eyes, processing the reluctance she felt inside. Then she thought of the characters in the fairy-tale cartoon movies she watched well into young adulthood and, admittedly, that she still watched from time to time. *So, this is how they felt when everything finally started working out for them. Why am I overthinking this? If I was comfortable handing my ideas over to my highly capable wedding planner and leaving everything to her to implement with occasional check-ins with me, it's not such a big stretch to embrace the possibility that she could still pull off the wedding of my dreams with no additional intervention from me.* Then she asked a remaining question aloud. "But what about my dress?"

Oji leaned back in his chair and crossed his legs as though he sat behind a desk overlooking the Atlanta skyline. "It's with an alterations team. There's a car at the front entrance of the restaurant waiting to take you, Mary, and Jasmine to your fitting. And before you ask, yes, we cleared your work calendar for today and tomorrow."

*

"ARE WE ALMOST there? Oji didn't mention anything about a blindfold. Is this really part of his plan, or are y'all just trying to get back at me?" Martha asked. She found comfort in incessant questioning as her sister guided her by her hand.

Jasmine trailed behind them with Martha's purse and heavy briefcase. She mostly held in her laughs but occasionally let one slip out.

"How many different ways are you going to ask me the same questions?" Mary asked joyfully. The sisters laughed, recalling their parents' similar response when Martha tortured them with questions as a child.

Jasmine and Mary had pressured Martha into putting on the blindfold before the car left The Alabaster Plate, but only after Martha was certain they'd retrieved her briefcase and laptop from her office. Although Jasmine and Mary tried explaining that she would have no time for work, Martha doubled down, holding on to what little control she had over the next thirty minutes of her life. The car's driver, a pleasant woman from Columbus, had let the expected arrival time slip, and Martha thanked her profusely.

From what Martha could tell, the driver had dropped them at a public place where they walked through a somewhat populated area and stepped on an elevator—with little wait—and arrived on whichever floor they were on now.

Martha assumed they'd walked through a lobby of some sort, but she couldn't figure out what building within a thirty-minute radius of Macon housed a tailor or who could ensure her wedding dress was ready in forty-eight hours. *But for all I know, we just drove fifteen minutes away, turned right back around, and are still in downtown Macon,* she thought.

"Why is it so quiet?" she asked. "Do y'all have your fingers on your lips, telling people to be quiet?"

Mary lifted Martha's hand and pushed her fingers down one by one around a cool metal lever. Martha gripped it for dear life.

"Is this a door? Please don't have me walking into a waiting room with people," Martha said. "Everyone will laugh at me, and I will be so embarrassed. Not that I could see them, but still."

Mary didn't answer.

Is Jasmine still here? Martha wondered.

Mary pushed Martha's hand down. As the door inched open, Martha grew impatient and added her own strength, taking a single step forward to expedite the movement. Then she ripped off her blindfold while standing in the doorway.

Ruth, Naomi, Nicholas, and the Greenwalds sat comfortably on a tan sectional sofa. "Congratulations to our bride-to-be," they said in butchered unison. Martha immediately recognized the bespoke furnishings and neutral color palette—in shades of cream and light gray—as the Edin Inn. Her eyes welled up at the sight of her current and future family members, and the tears became more plentiful as her loved ones rose from their seats and showered her with hugs and well wishes as Mary and Jasmine hurried into the suite from the hallway.

"Let us see the ring," Naomi demanded.

"Oh, haven't y'all seen it already?" Martha asked.

"Yes, but not on your hand, dear," Eve replied. The softness in her voice as she used the term of endearment conveyed favor instead of the haughtiness that had come through in the past.

Martha extended her left hand, eliciting oohs and aahs from everyone—including Mary and Jasmine, who'd shown the same reaction an hour earlier.

"I hate to cut our fun short," Ruth said, calling the group to attention. "Martha, please forgive us for rushing off, but we're only meant to greet you and swiftly hand you over to Mrs. Jones and the alterations team. But before we do that, M.J. asked me to tell you to check your phone."

"I was just thinking about him. He's the only one missing," Martha said with a sappy look on her face.

"Here you go," Jasmine said as she handed Martha her purse.

Martha retrieved her phone, unlocked it, and read M.J.'s message: *Im presenting at a conference. Flying home tonite. Remember our talk in the garden? Checkmate! The queen wins. But no more games okay? Luv u.*

"Awww! This is the sweetest," Martha said, wiping her eyes.

Jasmine nudged Mary.

"Oh," Mary said, nodding at Jasmine. "We forgot to tell you something on the ride over. Since we didn't have an opportunity to give you a proper bridal shower, we'll have one after the wedding."

"But before the honeymoon," Jasmine added with a wink.

Nicholas covered his ears. "Oh goodness!" he said. Then he laughed.

Martha put her arm around Nicholas and gave him a tight one-armed squeeze. "I heard you didn't have any complaints about the gift Mary and I gave Aunt Naomi at her shower."

"Martha!" Naomi said, playfully tapping Martha on her arm as the group giggled.

Nicholas covered his face amid the chuckles. Then he joined in.

"I may have some questions about that gift," Eve said, prompting more laughter.

Martha blushed at the thought of her aunt and future mother-in-law discussing lingerie.

Before the teasing went on too long, the gang received a polite but stern redirection when Mrs. Jones seemingly appeared out of nowhere, almost as smoothly as Oji had done earlier that morning. *I wonder if she taught him that. Maybe it's a secret military trick.*

"Martha, it's good to see you again," Mrs. Jones said. "I wish I could allow more time with your family, but we've got a long day ahead."

Martha's head spun toward Mrs. Jones, then back at her loved ones. Since none of them flinched when Mrs. Jones spoke, Martha did a double take and uncovered the secret to the planner's seemingly invisible appearance in the suite without using the front door. Mrs. Jones stood next to a closed door that Martha had previously overlooked. Martha had noticed an open bedroom door on the opposite side of the suite when she first arrived and assumed it was the only sleeping area.

"Is that another bedroom?" Martha asked, pointing to the door near Mrs. Jones.

"It used to be," Mrs. Jones said. She slid the door open to display two folding tables, each with a woman seated in front of a sewing machine.

Martha gasped.

"Hello," the women said, waving.

"Your suite is next door," Mrs. Jones said. Then she looked around the suite, making eye contact with Martha's loved ones and quickly nodding her head toward the front door.

Eve grabbed her purse. Then she and Adam walked hand in hand to Martha.

"We are delighted that you are joining our family. I always wanted a daughter," Adam said, pulling Martha in for a hug.

Water pooled in Martha's eyes. "Thank you," she replied. While they embraced, Martha remembered Adam's disappearance during Oji's first proposal and whispered a prayer of thanks that he would be present at the wedding.

Eve followed suit with a warm and lengthy hug. When Martha let go, it turned into one of those hugs where the other person isn't quite ready to let go when you release them so they grab your hand and hold it while they talk to you. "We'll see you tomorrow evening at the Stafford-Grant House," she said, squeezing Martha's hand lightly at the mention of the venue. Martha received the gesture as an unspoken apology for the tension between the two of them during their visit to the property.

"A rehearsal dinner!" Martha exclaimed. "I'm really touched that you would do this for me. Thank you both so much," she said, looking back and forth between Eve and Adam.

Eve's eyes welled with tears. "See you there, dear."

What amazing progress we've made! Martha thought.

As the Greenwalds made their way to the exit, Mrs. Jones pulled out her phone. She peeped at it, then quickly glanced at the Gardins and Jasmine.

Ruth spoke up on behalf of the remaining loved ones. "We'll be right behind them. Please forgive us for delaying your schedule, but we must have a brief moment with Martha before we leave."

"I'll go so y'all can have some privacy," Jasmine said.

"I would be so disappointed if you did," Naomi said with a toothy smile. "You were our secret weapon in this special little operation we helped Oji pull off." Then she directed her words at Martha. "As much as we all talked and strategized, it's fairly obvious that we didn't plan this part. Trust me when I say that Oji worked hard to convince us this was a good idea—all of us," she said as she briefly made eye contact with Jasmine before returning her gaze to Martha.

"As the two of you worked on your relationship," Naomi continued, "Oji went the extra mile to prove himself and get our buy-in for the wedding planning to proceed. But I decided to speak up because, in some way, each of us has noticed three things over the last few months as we've worked on this with Oji. One, we've never seen you happier. Two, it's obvious that your happiness isn't just because you and Oji found each other. And three, it's because you found yourself."

"Thank you, Aunt Naomi. And thank all of you. I'm not going to have any tears left for the wedding!" Martha said.

There wasn't a dry eye in the room, including Mrs. Jones and the alterations staff, who watched from the periphery of the suite.

Nicholas pulled two light-blue handkerchiefs from his pocket. He handed one to Martha and the other to Naomi. "I'm sorry I don't have enough of them to go around."

"Where's mine?" Ruth asked playfully. "I'm kidding," she said as she dabbed her eyes with one she'd brought from home.

"Is that Beau's?" Martha asked, tearing up again.

"Yes," Ruth said, taking Martha by the hand. "He would've loved to be here today. It's my way of having a little piece of him here—for me and for you. He'd have been so proud of you, Martha," she said with more tears in her eyes.

Tears streamed down Martha's face. "Thank you, Ruth. After Oji's proposal, I didn't think the day could get better, but finding out that I'm having a surprise wedding and that y'all have labored with him takes it over the top. My heart is so full . . . And, Ruth, Oji told me what you did to make this possible for us."

Martha placed her arm around Ruth before she continued. "I will forever treasure your investment in me over the past few months, your support of my relationship with Oji, and the sacrifice you made to make our wedding happen on the day that honors my parents . . . It means the world to me."

"It's what your parents and Beau would've wanted for you. It's my pleasure to stand in for them in such a special way."

"Oh, Ruth!" Martha said, sobbing and pulling Ruth closer for a hug.

"We all love you so much," Ruth said as Naomi, Nicholas, Mary, and Jasmine joined them in a big group hug.

Chapter Fifteen

November 7

"Oh my!" Naomi yelled as she opened the back door to the porch.

Martha jerked so hard in the egg-shaped basket swing that her sudden movement pulled the swing in the opposite direction. "We startled each other," she said as she planted her feet on the porch.

Naomi audibly exhaled. She gripped her mug of coffee with one hand and closed her back door. "It's seven A.M. You have a long list of pre-wedding-day tasks to get done. Mrs. Jones will be arriving at your suite at the Edin Inn soon, yet here you are in my backyard, all bright-eyed and bushy-tailed like the rabbits trying to get to my vegetables over there," she said, making her way to the sofa.

"I've been awake for hours, so I stopped at my cottage for a few things and then rushed here to watch the sunrise. It was a calming way to kick off the day," Martha said in a pensive voice.

"Is something bothering you?" Naomi asked before sipping her coffee.

Martha pushed herself back in the swing. "No. I'm just excited, and I wanted to see y'all. Is Nicholas coming out too?"

"Yes. He was on his way downstairs for his coffee. He won't be too long. Did you at least sleep well?"

"Maybe a few hours. I just have lots of things on my mind. Oji and I talked at dinner last night, and we've decided to stay on the estate after we get married. We'll either sell his condo or rent it out. Then we can save a little more money and build a house that we can grow into."

Naomi swallowed her coffee. "Obviously, that's fantastic news from my perspective, but how do you feel about it?"

"I'm satisfied with it. Before, I wanted a big house that would serve as a status symbol. But I figured out in therapy that was just part of the reason I didn't want us to stay in my cottage. Actually, I needed it as a safe place. I didn't feel secure enough in my relationship with Oji for it to become *his* home too. But I don't see things that way anymore."

"That's a pretty substantial breakthrough," Naomi said.

"Thank you," Martha said proudly as she pushed against the porch with her toes, causing the swing to sway. "That reminds me. Can we get a two-seater swing? I looked at some last night when I couldn't sleep. There are egg-shaped ones, but they also make some that look like a cross between a square and an oval. Would that make it squoval shaped?"

"I never thought I'd see the day," Naomi said.

Martha scrunched her face. "That I would get married? Really, Aunt Naomi?"

"No, I figured you'd marry someone, but I didn't see you sharing your swing with him."

Martha laughed. "I'd like to try to defend myself, but I can see how you'd feel that way. I only started thinking about it a few weeks ago. But growth is good, right?"

Nicholas opened the back door as Martha spoke. "Growth

is always good, but shouldn't you be having breakfast at the Edin Inn before your morning check-in with the alterations team?" he asked, looking at Naomi nervously as he sat next to her with his cup of coffee. Then he returned his gaze to Martha. "Martha, you don't want to fall behind. You've got to be ready when Oji picks you up to go for your wedding bands and marriage license."

"I see you've turned into Chloe," Martha said, sarcastically referencing the spunky executive assistant Nicholas and Ruth shared at Gardin Family Enterprises.

Naomi shook her head. "Child, this is only a glimpse of what I've had to live with since the wedding planning kicked into high gear," she said before taking another sip of coffee.

"I will not be shamed for my enthusiastic interest," Nicholas replied with his characteristic air of confidence.

Naomi and Martha chuckled.

"That's a great segue. Your 'enthusiastic interest' is precisely what brought me here," Martha said, parroting the way Nicholas pronounced the words. "But before you chastise me again, I promise to return to my room before Mrs. Jones notices I've escaped and sends her army of assistants to find me. I need to ask you something important, Nicholas. That's why I've stopped by so early."

She put her feet on the porch and stopped the swing from moving. "I'm wondering if you would be willing to walk me down the aisle."

Naomi drew her hands to her mouth. Then she quickly looked at Nicholas and then back at her niece again. Although Naomi's lips were covered and her cheekbones were relaxed, her eyes told Martha that surprise wasn't the only emotion her aunt felt. She was also elated by the request.

But Nicholas, a skilled negotiator, maintained his poker face. "I'm honored, but—"

"Forgive me for cutting you off." Martha smiled like a student who understood the material so well that she had anticipated the exact question her teacher included on the final exam. "I don't intend to be rude, but I know where this is going, and I'd like to get ahead of it. Please know that I'm not asking you to escort me down the aisle because of your partnership with Oji. While I'm delighted about the deal and can see how I will benefit from it, I appreciate that you and Oji didn't involve me in it. I'm asking you to walk me down the aisle because of your relationship with me."

Martha stole a peek at Naomi, who watched with bated breath, before she continued. "You came into our family ready to hold me accountable and challenge me but also to love and nurture me. And you did all those things in your own way. Even after you found out that Ruth is your daughter, you were so evenhanded with your love that I never felt threatened by your relationship with her," she said, dabbing her eyes.

"If I can be honest," she continued, "it baffled me that I felt that way. But then I began to recount all the ways you've shown up for me, never holding my insecurities against me. I could go on and on, but it occurred to me last night that I don't want to call you Nicholas anymore. If you don't mind, I'd prefer to call you Uncle Nicholas going forward," Martha said as her eyes filled with moisture.

Nicholas wiped his eyes. "I haven't cried like this since I asked your aunt to marry me," he said. "But I would love to be your uncle Nicholas, and I would be thrilled to walk you down the aisle."

Naomi patted Nicholas on the knee. Then she wiped away her tears.

Martha jumped out of the swing. Her vision was slightly obscured from crying, but she made her way to the middle of the porch, where she and Nicholas met in a warm, tearful embrace.

Then they joined Naomi on the sofa.

"Our coffee is cold, but this is worth it," Naomi said to Nicholas.

Nicholas turned to Martha. "In case you can't tell, I was bowled over by sentiment. That confirms for me that I made the right decision to partner with Oji."

Naomi nodded. "Me too."

"But to be clear, it wasn't about bailing Oji or you out," Nicholas said. "Oji's built a strong company, so he deserves to be compensated for that. It's also a smart investment for me, which makes our work together a glowing example of cooperative economics. He is one of the most exciting young entrepreneurs I've met in a long time, and I believe we'll have a tremendous amount of fun together."

ONLY A COUPLE of Martha's ideas for the rehearsal dinner came to fruition at the actual event, but she harbored no disappointment about it. The end result exceeded the high expectations she had of her future mother-in-law and wedding planner. With the decor and grounds of the Stafford-Grant House as the canvas, Martha was bound to be satisfied with whatever Eve and Mrs. Jones rendered. But instead of fulfilling Martha's requested theme highlighting

Oji's favorite things, they leaned into his surprise proposal, sprinkling the easels containing poster-sized images of the couple around the rose-colored tea room and adjacent gardens and tying them into a fun activity for the fifty guests.

"I am two photos away from winning the scavenger hunt," Jasmine said as she typed into her phone.

"I don't know that it's fair for my bridesmaid to win. The only prize you should get is my eternal gratitude," Martha said. She stepped away from the highboy table and quickly twirled around like a sassy five-year-old. But in place of a tutu, she wore a white A-line trapeze dress with large robin's-egg-blue ties at the end of her three-quarters sleeves.

Mary, who stood across the table from her sister, shook her head. "I hope you made an exception for your maid of honor, because no one told me that. I could've just gone to your wedding app and left comments on the photos. I didn't need to run around here looking for the specific photos first," she teased.

"The fun is in playing, little sister," Martha scoffed. "But don't worry—everyone gets a prize, even if they don't finish."

"You mean I'm not special? I was fully on board with this surprise wedding until now. I quit," Mary joked.

Jasmine placed her phone on the table. "I'll track down those last two photos later, after I drag Tony to the photo booth."

"That is why we're friends. You love the scavenger hunt and photo booth as much as I do. Those are the two elements that carried over from my initial requests for the rehearsal dinner," Martha said with a sentimental smile.

Jasmine blushed. "One of the many reasons we're friends.

But I'll save all that mushy talk for my toast tomorrow. For now, I'd better find my husband before he changes his mind about taking silly pictures with me."

"I just left Tony over by the cake table," Oji said as he walked up behind Martha. "He couldn't get over how much the cake looks like a real golf bag and clubs."

"I should've known," Jasmine said.

"So, *this* is the woman who squared off with Eve Greenwald and lived to tell the story?" asked a baritone voice Martha had never heard.

That could only be one person. Who else would feel comfortable saying that out loud? Martha pivoted with haste, but not so fast that she missed her sister staring in the voice's direction.

"You just got here, and you're looking for trouble already," Oji said. Then he made eye contact with Martha, slightly widening his eyes. "This is Nile, my brother."

Martha instantly understood her sister's facial expression. Although his photos gave some idea of his presence, they didn't do him justice. Nile looked to be around three inches taller than Oji, which would place him at about six foot five. While Oji's physique favored basketball players, Nile was much more Mary's type. He would fit right in with a lineup of professional football players. But from what Oji had said, these days he was more inclined to analyze the team statistics than watch or play the game. And it was just a matter of time before Mary would discover that he checked another box on her preference sheet.

Martha gave Nile a quick hug. "I've been looking forward to meeting you. I can already see you're gonna be fun."

Nile flashed a mischievous grin that matched his reputation. "I sure hope so, sis," he said with a booming laugh.

Mary giggled, stroking her long flowing hair lightly and tucking it behind her ear.

"This is my dear friend Jasmine. And *this* is my sister, Mary," Martha said, holding in a laugh.

"Hello. Very pleased to meet you both," Nile said, shaking Jasmine's hand first and then Mary's.

But Nile took his time greeting Mary, lingering as if he'd have said more if his brother—with whom he'd only recently resumed regular contact—and future sister-in-law weren't present. Mary looked as though she couldn't have been more delighted with the attention. She batted her eyelashes as her smile broadened, exposing all her teeth.

Jasmine seemed to pick up on the chemistry too. "Look at the time," she said, picking up her phone from the table. "Let me go make sure my husband didn't load your groom's cake into the car, Oji," she said immediately after the introductions were complete. But she gave Mary a knowing glance before she stepped away.

Nile suavely slipped into the spot Jasmine vacated at the highboy table.

And I thought Oji *was a handful when I first met him,* Martha thought.

While Mary and Nile chatted on their own, Martha stepped closer to Oji and whispered, "Did you notice the photographer floating around? I hope she got some shots of us talking."

"Of you meeting Nile?" Oji asked, speaking at a regular volume.

"Yes, but don't say it like that. He's your brother."

"How could I forget? My mother has said it every five minutes since I told her Nile agreed to come to the wedding. 'Your brother this. Your brother that.' It's exhausting."

Martha placed her hand atop Oji's on the table and rubbed it softly. "I know, babe. And you're handling it masterfully. There will be plenty of time for you, Nile, and your parents to work things out after the wedding. And you won't have to go through it alone this time. I'll be there with you every step of the way. But for now, let's just focus on us."

Oji closed his eyes and slowly nodded his head. "Thank you," he replied with his eyes still closed.

After a second, Martha caught a glimpse of the Greenwald matriarch approaching the table. "Here comes your mom," she said, nudging Oji. "Don't worry—she can't tell we're talking about her. She'll just think we were having a romantic moment," Martha continued as Oji opened his eyes.

Eve strolled up to the table with a look of victory on her face. "I love seeing my boys together again. It's been way too long. I want you to know that I put my heart into planning this for the two of you," she said, looking back and forth between Oji and Martha. "And now it feels like you've given me a special gift by giving my elder son a reason to come home. My only regret is that your father is missing our reunion, but sticking with his routine today will make for a better day tomorrow."

Nile and Oji wore plastic smiles.

Mary smiled politely.

"I'm sure it was a tough decision to hire a caregiver to stay with Mr. Greenwald this evening," Martha replied, hoping to shift the subject.

"Yes, dear. It's never easy," Eve replied in a pious tone.

Progress. Focus on progress, Martha thought. She recalled the advice Ruth shared about embracing progress over perfection in her relationship with Eve in the wake of Adam's disappearance. *Things between us don't have to be perfect, but I'm thankful for the progress.*

"Yes, we'll have some family time with Dad in the morning, before the wedding," Oji said.

"Nile, maybe you and your father could work on some crossword puzzles together," Eve said.

"Let's see how it goes, Mom. My main focus is assisting at the wedding," Nile said coolly.

What is this familiarity I'm feeling? Martha thought. Her eyes darted to Oji, but he looked unbothered.

"And, of course, I'll help Dad with handing you the rings during the ceremony if he develops any difficulty with it. And then Mom and I will tag team at the reception. So don't worry, okay?" Nile said, looking back and forth between Oji and Martha.

Mrs. Greenwald! Nile handles his mother with the same coolness she used for me, Martha thought. *How the plot thickens. This is going to be interesting.*

"Thank you, Nile. I'm glad you're here," Oji said. He seemed sincere, but Martha could tell he dug deep to say it.

"Yes, it's a gift that you could be here with us," Martha added.

Mary nodded. "Mm-hmm."

Chapter Sixteen

November 8

The classic cream interior of Martha's bridal suite provided a relaxing backdrop as she, Mary, Ruth, Jasmine, and Naomi prepared for the one o'clock wedding ceremony. The women debriefed on the previous night as they rotated through the five chairs set up in the living area, which were staffed by an efficient team of makeup artists and hairstylists.

"Nile followed me on social media after the rehearsal dinner—on *all* my accounts, both business and personal. And on all the platforms, too," Mary said as her stylist adjusted the loose curls cascading from the top of her head.

"He isn't subtle, is he?" Martha asked, turning to look at her sister. The makeup artist applying Martha's foundation paused. "Sorry. I forgot I'm not supposed to move," Martha said.

"Not at all, and I like it," Mary replied.

Jasmine traipsed back to her chair, having crossed the room to examine her freshly applied makeup in natural light, owing to the full-length mirror next to the terrace. "Oh, we could tell."

"Isn't he being a little thirsty?" Martha asked.

"Have you seen Nile?" Mary said with a loud laugh.

"When you look like that, it's not thirsty. It's called showing interest. I'm so glad you and Oji found each other, because you have absolutely no game."

Martha chuckled, shrugging. "You're not wrong about that. I'd never have been interested in Oji if he hadn't pursued me first. He generated too much attention from other women. I usually avoid those types of men. And from what I can tell of Nile so far, Oji's got nothing on him."

"But I can certainly see why people have said Eve has strong opinions about who her sons date," Naomi said as her stylist fluffed her silver hair. "She clearly had her hands full with those two when they were growing up."

That's an understatement, Martha thought. Although Eve and Martha were on pleasant terms, the awkward exchange with Eve after Nile's late arrival at the rehearsal dinner had placed Martha on high alert. While she was overjoyed about the apparent improvement in Oji and Nile's relationship, only time would tell if it would last past the wedding weekend. And Martha feared the subsequent strain that a budding relationship between her and Oji's siblings might introduce. Adding Eve's unpredictable nature on top of that could make for a combustible reaction, but Martha kept her concerns to herself.

She had shared enough with her sister about her journey with her future mother-in-law for Mary to make her own decisions, and she had also gained the required insight along her path to healing her relationship with Mary to know that it was essential that she respect Mary's boundaries about her romantic relationships.

"Don't worry—I can handle Nile," Mary said with a wink.

"Oh my goodness," Ruth said. She examined her newly applied eyelashes in a handheld mirror. After she fluttered them several times, she gave a thumbs-up to her makeup artist.

"Yes, Ruth! That's how you do it," Mary said with exaggerated sass.

Naomi stood up from her chair, stretching her legs as her hairstylist stepped away. "I can laugh about it now, but I don't know how I made it through your teenage years, Mary," she said with a laugh.

"I was there. I worried about you," Ruth said.

"We all did, even Mary," Martha said pensively.

"True," Mary admitted.

"Mrs. Dorsey, you should've seen her," Jasmine said, twisting in her chair to make eye contact with Naomi. "I'd forgotten that Mary was the one who got the attention from all the boys Martha and I liked. But once I saw her in action last night, I remembered why. Our girl is quick."

"When someone catches my eye, there's no need to waste time," Mary said.

"Next time you'll have to call me over," said Naomi, who sat down in the empty chair next to Martha. "I'd have been tickled to see all this in real time. I can take it now that Mary's all grown up. But I'm not going to be the one to tell Nicholas. He isn't ready for another one."

Martha placed her elbow on her chair's armrest and leaned toward Naomi. "Another what? What do you mean?"

"Another relationship. He almost didn't make it through you and Oji. He kept me up so many nights talking about y'all!" Naomi replied, shaking her head.

"He brought it up at the office, too," Ruth added. "Worrying about y'all has become like a part-time job for him. During his lunch break, I even caught him listening to a podcast about parenting young adults. And he doesn't usually take lunch breaks!"

Martha giggled. "Thankfully, all worked out well. But most of all, it's a reminder that Uncle Nicholas really loves us."

"He does. Not that you didn't already know," Naomi said.

"I know too, but it's still a sweet reminder," Mary said. "But he doesn't have anything to worry about. I'm not looking to get into anything serious. Work gets all my attention. Plus, I'm focused on my maid-of-honor duties today. But I might give Nile my number. We'll see." Mary laughed mischievously.

"After all that flirting y'all were doing, I don't understand how y'all haven't exchanged numbers," Jasmine said. "Clearly, I've been out of the dating game for too long. What am I missing?"

"Well, a lot has changed since 1922," Mary teased.

Jasmine chuckled. "So shady."

THE ORIGINAL SWINGING bell at the First Edin Baptist Church rang promptly at one in the afternoon on November 8, just as it had forty years prior. But instead of the momentous sound announcing the beginning of the ceremony to unite Mary Martha Crawford and Raymond Patrick Gardin in holy matrimony, it proclaimed the blessed union of their daughter Cadence Martha to Oji Christopher Greenwald, the son of Mr. and Mrs. Adam Greenwald.

Three hundred guests filled the pews to the sounds of a soulful string quartet and harpist. The decor in the historic church highlighted architectural elements adored by the bride and reflective of the Gardin family's rich history. An aisle runner—made of natural linen and embroidered with the couple's initials—separated two sections of wooden pews, the front portions of which were original to the church, having been constructed by the previously enslaved members of the Gardin family and others who founded the city of Edin.

Garlands containing camellias, daffodils, and ranunculus in shades of pink, purple, and white lined the aisles as well as the classical-style balcony on three sides of the church sanctuary. Prior to the ceremony, a spray made of similar flowers was placed on the first church pew in loving memory of the mother and father of the bride.

The musicians played Bach's "Air on the G String" to kick off the wedding processional.

Eve, escorted by Nile, looked regal in a floor-length brocade Esé Azénabor dress with a pink and blue floral pattern. After accompanying his mother to her seat, Nile joined his father and brother at the altar.

Naomi, escorted by M.J., wore a stunning floor-length emerald-green trumpet dress with ruche and a deep V in the back. She lit a candle honoring Martha's parents prior to taking her seat next to the flowers on the first pew, and M.J. sat beside her.

Jasmine, Mary, and Ruth filtered down the aisle single file to a rousing rendition of Handel's "Arrival of the Queen of Sheba." Dressed in the same off-one-shoulder satin Amsale gown with a draped bodice and bias column skirt, each bridal attendant wore a color of her choosing—Jasmine in platinum, Mary in fuchsia, and Ruth in gold. They carried delicate bouquets of peonies in shades of pink and purple. Immediately after Ruth entered the aisle, the wedding-planning team closed the arched wooden doors between the vestibule and the church sanctuary.

MINUTES BEFORE SHE would walk down the aisle, Martha chatted with Nicholas in the quiet room, an enclosed waiting space off the church vestibule that had served as a rest stop of sorts where she and the other kids who grew up in her church hung out after they tired of listening to the sermon and begged to go to the restroom.

Usually drafty, the room now felt warm and comforting. And it was anything but quiet. Nicholas and Martha laughed, talked, and made playful predictions about things that could possibly go wrong during the ceremony. Although she didn't feel nervous, their silly banter kept her well entertained. Martha was grateful she had deviated from her initial plan to walk down the aisle alone. She was certain she'd have played a different game of what-ifs, and she'd have been terrified if the examples she and Nicholas discussed had entered her mind without him for comfort. *This is what progress looks like,* she thought.

"Come in," Martha said to the soft knock at the door.

Mrs. Jones peeked her head inside the room. "Are y'all ready? It's time."

"One minute. Let me change my shoes," Martha said, having no regrets about turning down the assistant Mrs.

Jones had assigned to the quiet room to support her prior to the ceremony. Instead, she opted for quality time with her bridal attendants and Nicholas.

On cue, Nicholas carried over Martha's wedding shoes—robin's-egg-blue pumps adorned with shoe clips commissioned from her mother's wedding earrings. The footwear complemented the similar hue on the wall behind the altar where she and Oji would say their vows. But most important, the shoes provided a way for her to feel connected to her parents in their absence.

Martha slipped out of her white orthopedic slippers with arch support—which allowed her to stand comfortably and prevented her from wrinkling her dress by sitting for a long period of time—and into the pumps. "Now I'm ready," she said with an electric smile.

Mrs. Jones guided Martha and Nicholas to the vestibule, which was even draftier than the quiet room usually was. But since there had been a high of seventy degrees that day, Martha felt comfortable in the sleeveless ivory Amsale Archive gown that her wedding planner had miraculously procured on her behalf. The satin duchess dress featured a column silhouette, sheer illusion back, and row of rosettes atop the pleated train. Its classic elegance played into the Vintage Memories theme that Mrs. Jones selected for Martha's wedding. To complete her bridal look, Martha carried a cascade bouquet of white peonies and lush greenery that nearly touched the floor.

Martha felt giddy staring at the backside of the double arched doors to the church sanctuary, but her mood turned solemn when she heard the first note of the song that would accompany her down the aisle.

Instead of the traditional bridal march, Martha opted for a song of personal significance. As the string quartet and harpist played the first notes of a lullaby that Martha's father, a music enthusiast and amateur composer, wrote for her as an infant, the pastor asked the guests to stand. Martha was transported to the happy moments when the song brought her comfort, from childhood to the times before her parents' death. Only since she began dating Oji had she started to find joy through the song again.

Much to her surprise, there were no butterflies in her stomach. All she felt was calm. And as the doors opened, her eyes and heart searched for one person. Perfectly positioned at the altar, Oji—wearing a tailored black three-piece suit—locked eyes with Martha, and she teared up. She didn't see the rows of people staring at her. She didn't see the smiles or the mouths agape. She saw only Oji. She dried her tears with the handkerchief he gave her during his proposal, a keepsake she pledged to use on the special occasions they and their family would share going forward.

At the altar, Martha was again overcome with tears. Before Nicholas took his seat, he surprised her by quietly whispering a secret to her and Oji—a line from his favorite poem that served as guidance in his relationship with Naomi. Martha and Oji promised to keep it private, as Nicholas said that previously he'd shared it with only Naomi. Martha was deeply moved by this gesture because of the special approach she and Oji took to their vows.

Hand in hand, the couple exchanged traditional vows. Then the pastor temporarily stood with Adam and Nile as the string quartet and harpist played a special arrangement of "How Great Thou Art." Still facing each other and holding hands, Martha and Oji took a moment for a private prayer, during which they made an additional private vow between each other and God. Then the pastor led them through the traditional ring exchange. Adam produced the rings at the appointed time and without intervention from his sons, after which he moved Martha to more tears by surprising her with a tight embrace. Oji and Nile, who stepped aside momentarily to make space for the special moment, looked on approvingly.

After the pastor pronounced Martha and Oji husband and wife, the couple again joined hands. They both leaned forward toward each other—Oji a little more enthusiastically than Martha expected, which made her smile. As their lips met in a slow, sweet kiss, Martha felt the butterflies her mom had told her she would feel at her wedding. Moments later, she noticed her wedding guests' applause.

Martha and Oji interlaced their fingers as the pastor placed a straw broom—embellished with white peonies and ribbon—on the floor. The couple jumped the broom, eliciting another joyful round of applause and cheers.

Martha's eyes again filled as they met Oji's. *This is love. Wherever we are and whatever we go through, this is home. And because of it, I've found everything I've needed all along.*

Readers Guide

1. What traits did you notice about Martha that may have allowed her to miss any potential red flags about Oji before his confession in couples counseling? How might these traits have played into her inability to notice the similarities she shared with Oji? How could she manage the traits in the future?

2. Discuss the lessons *A Gardin Wedding* offers about navigating conflict with future in-laws. What do you think of Martha's approach to navigating the conflict with Eve? How did her approach evolve over the course of the story?

3. What do you think of Naomi's way of helping Martha deal with the conflict with Eve? What do you think of Ruth's? What would you have done differently, if anything, if you were in either of their shoes?

4. What does Martha's interaction with Eve after Adam locked himself out of the house show about Martha's growth and what she learned about herself?

5. How would you describe Martha's relationship with Nicholas? Why do you think the two of them developed a bond?

6. Given Martha's relationship issues with Ruth, were you surprised that Martha developed such a special connection with Nicholas? Why or why not?

7. How did Martha's experiences with her mother influence her relationship with Ruth?

8. How did Martha's overhearing what her mother said about her influence her view of herself? How did it influence the relationship she built with Oji?

9. What are your thoughts about the evolution of Martha's relationship with Jasmine?

10. In what ways did Martha and Oji's relationship change during the course of the story?

11. How did *A Gardin Wedding* influence your perception of vascular dementia? Why might the author have chosen to feature that type of dementia in the book? What are some things you can do to make sure your loved ones are aware of vascular dementia and its risk factors?

12. How did *A Gardin Wedding* influence your perception of dealing with unresolved childhood trauma?

13. How did *A Gardin Wedding* influence your perception of couples counseling? How do you feel about therapist Shari's verdict that Martha and Oji were in a healthy place for marriage because they recognized the need for change and were committed to progressing toward healing?

Acknowledgments

Many thanks to my editor, Jamie Lapeyrolerie. You are truly Martha's biggest cheerleader. Thank you for always seeing the best in her. Everyone needs a person in their life who cheers for them as much as you cheer for Martha. I also extend my sincere thanks to the other members of the WaterBrook team who worked on my book: Laura K. Wright, Cara Iverson, JoLeigh Buchanan, Rachel Kirsch, Diane Hobbing, Ginia Croker, Levi Phillips, Johanna Inwood, Douglas Mann, Oghosa Iyamu, Shauna Carlos, Ava Perego, Joseph Perez, Jaya Miceli, Kristopher Orr, Beverly Rykerd, Lori Addicott, and Laura Barker.

I am indebted to those who supported me over my debut year as I've juggled getting the word out about the first book in the Gardins of Edin series and writing the second one.

To my agent, Sharon Pelletier, thank you for stepping in during a tough time.

Lauren Cerand, my publicist, thank you for your wisdom and guidance.

A million thanks to JaNeen Molborn, the best mental health sensitivity reader and a true conduit of healing. It's always an honor to work with you.

Huge thanks to the library staff and booksellers who saw something special in the Gardin women and introduced them to readers. Thanks for all you do to champion reading and serve our communities.

Likewise, I am abundantly grateful to the authors, media outlets, book reviewers, book bloggers, Bookstagrammers, and BookTokers who gave my books favorable endorsements and reviews. I so appreciate the heart you bring to your work.

I offer special thanks to Becky Boerner and Jennifer Smith, two of the most supportive members on the launch team for *The Gardins of Edin*.

Johnnie (Chip) Allen, Antoinese Allen, Jayna Breigh, Jen Gilroy, M von Nkosi, and Rodney Sanders: I treasure your advice and support.

I am blessed to have a power team that I can always count on to share their opinions and subject-matter expertise, tell me when I'm doing too much (like Martha) or not doing enough, and keep me true to myself and my calling. I offer heartfelt thanks to Aurie, Lundi, Dill, Carol Riley, Chris Chanyasulkit, Dee McLeod, Hope Ferdowsian, Jan Buckner Walker, Janel Lowman, Karen Torres, Kristin Fields, Michelle Glogovac, Patrice Tyson, Sarah Laster, Terah Thomas-Faison, and Valerie Berry.

Finally, I offer my deepest gratitude to everyone who has read, borrowed, bought, and/or recommended my books. I am here because of you. Thank you for taking this journey with me and the Gardin family!

About the Author

ROSEY LEE is the author of *The Gardins of Edin* and *A Gardin Wedding.* She writes stories about complicated families and complex friendships, but a happy ending is guaranteed.

Rosey lives in Atlanta, Georgia, where she enjoys cooking, flower arranging, and occasional bursts of fanatical bargain shopping. She grew up on the Westbank of New Orleans and carries the area and her loved ones in her heart when she's away from them. Her essays have appeared in *Writer's Digest, The Nerd Daily,* and *Deep South Magazine.*

About the Type

THIS BOOK was set in Sabon, a typeface designed by the well-known German typographer Jan Tschichold (1902–74). Sabon's design is based upon the original letter forms of sixteenth-century French type designer Claude Garamond and was created specifically to be used for three sources: foundry type for hand composition, Linotype, and Monotype. Tschichold named his typeface for the famous Frankfurt typefounder Jacques Sabon (c. 1520–80).

A Battle for Control of an Empire
A Struggle to Conceal the Past
A Rift That Could Tear a Family—and a Legacy—Apart

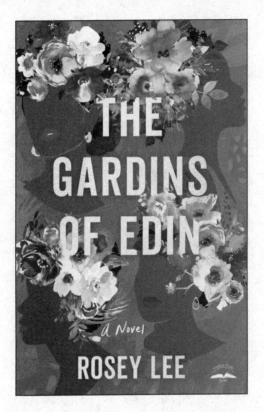

A multimillion-dollar peanut business in Edin, Georgia, was established by one family's formerly enslaved ancestors. But after Ruth's husband dies, tensions with Mary and Martha escalate, and the matriarch, Naomi, no longer wishes to serve as the peacemaker. Can the women find healing, make peace with one another, and save the Gardin family legacy?

Learn more about Rosey Lee's books at waterbrookmultnomah.com.